I0611154

LET US FIGHT IT OUT

The Chancellorsville Chronicles

Volume Two

C. L. Gray

The Stainless Banner Publishing Company

www.thestainlessbanner.com

For Tracy Clary – for his friendship and support.

General, if he does not give us good terms, come back and let us fight it out.

General James Longstreet
April 9, 1865

Chapter One

Room 5
Spotswood Hotel
Richmond, Virginia
May 5, 1863

Lieutenant General James Longstreet, commander of the Army of Northern Virginia's First Corps, pushed back the faded curtains and gazed outside. The cadet gray sky was streaked with vermilion. Last night's rain had moved out sometime after he had gone to bed. Puddles spotted the muddy streets. Quiet reigned except for a merchant across the way sweeping the sidewalk in front of his store.

Two days ago, the army had won a tremendous victory at a small village – no more than a crossroads in the Virginia wilderness – and sent the Union army scrambling back to Washington City to lick its wounds. A victory the army had won without him. He, along with Hood's and Pickett's divisions, had spent the winter in North Carolina securing food for Lee's starving soldiers.

In early March, Lee had sent a warning that the Yankees were preparing to cross the Rappahannock. Longstreet was to make immediate arrangements to return to Fredericksburg. It was an order Longstreet was in no hurry to obey. He had found something better to do than gather food. There were Yankees garrisoned in Suffolk, and he planned to seize the city and drive the enemy from North Carolina. But just as his plans were unfolding, the Yankees had crossed the Rappahannock in force. Urgent telegrams arrived from Richmond. Lee was in desperate straits and needed Longstreet and his men. Still, Longstreet took his time to move, hoping that the order would be rescinded and he could remain in North Carolina.

1

Voices in the hall. Longstreet turned from the window and listened to Jeb Stuart teasing his "good and gallant Jackson" to hurry up, for Stuart was starving. Jackson mumbled something in return.

Longstreet shook his head in amusement. That was one relationship he couldn't figure out: the boisterous Stuart and the puritanical, devout Jackson. They were polar opposites except Stuart was the only man in the army who could match Jackson's zeal for all things sacred. Longstreet gave the young cavalry leader credit though. Around Stuart's teasing ways, Jackson was almost human... and likeable. Their footsteps faded and the hall was silent.

Longstreet sat down at the desk and opened his portfolio. The leather notebook released its tight grip on papers and marked-up maps and splayed them over the scratched surface. He opened a map of Vicksburg and the surrounding vicinity. Right now, his old friend, Sam Grant, was poised to seize the city and, with it, control of the Mississippi River. The Confederates, under General James Pemberton, were scattered throughout the Mississippi country side trying in vain to stop the Union juggernaut. If Grant forced the Confederates into Vicksburg, both the city and army would be lost.

The situation cried out for the strong hand of a purposed commander who could rally the demoralized troops and stave off the disaster threatening to consume the South and end its bid for independence. It cried out for someone like him.

But Longstreet desired to go west for another reason. He was slowly suffocating in the shadows of Lee and Jackson. Over the past two years, both men had cheated him out of accolades that belonged to him. After all, it was his brigade that was responsible for the majority of the victories on the Peninsula when the Confederates had hurled McClellan's great army from the gates of Richmond. It was his corps that had withstood the bloody attack at Sharpsburg and the victory at Fredericksburg was due to his defensive line and nothing else.

2

But as a Georgian in an army named for Virginia, he received very little credit. Oh, Lee may affectionately call him "his old war horse," but in the past year, Lee had turned more and more to the taciturn Jackson to shape the army's strategy. Longstreet deeply resented being pushed aside in favor of the VMI professor.

He set the map aside and picked up the proposal he planned to present at this morning's meeting with President Davis. He was confident Lee would propose an invasion of the North, and, knowing Lee as he did, he was also certain that the plan would concentrate only on short-term remedies and not long-term solutions.

His plan, on the other hand, gathered up all the Confederate forces – the Army of Mississippi, the Army of Tennessee, and the Army of Northern Virginia – for an invasion of the North through Kentucky. This would force Grant to break off his attack on Vicksburg. The Confederates would cross the Ohio River, turn, dig in, and have the Yankees wreck themselves on the Confederates' strong defenses. He would assume command of the western armies and overall command of the invasion. Yes, even over Lee.

Humming tunelessly, he updated the maps with the latest intelligence. The sun came up, the candlelight faded, and his papers were bathed in rich, golden light. A knock at the door roused him from his task.

"General!" It was his adjutant, Moxley Sorrel.

"Come in, Major. Door is open."

Sorrel burst into the room. The young man, handsome with his dark hair and mustache, was a fellow Georgian and considered by many to be the best chief-of-staff in the Confederate army. Those in the Second Corps would vigorously protest that Sandie Pendleton was Sorrel's superior, but they would be wrong. "General Lee wants to know if you'll join him for a quick breakfast."

"Tell General Lee I'll be right down."

Sorrel backed out of the room and closed the door behind him. Longstreet jammed the papers into the portfolio and forced it closed.

✯ ✯ ✯

Longstreet sat in a rickety chair opposite the thick oak door of President Jefferson Davis' office. He gripped and released his portfolio until his knuckles hurt. He shifted in his seat and leaned back. The chair squeaked in protest. Burton Harrison, Davis' secretary, glanced up from his papers long enough to frown reproachfully.

Longstreet had been correct about Lee's intentions. The commanding general planned to go north. In the silence that followed Lee's announcement, and before Longstreet could open his leather case, Jackson, always Jackson, had spoken. Of course, the Presbyterian had his own plan – some nonsense about occupying coal fields and damaging the northern economy.

It was folly, but Jackson had gotten Davis' attention with high talk about defeating the Army of the Potomac, occupying Harrisburg, and perhaps affecting the presidential election. Davis was won over. Jackson left Richmond immediately to prepare his corps to march to Pennsylvania and Jeb Stuart went with him.

Longstreet sent word to a well-placed contact within Davis' office that he needed to see the president on an important matter. He warned his contact to approach the president only after Lee had left the White House.

Some might see such subterfuge as a betrayal, but Longstreet didn't care about appearances. He knew Lee's influence with Davis was so great that a simple shake of Lee's gray head would keep Longstreet forever chained to the Army of Northern Virginia.

His contact was true to his mission. He sent word to Longstreet that Davis would see him at three o'clock.

Longstreet sat at his desk and gutted his proposal. Gone was any mention of the Army of Northern Virginia. He would leave the East to Lee and Jackson. He would go west and prove two things: that Lee and Jackson were nothing without him and that his defensive strategy was far superior to Jackson's flank moves and Lee's audaciousness.

The door opened and Secretary of War James Seddon motioned for him to enter. Longstreet unfolded his long frame and soothed his jacket. He gripped his portfolio, cleared away all doubt from his mind, and marched into the president's office.

"General Longstreet," Davis greeted him warmly. "I hope you don't mind, but I thought it best if Secretary Seddon joined us."

"Yes, sir." Longstreet waited at the round table, his portfolio clutched in front of him.

"Sit, sit!" Davis ordered, settling back in his chair. "Now what's so important that you had to see me immediately? I do wish you'd have given me more notice. I'd have liked General Lee to sit in on this meeting as well."

Longstreet held his breath. Had the president sent for Lee?

"But my runner informs me that General Lee is unavailable. So, you'll have to settle for us."

"I'm very happy to do so," Longstreet said in relief.

"Now what can I do for you?" Davis asked.

Longstreet cleared his throat and spoke quickly. "I believe the situation out west is critical. If we don't do something in the next few days to change it, the war will be lost."

Davis folded his hands on the table. "What do you suggest?"

"Consolidate all the commands scattered throughout the Department of Mississippi into a single army under my command."

Davis shot Seddon a wary look.

Longstreet also glanced at Seddon, but the Secretary's face didn't give away what he was thinking. Seddon gestured for Longstreet to continue. "I believe I've proven my worth as both a corps and an independent commander."

"You're one of the best," Seddon responded.

"General, how developed are your plans?" Davis asked.

Longstreet stared at the president for a long moment. How many letters had he sent Davis since the first of the year? At least a dozen, if not more. He opened his portfolio and selected a map. Unfolding it, he set it before the commander-in-chief. "There's only one way to prevent Vicksburg from being captured. We need to concentrate our forces in Tennessee. I'm talking about gathering them all in. Pemberton's army, Taylor's small force, the army General Johnston is assembling in Jackson, General Gardner's force at Port Hudson, and Bragg's army at Tullahoma."

Davis folded the map and handed it back to Longstreet. "Absolutely not! That will leave the entire river open to the Yankees."

Longstreet appealed to Seddon but the Secretary sat impassive.

Longstreet cleared his throat. "The river is threatened because Grant's army is between Pemberton's scattered forces and Bragg's inactive one."

Davis held up his hand. "I've heard all of this from General Johnston."

"General Johnston is essentially correct," Longstreet insisted. He reopened the map and slid it over to Davis. "If we don't concentrate our forces, Grant will drive General Pemberton into Vicksburg and besiege the city. Then he will march to Murfreesboro and combine his forces with the Army of the Cumberland. A quick march to capture Chattanooga and from there, Atlanta and Savannah."

"But Vicksburg!" Davis lectured like a college professor with Longstreet as his lowly pupil.

Longstreet unfolded another map. "Vicksburg isn't Grant's true target."

Davis turned his head to stare out the window.

"Go on, General." This came from Seddon.

Longstreet turned his attention from the President's averted head to the approving face of the Secretary of War. "Before General

Grant can take Vicksburg, he must defeat Pemberton or risk being shut up in Vicksburg himself."

Davis turned back from the window and stared at Seddon, who slowly nodded.

Confidence shot through Longstreet. He had an ally. He passed another map to the Secretary. "I know Sam Grant. Before the war he was one of my best friends. I know the way he thinks and how he will react in most circumstances."

Davis leaned back down in his chair. "Really?"

Longstreet's nod in response was authoritative. He did *know* Sam Grant. "Grant will push Pemberton into Vicksburg and starve him out. We can't allow that to happen. If we combine all our forces, we can match the Yankees in manpower. We move swiftly against Rosecrans, defeat his army, then march through Tennessee and Kentucky and invade the Ohio Valley. Grant will have no choice but to leave Mississippi and chase us. We maneuver around him, find good ground, and make him attack us."

Davis pulled on his iron gray goatee as he contemplated Longstreet's words "No, we can't lose Vicksburg!"

From the expression on Davis' face, Longstreet knew he was in danger of being dismissed. "We can if it helps us drive the Yankees from our land."

"You sound more and more like General Johnston," Davis declared. "His telegrams are filled front to back with tactical retreats and dire warnings."

"Except General Johnston's strategy is to only retreat. He never commits his troops to battle. I do and I will."

Davis' gaze returned to the window.

"That's true," Seddon said.

What was true? That Johnston didn't put his troops into the fray or that he, Longstreet, would fight. Longstreet wasn't sure.

"The Army of Northern Virginia is heading north," Davis said to the window.

"Public relations." Longstreet was dismissive.

It was the wrong thing to say. Davis went rigid with anger. Another surreptitious glance at Seddon revealed that his remark had also angered the Secretary.

"Don't get me wrong," Longstreet swiftly backpedaled. "I believe Lee's march is the right strategy for the Eastern Theater, but west is where we'll win our independence."

Davis relented. Longstreet handed the President his proposal.

Davis quickly read the first few pages and handed them to Seddon. "Why not just give this plan to General Johnston. He's already in Mississippi."

Longstreet's blue eyes revealed his fear. What if they accepted his plan but rejected him?

Before he could speak, Seddon did. "I think the most important component of any winning strategy is the commanding general."

Davis opened another map and studied the Mississippi's winding curves. "General Johnston feels that the department is too much for one man to handle."

Longstreet sensed a trap. Either Davis was planning to dilute his command from the outset or seeking assurances that Johnston was the man for the job. He leaned back in his chair. His fingers rifled through the edges of his papers while he thought his way clear of the snare. "I'd have to disagree with General Johnston's assessment. I believe the situation calls for one commander."

Davis studied Longstreet. "Is General Johnston that one commander?"

Longstreet paused. Johnston was a good friend, and he didn't want to harm Johnston's reputation. "If General Johnston had fully recovered from his wounds, then, yes, he'd be that commander," he said slowly, "but he hasn't and that hinders him."

Davis seemed to agree with Longstreet's assessment. He picked up the proposal and scanned it again. "Having a steady leader would certainly solve an enormous problem," he said to Seddon.

"As I have suggested several times," Seddon replied.

"Yes, you have," Davis said tightly. "General Longstreet, whereas I appreciate this proposal, I do have to say that with the army headed north, I believe your place is with your corps."

Longstreet swallowed deeply. "There are many capable generals in the army who can lead the First Corps: A.P. Hill, Generals Ewell or Hood. I'm needed out west." He swallowed again. That last sentence made him sound desperate.

Davis chewed on the remark as he reread the proposal. "Have you spoken to General Lee about this?"

Longstreet stepped warily around the subject of Lee. "Since my detachment from the army, my communication with General Lee has dealt mainly with supplies. I left any talk of strategy for a face-to-face meeting. Due to the extreme emergency we find ourselves in, I haven't had the opportunity."

"What do you think he'd say?" Seddon asked.

"I think he'd agree with me."

Davis sighed. "The Confederacy is in extreme emergency, and I have no confidence in General Johnston or General Bragg to successfully deal with the Yankees." Davis' head dropped down on his chest. He closed his eyes. "What do you think, Secretary Seddon?"

"I believe General Longstreet's an answer to prayer," Seddon said, smiling at Longstreet.

Longstreet held his breath.

"I agree," Davis replied, opening his eyes and raising his head. "General Longstreet, I approve your proposal. How soon can you leave for Tennessee?"

Longstreet wasn't ready to accept Davis' offer just yet. He hadn't received everything he wanted or needed. He splayed his large hands on the table. "Sir, I am a lieutenant general..."

"Yes, yes." Davis waved his hand dismissively. "I'll recommend your promotion to full general to the Congress."

Longstreet swallowed his triumphant smile. "Then I can leave for Tennessee at first light."

"Excellent!" Davis stood, followed promptly by Seddon.

Longstreet kept his seat.

"What else?" Davis questioned impatiently.

"General Lee."

"I'll inform General Lee of my decision at dinner."

Longstreet stood.

Davis offered his hand. "General, I don't need to tell you what's at stake."

Longstreet gripped Davis' hand. "No, sir, you don't."

Robert E. Lee stood across the street from the Spotswood Hotel and stared at the hectic activity in the lobby through the hotel's wide windows. He spied Major Sorrel hurrying through the room. Where was Longstreet? He wasn't visible, but Lee was certain his old war horse was in the middle of the crush of men, orchestrating the commotion.

Two couriers exited the hotel on the run and headed toward the telegraph office. They clutched slips of papers in their hands; most likely orders to Longstreet's new subordinates out west – the most fractious and ambitious bunch of men in the entire Confederate army. Well, Longstreet was welcome to them.

Dinner was winding down when Davis had brusquely informed him that late this afternoon, the Congress had approved Longstreet's reassignment to the Department of Mississippi and promotion to full general. Davis paused so Lee could object, but Lee said nothing. In the silence, Davis stammered out justification after justification for snatching away Longstreet on the eve of the army's invasion of the north.

As Davis stumbled through his list of reasons, Lee could only nod in agreement. The situation out west *was* deteriorating rapidly. But if there was going to be a change in command, then Jackson was better suited to lead an army against the aggressive Grant. Lee was preparing to offer Jackson but stopped before he did. It was a selfish impulse, yet it snatched the words clean from his throat. He didn't want Jackson to leave his command. He would miss the reticent professor. Over the past winter a friendship had grown between the two men – a friendship Lee took pleasure in.

When Davis' last reason had faded away, Lee acquiesced because he didn't really have a choice. The decision had been made and the orders given. All Lee could do now was make a list of candidates to replace Longstreet.

Another courier dashed down the street. Major Sorrel stood framed in the doorway. As he turned to go back inside, he spied Lee and waved. Lee waved back and headed across the street toward the hotel.

"Sir, General Lee is coming," Sorrel announced.

Longstreet suddenly felt like a disobedient child about to face a disapproving father. He steeled himself and forced the panic away. He had no reason to be intimidated. This afternoon he had become Lee's equal. When he chased Grant from Mississippi, he would finally usurp the Virginian in the public's affection.

He drained the whiskey from his glass and set it down on the table with a thud. He stood as Lee approached.

Lee waved him back into his seat and fell wearily into the chair across the way. In the candlelight, Lee looked older than his fifty-six years.

"Robert," Longstreet said in greeting.

"General Longstreet."

Longstreet ignored the reprimand in Lee's voice. "When will you be returning to the army?"

"I've a few things to wrap up here first."

"I'm headed for Tennessee tomorrow morning," Longstreet said, careful to keep his voice free of triumph.

"So I've heard." Lee rose. "Well, it's late."

"Robert, before you go, I want to talk to you about Stuart."

Lee frowned and retook his seat. "What about General Stuart?"

"I'd like him to come to Tennessee with me."

Lee's frown deepened. "I don't think I could do without General Stuart's services."

"Now, don't be stingy, Robert," he scolded. "You've plenty of officers to take Stuart's place."

Lee pulled hard on his shirt cuff.

Longstreet gave him a stare. "Are you not even open to the possibility that my need for Stuart could outweigh yours?"

"No." Lee was abrupt.

Longstreet chuckled. "Perhaps we should bring the matter up to the president."

Lee raised an eyebrow. "You've had quite a day, General. Why not be satisfied with the victories already won?"

Longstreet wanted to speak angry words but Lee was on his feet.

"I wish you success in your new command. I know how much you longed for it and what was involved in securing it. I hope all your corps commanders obey your orders as swiftly as you obeyed mine last week. Good night."

Without turning back, Lee disappeared from the lobby.

Chapter Two

The Big Black River
East of Vicksburg
May 7, 1863

L ieutenant General John Pemberton read the telegram again. "You're sure this is the *latest* telegram from Richmond?" His northern accent was a stranger in the sea of soft, drawling voices that constantly surrounded him. He was Pennsylvanian by birth but had married a Virginia girl. When the war came, he faced a difficult choice. Go home to Pennsylvania or remain with his adoptive state. He chose the latter and though he had served with honor in both South Carolina and Mississippi, to many in the South, his *foreign* birth caused his every move and retreat to be viewed with suspicion.

"Yes, sir," his adjutant, John Waddy, replied. "I verified it myself. Twice."

Pemberton rubbed his brow and reread the telegram. Since Grant had crossed the Mississippi River in mid-April, Davis and Seddon had bombarded him with hourly telegrams ordering him to defend Vicksburg at all hazards.

As if he needed Richmond's constant hectoring. He was fully aware of the stakes. If Vicksburg fell, the Union navy would take control of the Mississippi River, split the Confederacy in two, and deny the armies much needed supplies from Arkansas, Louisiana, and Texas.

That is why this latest telegram made no sense. It was from General Longstreet, one of Lee's lieutenants. Pemberton had served under Lee in South Carolina and knew Lee to be an aggressive commander. But Longstreet's first order was the opposite of aggressive. The telegram instructed him to abandon Vicksburg, march to Tullahoma, Tennessee, and join up with Braxton Bragg's

Army of Tennessee. No reason was given for the order; just a time frame – immediately.

"What do we do, General?" Waddy asked. He pointed at the telegram crumpled in Pemberton's hand.

Pemberton released his grip on the slip of paper and smoothed the wrinkles. He handed it to Waddy. "We have our orders. We obey them and pray to God that Longstreet knows what he's doing."

Tullahoma, Tennessee
May 7, 1863
Evening

General Braxton Bragg stared down at the recent telegram from Richmond, not really thinking what it meant for the army but what it meant for him. General Johnston had been replaced and one of Lee's lieutenants was rushing to Tennessee. Did this Longstreet finally bear the orders that would relieve him from command?

Bragg knew his position at the head of the Army of Tennessee was tenuous. When he had inherited the army from the ailing Beauregard, he had immediately written to Richmond asking that the rules of promotion by seniority be set aside so the higher-ranked, politically appointed generals, dead weight was his precise phrase, could be removed from command in favor of younger, harder fighting generals who were quick to obey their orders. Richmond refused.

This refusal bore its fruit at Perryville last summer. Bragg ordered General Leonidas Polk to attack the Union forces at Bardstown, Kentucky. Instead, Polk held a war counsel and convinced his fellow generals that they, in good conscience, couldn't obey Bragg's order.

To disguise their insubordination, the generals wrote Bragg lengthy letters instructing him on correct army protocol. "Never divide your army in the face of a larger force," General William Hardee had intoned. Bragg had to wonder if it ever occurred to Hardee that his insubordination was the direct cause of the army's division. Bragg's letters to Richmond asking for Polk and Hardee to be reassigned went unanswered.

Last December, his commanders had urged him to retreat after a hard won victory at Stones River. At first Bragg refused, but Polk and Hardee insisted. Against his better judgment, he accepted their counsel and retreated to Tullahoma.

The two generals began a new letter writing campaign. This time, they directed their complaints to Davis, the War Department, and members of Congress. Oh, no, it wasn't their choice to retreat, the two assured the letters' recipients. They had wanted to stay and fight, but Bragg's ineptitude had cost the army a sure victory. If the Confederacy's fortune was to change, Bragg had to go.

Bragg was stunned by this blatant betrayal. He circulated a letter throughout his command, asking his corps and division commanders if they had confidence in his leadership. Their frank replies caught him by surprise. Most of his generals thought it'd be best for the army if he resigned.

Bragg wrote an angry letter resigning his command. He never mailed it. He refused to be forced out by his back-stabbing lieutenants.

Joe Johnston arrived in Tullahoma with instructions from Davis to relieve Bragg if Bragg's leadership had been damaged. Fortunately for Bragg, Johnston didn't believe a change of command was necessary.

Now Johnston had been relieved and another general was coming from Virginia. If Damocles' sword was going to fall at last, Bragg prayed it would do so quickly and mercifully.

A knock at the tent door roused him from his musings. "Yes, come in," he barked irritably.

The flap opened to reveal General Polk. Bragg grimaced. There was only one reason the tall, lean Polk had come to his tent. He must have heard the news about Longstreet and had come to gloat.

Without waiting to be asked, Polk collapsed in the chair opposite Bragg. He brushed the silver gray hair from his forehead, placed both elbows on the small table, leaned across, and tried to read the telegram.

Annoyed at the antic, Bragg retrieved the telegram and stowed it inside his jacket pocket.

"I hear the army is getting a new commander," Polk crowed.

Bragg refused to take the bait. He shrugged and poured a cup of coffee.

Polk was speechless; a rarity for the Episcopalian Bishop turned warrior, but he quickly recovered his tongue. "Personally, I think Richmond has a shake-up of the entire command structure in mind. About time, if you ask me."

Bragg hadn't asked.

Polk pointed to the coffee pot in the center of the table. "May I?"

Bragg consented.

"As you know, President Davis is an old and dear friend…"

It was this friendship between Polk and Davis that was directly responsible for the rancor that now existed in the army. Davis refused to hear any criticism against his friend, no matter how egregiously Polk behaved. This gave Polk immunity to act anyway he chose, knowing he was safely protected by presidential favor.

"Did you want anything in particular?" Bragg asked impatiently.

"Just came to flesh out the rumors floating through the army. General Hardee…"

Bragg flushed angrily. Hardee was the Bishop's most devoted acolyte. He dissimulated Polk's lies through the army with stunning zeal. Polk must have asked a question, for he had stopped yammering and was looking at Bragg expectantly.

"Do you know when General Longstreet is to arrive?" Polk repeated his question.

"I'm sure he's coming with all haste."

Polk drained his tin cup. "He can't come quickly enough for me."

The nerve of this man! To come into his tent and insult him so! Bragg's mind raced for a retort, but wrath choked out all thought. "It's late, General." He stood, giving Polk no choice but to say goodnight.

Northern Alabama
May 9, 1863

General Nathan Bedford Forrest rolled over and shut his eyes against the invading rays of the rising sun. He had spent the last eight days chasing a Union raiding party through Tennessee and Alabama and had finally caught up with the Yankees at Cedar Bluffs, a small town near the Georgia border. Forrest employed some trickery and convinced the worn-out Yankees that he had numerical superiority. They surrendered twenty miles from their goal of Rome, Georgia.

He rolled back over. His eyes were filled with the sight of scarred cavalry boots. He glanced up. "It had better be important, Major Kelley," he growled.

"Courier came in late last night." Kelley collapsed on the ground next to Forrest. He held up two telegrams. "From Bragg."

"What's that numbskull want?" Forrest gave up on the idea of sleep. He sat up and jerked his fingers through his graying hair "Well?" His fingers combed through his jet black goatee. He was in desperate need of a hot bath and some breakfast.

Kelley read the telegram out loud. "Report to me at Tullahoma immediately. General Johnston replaced by General Longstreet."

Forrest snatched the telegram from the adjutant. Reading and writing weren't skills he had mastered, but between the two, he knew enough words to understand the gist of the telegram.

"Longstreet? Ain't he one of Lee's generals?" He handed the telegram back to Kelley and pulled on his boots. He could smell coffee brewing and felt a powerful thirst deep in his gullet.

"I believe he was a corps commander. At least that's what I read in the newspapers once."

"If Richmond was gonna go through all the trouble of sendin' us another general, why didn't they send us that Stonewall feller. Now there's a man who knows how to fight. And we certainly need us one of them."

Kelley chuckled. "Why don't you ask our new commander that very thing when you see him?"

"I might just do that," Forrest snapped. He had run out of patience for incompetent, cowardly generals, who surrendered forts and field armies whenever the going got a little tough. If Richmond had sent another sissified general who gave up wide swathes of ground instead of fighting, he was going to raise hell. "What does the other telegram say?"

Kelley ripped open the envelope. He turned as pale as his shirt front. "General Van Dorn is dead."

Once again, Forrest snatched the telegram out of Kelley's hand. He saw nothing about how the dashing general had met his untimely death, but if he had to make a wager, he would put his money on a cuckolded husband finally getting his revenge.

The blood returned to Kelley's face and he grinned. "Do you know what that means? You'll be given the cavalry. Longstreet may even promote you to major general."

Forrest made a face. "I don't want to be no major general in an army that don't fight."

"But…"

"I don't want to talk about it no more." He gave up on the idea of breakfast. "Get the men up and in the saddle. We'll be headin' out in the next fifteen minutes."

Kelley nodded and pocketed the two telegrams. Forrest could hear him shouting orders to the men. With a groan, he stood and stretched wide his arms. He was so tired!

Chapter Three

B ragg stared across the table at an exhausted John Pemberton and watched him drain his fifth cup of coffee. Next to Pemberton sat a dusty Forrest snoring quietly, sound asleep in the chair he had plopped down in.

Bragg and Pemberton made surreptitious glances at the tent door. An hour ago, word had arrived from Longstreet's adjutant that Longstreet wanted to meet briefly with his commanders. Bragg had a million questions about the future, and he was sure Pemberton did too.

Obviously, the assembling of the two armies meant one thing. The Confederates were going on the offense. But against whom? Grant, who had seized Vicksburg two days ago, or Rosecrans' Army of the Cumberland now encamped at Murfreesboro?

The sound of horses. Forrest woke with a start. The tent flap opened. A captain entered followed by a major. A brief moment passed, as if staged for dramatic effect, then General Longstreet strode into the tent. The moment of truth had arrived. Here was Richmond's champion! The generals rose.

Longstreet handed his hat and gauntlets to the captain and accepted a weather-beaten portfolio from the major. He faced his gawking generals and took them in with one sweeping glance.

Bragg stepped forward. "Good evening, General Longstreet. I'm General Bragg." He held out his hand. Longstreet's grip was firm. Bragg turned toward Pemberton and Forrest, both standing somewhat at attention. "This is General Pemberton and General Forrest."

"General Pemberton," Longstreet said, "General Lee wanted me to give you his warm regards."

"How is the General?" Pemberton asked. A smile graced his weary face.

"Preparing to follow General Jackson's corps into Pennsylvania."

Forrest sat back down and grabbed a coffee cup. "We shoulda done that a year ago," he snorted.

"General Forrest!" Bragg snapped, irritated by the cavalry leader's bluntness.

Forrest glared at him before splashing the rest of the pot's contents into his cup.

Longstreet gestured toward the table. "Let's sit, gentlemen." He sat next to Forrest and opened his portfolio. Pemberton and Bragg returned to their places.

"You may not be aware of it, General Longstreet, but Vicksburg has fallen," Pemberton announced.

"Yes, I did know that."

"It needn't have happened. My army could have protected the city." Pemberton was defensive.

"Perhaps," Longstreet replied with a casual shrug.

Pemberton bristled. "Perhaps!" He jerked back in his chair and folded his arms.

Longstreet gave a small smile and held up his hand. "General Pemberton, smooth your ruffled feathers. I'm not belittling your men or their fighting prowess. I'm sure they are the finest in the Confederacy. But, gentlemen, let's not deceive ourselves. The war is being lost, here, in the West. Richmond has sent me to right this sinking ship. And I mean to do just that."

Bragg took umbrage at the statement. Maybe not with the statement's truth but certainly with the cold, hard way it was delivered. He followed Pemberton's lead, leaned back in his chair, and folded his arms across his chest.

Longstreet didn't seem to notice that he had offended two of his generals. "Gentlemen, the blame doesn't belong with you or with

21

your men," he continued, "but to a strategy devised in Richmond that has tried to defend too much land with too little men."

Bragg repented of his hasty judgment. Longstreet had pinpointed a major source of the failure suffered by the commands in the West. He unfolded his arms.

"It's time to change that strategy and give our armies the opportunity to show the Yankees their mettle," Longstreet finished.

"What do ya have in mind?" Forrest asked. He emptied his cup.

Longstreet opened his portfolio and drew out a map. He unfolded it and slid it over to Bragg.

Bragg placed a finger on the map. If he was to be relieved, then he wanted to be relieved now, before Longstreet unfolded whatever plan he had been sent west with. "Sir, before you go on, what happens to the armies and their commanders?"

Pemberton leaned forward. "That's a question I'd like an answer to."

Longstreet looked Bragg in the eyes. "As far as I'm concerned, everyone begins with a clean slate. Obey my orders, and you'll keep your commands."

At the news, relief swept through Bragg. He raised his eyes to Heaven and uttered a silent prayer of thanksgiving.

Longstreet unfolded another map and set it before Pemberton. "We're going to push Rosecrans out of the way and head toward the Ohio River."

Forrest slapped his hand on the table. "It's about time!"

Bragg raised a hand. "Hold on," he said to Forrest. He turned his attention to Longstreet. "Push Rosecrans out of the way, where?"

"Toward Shelbyville," Longstreet answered. "We're going to force him to either do battle with us as we pour through Guy's Gap and Bell Buckle Gap or retreat."

Bragg shook his head in disagreement. "He can easily flank us through either Liberty Gap or Hoover Gap."

Longstreet pointed at the map. "Not if we cut the Nashville and Chattanooga Railroad." He reached over and drew Bragg's map to him. "For Rosecrans or any other Union commander, their most pressing concern is protecting their supply lines. It's their Achilles' heel."

"That's how we stopped Grant cold last December," Forrest said. "When Van Dorn burnt the Yankees' supply depot at Holly Springs, Grant had no choice but to break off his attack on Vicksburg."

"Thank you for the history lesson," Bragg sharply rebuked.

Forrest warded off the reprimand with a shrug of his shoulder.

"We cut the railroad and Rosecrans will have to attack or retreat. The Barrens will protect us from an attack through Liberty or Hoover Gaps," Longstreet explained.

"That made sense," Bragg thought. His army had stripped The Barrens of what little it had produced months ago.

"Once we dispatch Rosecrans, the way to the Ohio will be wide open," Longstreet continued. "Mr. Lincoln can't have both the Army of Northern Virginia and our combined forces tramping unopposed through the North. He'll have no choice but to send Grant after us."

Bragg reclaimed the map from Longstreet. "I think it's a mistake to plan a strategy based on what Lincoln will or will not do. He could easily order Grant south toward Atlanta. We would have no choice but to break off our invasion."

Longstreet took a cigar from his pocket. He twirled it between thumb and forefinger. "There is that possibility and I won't deny it." He bit off the end of the cigar and spat it on the ground. "But we have two choices. We can wait for Grant to combine with Rosecrans and then push toward Atlanta, or we can take the initiative and force the Yankees to dance to our tune." He lit the cigar and puffed out a cloud of smoke.

Of the two scenarios, Bragg preferred the latter. "When do we go?"

"General Pemberton, when will your men arrive?" Longstreet asked.

"They're about two days away. But sir, they've fought hard for the past six months and have marched hard for the last few days. They'll need rest."

"They'll have it." Longstreet rounded on Forrest. "General, I'm going to give you the task of cutting and holding the railroad."

"I'll need Morgan's and Wheeler's brigades put under my command."

"Major Sorrel," Longstreet called. The adjutant took out a piece of paper and wrote quickly. He handed the note to the captain, who exited the tent. "Gentlemen, I know it's late and General Pemberton and General Forrest have ridden many miles today. Let's meet here tomorrow morning after we've all had a good night's sleep and discuss the particulars. I will give out specific assignments then and answer any questions you may have." Longstreet stood. The generals followed suit. "If there's nothing else." Longstreet didn't wait for answer. He exited the tent.

Chapter Four

M ajor General Philip Sheridan sat on his horse scowling in the general direction of the Confederate army, which was somewhere south of the gap his division was guarding. For the past two weeks, deserters had appeared through the gap with tales of a grand offensive. Whereas Sheridan took the reports seriously, General Rosecrans and his staff dismissed them. The Rebs often sent deserters through the lines with disinformation, and Rosecrans believed that's what they were doing now.

Stodgy fellow, Old Rosy. Too cautious for his own good. Believed Bragg was a threat. Believed Pemberton's arrival in Tullahoma didn't alter the Army of the Cumberland's circumstances. Believed Grant's decision to rest his men in Vicksburg meant that Grant's army protected Rosecrans' right flank, while the Barrens protected his left. After all, any move the Rebs dare make would bring the Army of the Tennessee on the double-quick. Rosecrans was convinced that Longstreet only had the strength of arms to react to whatever the Union forces proposed to do, whenever they proposed to do it.

Then came news that Reb cavalry had severed the Nashville and Chattanooga Railroad. Rosecrans saw it as a raid – a nuisance. Since the army had enough supplies to last a week, Rosecrans sent word to the War Department not to send any trains until further notice. He was sure that the Rebs would soon get bored and wander off to strike another target. The trains would rumble down the tracks once more delivering the supplies and ammunition necessary to push the Rebs out of the way. Then it would be just a summer stroll to Atlanta to end the war.

Not even reports that the famous, or infamous depending on your viewpoint, Stonewall Jackson was in Pennsylvania could budge Rosecrans. As Sheridan pondered the stupidity of commanding generals, his scowl grew deeper until his face contorted into a mask of hate. The Rebs were coming as sure as the sun was rising on his left. All the signs pointed to this reality, which Rosecrans ignored to the peril of them all.

Gun shots! Sporadic, but drawing nearer. Must be Confederate skirmishers pushing back his picket line. He sent word to General McCook. The army would be in a fight by mid-afternoon. Whether or not General Rosecrans was prepared for that eventuality.

Lieutenant General William J. Hardee, commanding the Army of Tennessee's Second Corps' assault on the Union troops at the northern end of Bell Buckle Gap, stood beneath a fly tent pitched between two poplar trees. His skirmishers had scattered the Yankees' pickets in a confrontation that lasted a little less than thirty minutes. It was a good start to the work ahead.

Behind him, Hardee heard his adjutant conversing with one of Longstreet's aides – Captain Goree to be specific. Goree was nothing more than Longstreet's spy in the midst of his headquarters. Hardee bit his tongue to keep from snapping at the likeable young Texan. It wasn't Goree's fault that the man he worked for was a complete idiot.

During a dinner that also served as a staff meeting, Hardee had sat dumfounded as Longstreet stated that he was not prepared to make any changes to the armies' command structure. The announcement evaporated what little appetite Hardee had for the tough beef and soupy potatoes.

General Polk had quickly challenged Longstreet's decision. After the defeat at Stones River, the army was disillusioned with Bragg's leadership. If he remained in command, the men would be demoralized. Longstreet dismissed Polk's counsel with a smile.

Next, Longstreet proposed sweeping changes to the armies' structure. No longer did Hardee lead the left wing of Bragg's army. Now, he commanded the Second Corps of the Army of Tennessee. With a chuckle, Longstreet quipped that he hoped Hardee would prove as formidable as Lee's Second Corps commander. Hardee flushed scarlet with mortification. He would put his record up against Stonewall Jackson's any day.

"Longstreet's a fool," he railed to Polk after the meeting. "I can understand why he didn't want to clean house. But to keep Bragg!"

Polk smiled. "No, no," he soothed. "Longstreet will learn all about Bragg soon enough."

Hardee wasn't in the same generous mood as Polk. "Why are you defending him?"

"I'm not defending him," Polk replied. "We owe him a chance."

Hardee huffed in exasperation.

"A chance," Polk reiterated. He held up one finger. "After all, if the august Lee has confidence in Longstreet, perhaps we should too."

Hardee shook his head. "And if Bragg leads us into disaster again? Then what?"

"We cut Longstreet off at his knees and send him packing to Virginia."

Hardee calmed down. "One chance."

Thankfully, Polk had agreed.

Hardee spat on the ground and rubbed his arm. In the damp, the wound he had suffered at Shiloh bothered him.

An aide appeared out of the drizzle. He saluted and handed Hardee a small slip of paper. It was from General Cleburne. If there was going to be any success this day, Hardee was determined that it would belong to him. That's why he had sent Cleburne's division to lead the assault. Not much terrified the Yankees about the Army of Tennessee, but the blue flags of Cleburne's division did.

"May I see the message?"

Hardee whirled around. Goree had his hand out. Hardee stared hard, but the young man didn't flinch. He wasn't in command of his corps, this Texan was. He spoke for Longstreet and acted for the Georgian as well. "Just a note from Cleburne." Hardee didn't pass the paper over.

Goree didn't retract his hand. "Sir, please." It was almost a plea.

Hardee softened. Perhaps the young man did realize that he had no business peering over a lieutenant general's shoulder. He handed over the message.

Goree folded the paper without reading it. "Any thing I need to know?" He smiled and slipped the note into his haversack.

Hardee fought hard not to return the smile but he wanted Goree to remain uncomfortable in his presence. "Cleburne's reporting contact with the enemy."

"Splendid!"

Hardee gestured to the aide. "Tell General Cleburne to press forward immediately."

★ ★ ★

A cannonball slammed into the stately mansion General William S. Rosecrans had called home for the last six months, shaking the general from his bed. He fell onto the floor in a heap, not quite sure what was happening. The distant cannon fire sounded like a fast approaching storm that was moving fast indeed if his peaceful sanctuary in the center of Murfreesboro found itself under enemy fire.

Footsteps dashed up the stairs and ran down the hall. A frantic knock before the door crashed opened. "Sir, the Rebels are attackin'," a sergeant said with a hint of panic in his voice. He ducked as another cannonball screamed toward the house. The range was long.

28

The missile sailed over the house and crashed into the chicken coop in the backyard.

"I'm very well aware of that, Sergeant," Rosecrans answered calmly. *Where was his jacket?* He searched the bed but it wasn't there. Stymied, he put his hands on his hips. Well, he couldn't waste any more time searching. He took two steps and tripped over an unexpected barrier. He looked down. His jacket! It had suffered the same fate as he – unceremoniously dumped from the bed. He donned it and followed the sergeant down the stairs. Another barrage shook the mansion.

"General Garfield's settin' up a makeshift headquarters two blocks away," the sergeant reported, the panic in his voice growing more acute.

Rosecrans nodded and stepped out onto the porch. A cannonball careened against a porch column, showering splinters. One nicked his face. He winced in pain and fished out a handkerchief to staunch the bleeding.

"Are you hurt?" The sergeant asked.

"It's a scrape." Rosecrans stuffed the handkerchief back into his pocket. "Let's go see General Garfield." He followed the sergeant down the steps and through the chaotic streets.

The sergeant suddenly threw a strong arm across Rosecrans' chest, stopping him dead in his tracks. A runaway team careened past, its limber of ammunition smoldering. The strong arm was lowered and the two men continued on their way.

In the wake of the Confederate surprise attack, Rosecrans had been pleased with the way his army had stiffened its spine. The men had pushed the Rebs back, but the victory was short-lived. Within the hour his lines had been broken, and soldiers had poured back into the trenches around Murfreesboro.

Yesterday afternoon the Rebs arrived in strength. Pemberton's army poured through Liberty and Hoover Gaps, taking its place on the right of Polk and Hardee. The city was almost encircled. By night fall the first line of trenches were evacuated. His men were holding on to the city with their fingertips.

The sergeant crossed the street and entered a small park. Rosecrans caught sight of his golden-haired chief-of-staff ruling over bedlam. Couriers dashed in and out of the tent relaying frantic messages to overwhelmed aides.

"Attention!" James Garfield shouted when Rosecrans entered the tent.

The confusion ebbed away as soldiers came to attention.

"At ease. Garfield, what's the situation?"

"The Rebs are attacking on all fronts. The men are overwhelmed and falling back." Garfield impatiently swept some papers aside to reveal a map of the city.

In the lantern light, Rosecrans saw that only the roads north remained in his army's hands.

"Right now General Stanley's cavalry is maintaining a perimeter five miles out," Garfield said.

Rosecrans studied the map. "Send orders to General Crittenden to reinforce Stanley. I won't allow us to be besieged. Tell Crittenden he must hold the roads at all cost."

Garfield sprang away from the table and spoke in low tones to an aide. The aide sprinted from the tent.

"Have we heard from General Grant?" Rosecrans asked.

"We received his reply right before the telegraph lines were cut," Garfield replied. He searched through a stack of papers, found the telegram, and handed it to Rosecrans.

Rosecrans moved closer to the lantern and read the slanted handwriting on the telegram. Grant's message was succinct. The Army of the Cumberland was to retreat north, remaining in front of the Rebs. Grant was preparing his army to hurry to Rosecrans' aid, but it would take four to five days before he would be ready to march.

Rosecrans returned the telegram to Garfield. "Did you say the lines were cut?"

"About an hour ago." Garfield placed the telegram in Rosecrans' order book.

That fact made Rosecrans next decision very easy. "Sound the retreat."

"Where to?"

"Nashville."

Garfield dropped the order book. It clattered loudly on the table. "Nashville?" He stared at Rosecrans in disbelief. "Nashville?" He repeated. "But... but... General Grant ordered us north."

"General Grant isn't in command of this army."

Garfield retrieved the order book. "No, sir, he's not. But we can't let the Rebs get past us."

"I must think of my wounded and find a way to resupply the men," Rosecrans said severely.

"Sir, I'll get the wounded to Nashville. We can re-supply as we march."

Rosecrans glared at the argumentative young man. "General Garfield, I know you're new to my staff, but it's not your place to question me or my orders. Are we clear?"

Garfield nodded.

"Sir."

Sheridan turned and saw a nervous young corporal backlit by the smoldering trees. "What?" He snapped.

"Message from General McCook. We're retreating."

"Repeat the message!" Sheridan hollered.

The corporal shrank into the shadows. "We're retreating," he squeaked.

"Where to?" Sheridan was still hollering.

"Nashville. General Crittenden is holding the way open. General McCook says to withdraw your men as quickly as possible."

Nashville! What was that dunderheaded Rosecrans doing! Losing the war, that's what! Oh, what Sheridan wouldn't give to fight for a general who didn't turn tail and run whenever the fighting got too hot or the odds looked a little long.

The corporal timidly shook Sheridan's arm. "Sir? What should I tell General McCook?"

"Tell him I'm tired of running away," Sheridan fumed silently. He checked his anger. "My men will be on the road as soon as I can extricate them from the battle."

The corporal turned to go.

"Corporal," Sheridan called out, "are you sure General McCook said Nashville?"

"Yes, sir," the corporal replied.

Sheridan lifted his eyes toward the sky. Where was the general who would stand and fight?

Chapter Five

The Executive Mansion
Washington City
June 11, 1863

President Abraham Lincoln heaved a weary sigh. The bottom was out of the tub. This morning a wounded Army of the Potomac had limped from the capital on its way to Pennsylvania. Lee was marching toward Harrisburg while Jackson was in the coal fields destroying the rail lines and canals that brought coal to the Eastern Seaboard. In Tennessee Rosecrans had been defeated by a combined force of Pemberton and Bragg. A retreat to Nashville, of all places, had left Kentucky defenseless. Governor Robinson sent hysterical telegrams twice a day demanding Lincoln do something abut the Confederates who were stripping the fertile Bluegrass Region like a swarm of locust.

"Where's General Grant now?" Lincoln asked.

General Henry Halleck leaned forward, eager to answer. "He's ferrying his men up the river to Louisville."

"When will he arrive?"

"I don't know." Was the reluctant reply.

Lincoln felt his frustration mounting. Halleck and the man seated next to him, Secretary of War Edwin Stanton, never seemed to know what was happening with the armies. Or if they did know, they didn't share their knowledge with him unless he forced it from them. "But you're still convinced Longstreet's goal is the Ohio River?"

"His course hasn't changed," Halleck replied.

"Did Rosecrans give any indication why he ignored General Grant's advice?" Lincoln asked Stanton.

"Rosecrans doesn't include me in his thinking," the portly Stanton replied. He settled his clasped hands on his rotund stomach.

"Under no circumstance can Longstreet join up with Lee. If he does, the war's over," Lincoln fretted.

"I wouldn't write off General Hancock so quickly," Halleck said.

Lincoln swallowed his contempt for the man nicknamed "Old Brains." Some in the War Department considered Halleck a military genius, but Lincoln thought Halleck's talents were more in line with a first rate clerk. "General Hancock, for all his talent, leads an army that has been thoroughly decimated. Wishful thinking isn't going to change that fact."

He took a deep breath and reached over to a bowl of fruit sitting on his desk. He plucked out a peach and took a deep bite. He chewed until his temper was under control. The two men stared at him, not blinking, not moving, waiting for him to act. So, he would. He knew of only one man who fought to win. Who didn't let the odds influence him. Ulysses S. Grant just moved forward, ever forward, to his goal.

Lincoln set the peach down and wiped his sticky fingers on his pants. "Relieve General Rosecrans from command."

Halleck jerked back in his chair. "Relieve him?" He gasped.

"Yes," Lincoln said coolly. "I'm just a Springfield attorney, but even I know that Rosecrans should not have let Longstreet by him. I don't need a man like that leading an army." He picked up a file and handed it to Stanton. "Place General Thomas in command."

Halleck jerked forward. "Thomas is a Southern!"

"A Southern who stayed with the Union and fought bravely at Mill Springs, Perryville, and Stones River," Lincoln remarked. "He'll do."

Stanton unclasped his hands and raised one in the air. "General Thomas' reputation is one of deliberateness and caution."

"Would he know enough not to let Longstreet past him?" Lincoln demanded.

With a nod Stanton conceded the point.

"I'll solve any problems of caution by giving General Grant command of the Western Theater."

Halleck sucked in his breath with such force that Lincoln believed the general would empty the oxygen from the office.

"Are you sure about Grant?" Halleck asked.

"He fights," Lincoln replied, leaning back in his chair. He put his feet up on the desk and stretched his long arms forward.

"He drinks," Halleck sniped.

"Then send every officer in the army whatever he's drinking," Lincoln retorted to Stanton's amusement.

Halleck shifted uncomfortably in his seat and looked longingly at the door. Lincoln wondered if he would have the courage to bolt.

Halleck rallied. "Before the war, Grant was discharged from the army because of rumors of hard drinking. And those rumors have haunted him ever since. I don't think we should give such responsibility to a man enslaved to whiskey."

Lincoln's feet hit the floor. Was Halleck genuinely concerned about the army's fortune, or was he continuing his smear campaign against his former rival. Lincoln wished he could read minds so he could better discern the motives behind what little advice these two men offered. "Have you ever seen Grant drunk?" His stare bore into Halleck, hoping to find the truth in Halleck's eyes no matter what statement came out of the general's mouth.

Halleck's eyes held Lincoln's for a long moment. Then he lowered his head. "No."

"Do you know anyone who has seen Grant drunk?"

Halleck shook his head.

"Then he's our man. Send orders to Louisville. Tell Grant that under no circumstance is he to permit Longstreet to join up with Lee or cross the Ohio River."

He plucked another peach from the bowl and chewed contently while the two men scurried to make his orders law.

★ ★ ★

Near Lexington, Kentucky
June 16, 1863

Longstreet rode down the dusty road, beneath shadowing trees and along side white rail fences. His aides trailed behind, chatting and laughing. Longstreet was alone with his thoughts, which he preferred since his thoughts were congratulatory in nature. His hard work this winter had paid off. Rosecrans had been thoroughly whipped and his unexpected retreat to Nashville allowed the Confederates to escape to Kentucky unscathed and, better yet, not pursued.

Longstreet scattered his men through the rich farm land and instructed them to take only what the army needed. Any reports of looting would be punishable by death. So far that threat seemed to hold most of the men in line, though a few thought to test him. They were punished as promised, and the dread of the new commanding general spread quickly through the ranks.

His musings were interrupted by a shout. He saw General Forrest galloping toward him. He drew up and waited for the cavalry leader.

"General Forrest, what a grand looking animal," Longstreet said, admiring the long-legged bay. What was it about cavalry leaders and horses? Stuart also managed to procure the most magnificent animals.

Forrest patted the animal and cackled in response. "I figured you'd want the eyes and ears of your army ridin' only the very best."

"That I do." Longstreet dismounted and walked over to a large oak tree. He leaned against the trunk, withdrew a cigar from his pocket, and lit it. Forrest joined him.

"Well, General," Forrest said. A puff of wind blew smoke into his face. He coughed and moved upwind of Longstreet. "When will we be joinin' with Lee?"

"We aren't."

A frown creased Forrest's face. "Well, why not? If we joined up with Lee, we could win the war."

Longstreet flicked an ash. "General Forrest, you make it sound like I don't want to win the war. This, after I just won a great victory."

Forrest reached up, twisted a twig from an overhanging branch, and proceeded to strip it of its leaves. "But we ain't profitin' on that victory. We just let the Yankees retreat to Nashville unmolested. Now, you seem to be plumb happy to make ten miles a day. If you pressed the men, we'd be across the Ohio already."

Longstreet glared at Forrest only to find Forrest unaffected by such displays. Forrest stood his ground and waited for an answer. "I know what I'm doing," Longstreet snapped.

"You'll just have to forgive me if I'm a tad flummoxed." He threw the bare twig on the ground.

"What flummoxes you?" Longstreet asked in exasperation.

Forrest gave him a disbelieving look. "Why we don't whip Yankees when we have the chance. Now we'll have to fight Rosecrans again, plus all them other Yankees that left Vicksburg and are headed our way."

The cigar stopped halfway to Longstreet's mouth. "How do you know the Yankees left Vicksburg?"

Forrest grinned. "You wouldn't want me to reveal my secrets, would ya? General, my sources are solid. Grant loaded his whole army on transports and steamed away from Vicksburg. I say we fight Rosecrans before Grant joins him. No reason to fight the whole kit-n-caboodle if we ain't gotta."

Longstreet clamped his cigar between his teeth. "What's wrong, General, you're not scared, are you?"

Longstreet thought Forrest was going to punch him, but the cavalry leader settled for scowling instead.

"I ain't sceered of Yankees. I don't care how many of 'em there are."

"Neither am I," Longstreet said.

"Glad to hear it. That makes you different from most of the generals 'round here. They're sceered of Yankees and victory." Forrest spat on the ground. "They avoid both like the plague. Cleburne fights, though. He's Irish, you know, and a man worth countin' on in a pinch. Don't be afraid to."

"I'll remember that."

Forrest faced him. "You can count on me, too."

Longstreet smiled. "Thank you."

"Now, if'n you'll excuse me, I'll be checkin' on my men." Forrest remounted and rode down the road at a gallop.

Major General Ulysses S. Grant stood on the pier and waited until the ground beneath his feet stopped rolling and swaying. All around him, Admiral Porter's transports belched forth soldiers. Shouts and commands herded the men from the river and through the streets of Louisville. Grant saw his adjutant fighting his way through the flood of soldiers, waving a telegram high in the air. "Colonel Rawlins!" He called.

Rawlins squeezed through a group of boisterous solders and joined Grant. "From Halleck, sir," he reported breathlessly.

Grant opened the message and read it quickly. "Rosecrans has been relieved of command. Thomas has his place."

"Are you surprised?"

Grant didn't reply. He re-read the telegram. "And it appears I've been given command of the armies in the West."

Rawlins retrieved the telegram and read it. He whistled in appreciation.

A golden-haired officer approached. "General Grant?" He questioned. Grant nodded. "I'm General Garfield, General Thomas' chief-of-staff."

Grant reached into his pocket and withdrew a cigar. "Where's Thomas now?" He lit a match and applied it to the cigar.

"The army is north of Elizabethtown."

"Do you know where the Rebs are?" He blew a stream of smoke into the air.

Garfield took a map from his rucksack. He glanced about for a place to unfold it. Not finding one, he knelt down and spread the large map at Grant's feet. "Here." With his finger he drew a circle around Lexington.

Grant squatted down and traced the route from Murfreesboro to Lexington. "They haven't turned east?"

"No. It appears they're driving toward the Ohio River."

Grant didn't understand Longstreet's strategy. The logical thing for him to do was march east and join up with Lee. It didn't matter now. He had his orders. He wasn't to allow Longstreet across the Ohio River. He stood. "The rest of my men should be here before nightfall. I'll make it my responsibility to rendezvous with General Thomas."

Garfield folded the map and slipped it back in his rucksack.

"Tell me, General Garfield, what kind of man is General Thomas?"

"Sir, I really don't know. I was General Rosecrans' chief-of-staff. General Thomas kept me on, but he'll probably replace me with his own man soon enough. I can tell you this much. Under Rosecrans we were making fifteen miles a day. Under General Thomas, we're making thirty."

It was just the thing Grant needed to hear. He plucked a small notebook from his pocket and scratched a hasty note. He handed it to Garfield. "Give this to General Thomas."

Garfield stuck the paper in his pocket. "Is there anything else?" Grant's reply was negative. "Then I'll return to General Thomas." He saluted and ran up the pier.

"Colonel Rawlins, let's get some breakfast." Grant threw his cigar into the river and followed General Garfield up the pier and into the city.

Chapter Six

L ongstreet stood in his tent door, sipped a cup of hot coffee, and waited for his artillery to open up on the Yankees entrenched about two miles west of his position. The coffee was bitter, but, then again, so was his mood.

Four days ago, Union transports had belched forth the Army of the Tennessee onto Kentucky soil. Longstreet shrugged when Forrest brought him the news. There was no way Grant was going to beat him to the river. The army continued on its unhurried way through central Kentucky. But Grant marched his army with all the speed of a brigade, leaving Longstreet gasping for breath. He hastily gathered up his far-flung divisions and drove them hard toward the river.

He ordered John Hunt Morgan to seize the unfinished suspension bridge linking Kentucky with Cincinnati. Morgan's brigade rode down the long, sweeping hill into the small city of Covington only to find the Yankees waiting. Recruits from Camp Dennison, militias from southern Indiana, southern Ohio, and northern Kentucky formed a formidable gauntlet. The batteries guarding the Queen City and the mouth of the Licking River shelled Morgan's troopers, decimating the brigade.

Morgan sent word to Longstreet. If he was to take the bridge, he needed both Forrest and Wheeler. The two cavalry brigades were unavailable. Longstreet had sent Forrest south to spy out Grant's position, and Wheeler's brigade was skirmishing with Union cavalry at the rear of the columns. Morgan had no choice but to withdraw.

Then two nights ago, right before dusk, a dusty Forrest rode into Longstreet's headquarters.

"Them Yankees are at Glencoe." Forrest removed his hat and beat it against his leg. Clouds of dust glinted in the fading sunlight. "Ain't no more than a day's march away."

Longstreet gasped. "A day! Are you sure?"

"Yes, sir, the roads were blue as far as the eye could see." Forrest settled his hat back on head.

A day! Longstreet couldn't think. He took a deep breath. Then another.

Forrest was watching him intently. "What do you plan to do, General?"

"I plan to give battle."

In the morning, he rode over the rolling hills between Walton and Crittenden and was satisfied with the ground. He ordered Pemberton to turn his army west and anchor his right behind a high-bank creek that wound its way through a thick cover of trees. The line stretched down the creek, ending north of the small hamlet of Piner where Bragg took responsibility for the left. Forrest had Morgan's and Wheeler's brigades ranging on both flanks for added protection.

Thunder! Longstreet's heart thudded heavily. Then he laughed at his foolishness. It wasn't thunder but the artillery. His heart settled back down into its normal rhythm. He took out his watch and noted the time. The artillery had opened fire on schedule.

"General Longstreet!"

Longstreet squinted into the gray light. It was Sorrel. "Good morning, Major."

"Cook has some eggs and ham frying."

Longstreet shook his head. He had no appetite. "How are the men?"

"Coming to the line now."

Another burst of artillery.

Longstreet tossed out the lukewarm remains in his cup. "I want to ride the line, but first let me grab another cup of coffee."

★ ★ ★

Sheridan knelt in the thick brushwood. He raised his fieldglasses, careful to keep the sun from reflecting off the lenses and alerting the Rebs of his position. Across the creek, the regimental flags of Stewart's brigade waved in the breeze. Stewart had picked good ground to defend. The opposite bank was a steep incline of about four feet and void of roots or other things his men could utilize to climb out of the creek. On top of the bank, the Rebs were well entrenched – three men deep behind a breastwork of logs and saplings.

Sheridan wriggled back through the brush. A direct assault against those fortifications would result in the slaughter of his men. He stalked back to the small sapling that served as his field-quarters. A courier from McCook was waiting.

"Well?" Sheridan snapped.

The courier handed Sheridan a slip of paper. "I'm to wait for a reply."

Sheridan tore open the message. His scowl turned into a smile of delight. On a signal of three quick cannon shots, the whole line would surge forward and test the Rebs' resolve. "My men will be ready."

★ ★ ★

Boom! Boom! Boom!

Sheridan drew his pistol from its holster and sprinted into the calf-high water. His men splashed after him and quickly formed up. Bullets splintered bark off the log fortifications. Stewart's Tennessee brigade stood and lowered their guns. Blue flame lit up the woods. The dead dropped into the creek, turning the clear water red. Sheridan ordered another volley, but the Rebs held their ground and returned a deadly fire. His men were trapped in the creek.

Artillery crashed into the woods – solid shot and canister drove the Rebs from their fortifications. Sheridan crawled out of the creek and began a careful advance. Artillery continued to pound, felling trees that slowed Sheridan's progress.

The Rebs melted away without a fight. Sheridan could see the gray figures threading their way through the pines and scrub. Musket fire bounced all through the woods, confusing the ear. He couldn't get a sense of the battle.

Smoke blew in from the right – too thick to be from gunfire. He snatched his fieldglasses from their case and surveyed the ground. All he saw was smoke and dense underbrush. Half his men lagged behind, while the other half was drifting left. He sent orders to close up ranks, but after an advance of another fifty yards, the men were drifting left again.

"General Sheridan! General Sheridan!" At the sound of terror in the voice, Sheridan pulled up short. A private burst through the trees. "The woods are on fire! Captain Bridge sent me! He said to tell you that we have men trapped in the flames."

Leaving orders that the line should press forward, Sheridan threaded his way through the thick undergrowth. Smoke limited his visibility. He could smell burning leaves and wood and hear the flames cracking and popping.

His lungs filled with smoke. He coughed, but that only made it worse. He stopped running, bent over, and coughed and coughed until he thought he was going to cough up a lung. He straightened up and slowly started on his way. As he came across small pockets of men, he sent them to left, away from the fire.

Screams! Indescribable! Like nothing he had ever heard before! It cut through him like a knife. The next ten steps brought him into hell. Before him, three men were encircled by a wall of flames. From inside, a myriad of sounds: screams of pain, cries for help, and prayers for deliverance.

"TOMMY!" A sergeant emerged from the woods, surprising Sheridan by his sudden appearance. He rushed toward the men trapped in the flames. "TOMMY!" He screamed again.

Two burly soldiers caught him by the arms and dragged him to safety. He fought them like a wildman. "Leave me be. That's my little brother! I have to help him!" The soldiers refused his entreaty.

Musket fire brought everyone back to the battle. Sheridan hit the ground. The soldier standing next to him collapsed – half his face missing.

Sheridan stood on shaking legs. The sergeant continued his frantic pleas; the men trapped inside the fire continued theirs. Sharp reports from behind. Startled, Sheridan whirled around; his eyes taking in the scene one piece at a time: smoking rifles, soot-covered soldiers, tears streaming down dirty faces.

Anguished wailing replaced the screams. The sergeant was on his knees. "He was my brother." Sobs overtook him and he fell to ground, his body convulsing in agony.

The weeping was more heart-wrenching than the screams of terror. Sheridan turned back toward the soldiers. They had not lowered their guns. Finally, an old grizzled veteran did. "It was the merciful thing to do." He turned away and headed back toward the battle.

Sheridan didn't disagree.

For convenience and control, Longstreet had located his headquarters near Piner and the center of the Confederate line. Couriers made circuitous routes from corps headquarters with updates. The Yankees opposite Pemberton showed no interest in attacking on this hot and humid day. Unfortunately, that was not the case on the left. The most recent message from Sorrel reported that the Yankees had attacked across the creek. Polk had been driven back about three hundred yards, but the Fighting Bishop had rallied his men and was pushing the Yankees back.

Goree rode up and threw himself off his lathered horse. "General Pemberton reports that the Yankees still haven't advanced." He grabbed a loose canteen sitting on the table and took a long drink.

"Did you warn him to remain alert?" Longstreet asked. He took a message from another aide and read it quickly.

Goree swallowed. "Yes, sir."

"Okay." It was a dismissal.

Goree took one more swallow of water and headed toward the corral and a fresh horse. He had no sooner disappeared when Moxley Sorrel galloped up, waving his hat, and hollering at the top of his lungs. "General! General!" He wheeled his gelding and pulled up. "Sir, General Polk is pulling out. His men are already on the road, heading south."

Anger burned through Longstreet's veins. He was well aware of Polk's past treachery but believed Sorrel's presence would keep Polk in line. He should have set his headquarters right next to Polk's and taken all decisions from the Bishop's hands.

He called for Hero. An aide brought the gelding forward. Longstreet practically jumped into the saddle. A sharp jab in the ribs sent Hero pounding down the road toward Polk's headquarters. Hopefully he could reverse the damage before the battle was lost.

"Major Sorrel, go fetch General Forrest," he ordered the adjutant, who was riding along side.

Sorrel shouted his agreement, left the road, and disappeared into the trees.

Men! Fleeing the battle! At least they weren't running, Longstreet noted with gratitude. He drew up sharply, scattering pebbles and dust. "Stop!" The first line of men stopped short, the rest bunched up behind them. "The battle is that way!" He pointed toward the creek.

"We've orders to reassemble at Morning View," a dusty corporal informed him.

"Do you know who I am?" Longstreet questioned. The men in front nodded. "Then turn around and return to the line."

"Yes, sir," the corporal said.

Longstreet threaded his way through pockets of men, turning them around, and ordering them back to the fight. There must be at least three brigades on the road. If all of Polk's men were on the move, then there was nothing to prevent the Yankees from falling on Hardee's flank and rolling up the rest of his line. And if Grant sent the Army of the Tennessee across the creek...

He cursed. A good, satisfying curse. He would not become a Beauregard, a Kirby-Smith, or any of the other generals that had been disgraced on the battlefield and sent to the backwaters of the Confederacy to wait for the war's end.

When he arrived at Polk's headquarters, the odor of burning wood was overpowering. He covered his nose with the back of his hand. The only thing he could see that would account for the stench was Polk's aides burning papers in the campfire. The swirling breeze blew smoke from the fire directly into his face. His eyes watered and he began to cough. He turned his back to the fire and waited for his vision to clear. When it did, he spied Polk standing next to a table, calmly drinking a cup of coffee, aloof from the frantic action whirling about him.

"General Polk!" Three long strides and he came upon the Bishop. It took great effort not to throttle the man. "What are you doing? You've no orders to retreat."

"My men were beaten badly," Polk answered calmly. "It would have been suicide to stay. The Yankees had driven my left flank at least a half-mile."

"I've turned the men around. Have them reassume their position and push the Yankees back."

"That would be very unwise."

Polk was arguing with him! Longstreet pushed his finger into Polk's chest. "If you won't follow orders, I'll find a general who will. You, there!" He pointed to one of the aides. "Put those papers down and go fetch me General Cleburne."

The aide glanced at Polk for permission.

"Don't look at him!" Longstreet thundered. "Do as I tell you!"

The aide nodded meekly and ran off toward a string of horses.

"General, I must protest your treatment of my aide," Polk admonished gravely, his face one of sadness at Longstreet's rudeness.

Forrest appeared from the woods, Sorrel following behind him. Forrest dropped from the saddle and ran over. "The woods are on fire," he choked out. "This breeze is whippin' the flames up something fierce. Men are burnin' up, sir. The wounded are beggin' my men to shoot 'em before the fire arrives. It's awful." His eyes filled with tears. He cleared his throat, but the horror remained etched on its face. "It's comin', sir. Within the hour, this whole place will be ablaze."

"Sir," Sorrel interjected, "the fighting is in front of the fire, so we do have room to maneuver. Our immediate problem is that only Withers' Division is preventing the Yankees from rolling up the line. They can't hold much longer."

More horses coming from the south. All turned and waited to see who would appear. "I've ordered Bate's Division to assist General Withers," Bragg shouted as soon as he emerged from the trees. He pulled up in front of the clutch of men. "General Hardee is being pressed but is holding. General Pemberton reports that the Yankees are crossing the creek in force."

It was all falling apart! Longstreet frowned at the man responsible, only to realize that Bragg was also glaring at the insubordinate Bishop.

"Major Sorrel, I turned General Polk's men around about a mile from here. Please direct them toward Withers' division," Longstreet said.

Sorrel remounted and galloped away.

"You need to get the men away before the fire reaches them," Forrest warned. "In this wind, the flames could encircle us and cut off our retreat."

"The same thing could happen to the Yankees," Longstreet replied. "If they can stand the fire, so can we."

"I think General Forrest is correct," Polk commented.

"That's enough from you!" Bragg growled.

Longstreet silenced both men with an angry gesture.

"General Forrest, I need your men to keep an eye on the fire. Keep me posted."

Forrest headed back to his horse.

"General Bragg, take command at Withers' position," Longstreet said. "Hold the line until you hear from me."

Bragg wheeled around and rode off.

"What do you want me to do?" Polk asked. He stood eagerly, waiting for Longstreet's command.

Now wasn't the time to discipline the Bishop. "Get your men to safety."

★ ★ ★

The night sky glowed orange. Grant leaned against a tree and wrinkled his nose. The stench of burnt flesh turned his stomach. He lit a cigar and smoked in silence.

General Thomas approached: his face dirty with soot and his uniform reeking of smoke. He wearily fell against the tree then slid down the rough bark to the ground. He dropped his head in his hands.

"We're back over the creek away from the flames." His voice shook with fatigue and emotion.

Grant reached down his hand.

Thomas grabbed it and allowed Grant to haul him to his feet.

"I can't imagine what agonies you've had to endure this afternoon," Grant said.

"What my men endured," Thomas corrected, his voice strained. "I had to finally order my medics, orderlies, clergy...all of them to the rear." He turned away from Grant. With a trembling hand he took out his handkerchief and wiped his eyes. "The men didn't want to stop trying to reach the wounded and those trapped by the flames, but I had no choice. It was the hardest decision I ever had to make." He turned back toward Grant, his face bleak and haunted. "But we are in place and ready to go tomorrow."

Grant smiled. Thomas had a reputation for toughness. "Good." He pushed off against the tree and headed toward his tent. Thomas followed at his heels.

A map lay open on the table. "At dawn, march your men down this road." Grant's finger traced a road leading through Crittenden. "Then swing east."

Thomas puffed out his cheeks. "I haven't been able to determine Bragg's location," he confessed.

"That's okay," Grant assured the weary commander. "We know Bragg can't remain where he is. Not with the woods on fire and his left flank badly damaged. What I want you to do is cut off his retreat south. Get your men in place as quickly as possible. When done, I'll press Pemberton."

Thomas examined the map. "You plan to drive Longstreet east?"

"East. North. I don't care. As long as he can't escape south."

"But what if he gets away and joins up with Lee?" Thomas questioned sharply.

"We'll catch him at the river before that happens." Grant was confident.

A small smile crossed Thomas' lips. "I'll have my men on the road as soon as practicable."

Grant folded the map. "General Thomas, how many men did we lose to the fire?"

"Over 3,000 at last count."

Grant had no words. He reached into his pocket and took out another cigar. In the distance, thunder echoed. At any other time, he would have dreaded the approaching rain. But not tonight. "I'll wait for your report." He escorted Thomas from the tent.

"I'll send it," Thomas promised.

Grant waved good-bye and headed back to his tent.

Chapter Seven

Outside, rain fell. Not hard enough to put out the fire, but a constant drizzle that only promised to increase the humidity. Longstreet paced the small space between the walls of his tent, fighting against the many emotions threatening to overpower him. He was able to hold most of them back, but he couldn't hold back the fear. It engulfed him, making it impossible to think, and right now, he needed to think. Much had gone right today. Pemberton had held against Grant's repeated charges. Longstreet knew his old friend well enough to know that tomorrow morning, when Grant came across the creek, he would smash against Pemberton with fury.

Then there was the disaster that was Bragg's army. The First Corps was strung out on the roads headed south. In the hasty retreat, Polk had abandoned his supply wagons, artillery, everything. By time he sent orders for the wagons to be removed, the fire had consumed over half of them, though the artillery had escaped the flames with only a bad scorching.

The fire continued to burn up acreage. Hardee moved brigades to the rear to keep them from the fire's grasp. Unless the night skies became serious about pouring rain and extinguishing the flames, Hardee would have no choice but to abandon his lines. This would make Pemberton's left flank vulnerable.

What should he do? He could pull his army out and head south but he wasn't willing to admit defeat. If only Polk had obeyed!

A memory flashed. Not a particularly pleasant one. Lee in the lobby of the Spotswood Hotel. *"I hope your corps commanders obey your orders as quickly as you obeyed mine this week."*

Longstreet tried to push back the rebuke, but he couldn't. It wasn't the first time he had disobeyed Lee. While Jackson fought the Yankees with rocks at Manassas, Lee ordered Longstreet to sweep the field. Longstreet refused. Instead, he enfiladed the Yankees with canister and won the battle.

Longstreet threw down the condemning memory. There was huge difference between what had happened at Manassas and what Polk did this afternoon. Longstreet hesitated in unfurling the attack that Lee had desperately called for because he knew a better way to relieve Jackson. Polk was simply insubordinate. End of story. And Polk would pay for his disobedience.

"Sir." It was Sorrel. "Generals Pemberton and Forrest have arrived."

"Bragg?" He questioned. Sorrel shook his head. "Show them in."

Sorrel backed out of the tent. Longstreet heard voices then Pemberton and Forrest entered.

"There's hot coffee on the table," Longstreet said.

Both men took advantage of the invitation.

"General Pemberton, how are the men?"

"I left them digging a firebreak just in case the rain doesn't put out the fire. Other than that, they're in high spirits. Is General Bragg going to join us? I need to ask him about Hardee. If Hardee pulls out, my flank will be vulnerable."

"I'm fully aware of the difficulties you face."

An uncomfortable silence fell. Forrest drummed his fingers on the table. The quiet was finally punctured by Bragg's arrival. He entered the tent and apologized for his tardiness.

"Right as I was leaving, word came that the Yankees were pulling out." He stripped off his gauntlets and threw them down on the table. "I sent a few men over the creek to check it out. It's true. Yankees are jamming the roads south."

"Do you know where?" Longstreet questioned.

"I think that's a question General Forrest can answer," Bragg replied. He picked up the coffee pot. A few drops of the dark liquid dribbled out. With a disappointed sigh, he set the pot down.

"I agree," Longstreet said. He gave Forrest a pointed look.

Forrest drained his cup. He dropped it on the table with a clang, swept up his hat and gauntlets, and exited the tent.

"Should we retreat?" Pemberton asked.

Everything inside Longstreet rebelled at the question. Fear returned with a vengeance. "Think!" He ordered himself. He unfolded a map and spread it out on the table. Bragg rose, moved behind him, and studied the map over his shoulder.

Bragg's closeness made Longstreet feel claustrophobic. He shifted his chair to the right. "We could make a break for the river."

"And join up with Lee?" Pemberton volunteered.

Longstreet ignored the question by asking Major Sorrel for more coffee. Bragg returned to his seat.

"So, do we join up with Lee?" Pemberton asked again.

Sorrel arrived with the coffee pot. As soon as the pot hit the table, Bragg claimed it. He filled his cup and took a long drink. "There's no need to retreat," Bragg said, setting the cup on the table. "We flank Grant before Thomas can flank us."

Even though Longstreet was grateful for a way out of the fix, he still resented Bragg for offering up strategy without clearing it through him first.

"Exactly," he said, hoping to gloss over any indecision that might have been evident. "General Bragg, how fast can you get your men on the road?"

Bragg settled back in his chair, a frown on his face.

"Problem, General?" Longstreet asked.

"With Polk's corps strung out for miles, I think it'd be more expedient to slide General Pemberton's forces around Grant's left and catch Grant marching the wrong way."

Longstreet turned in his chair and directed his gaze upon Pemberton. "Can your men do it?"

"Of course. But what prevents Grant from wheeling right and flanking me."

"My men will fill in your line," Bragg said.

"Hold up, General," Longstreet barked, angry at Bragg for speaking out of turn again. "That's not your call to make."

Bragg held up his hand in apology.

"General Pemberton, when can your men be on the road?" Longstreet questioned.

"Within the hour if need be."

"General Bragg, I'm concerned about your left flank. It'll be in the air," Longstreet said.

A look of puzzlement flashed across Bragg's face. "My left is protected by the fire. The Yankees won't brave the flames."

Longstreet examined the map. He didn't want to give the appearance that Bragg was setting the army's strategy, even if that strategy was sound. "General Pemberton, get your men on the road as quietly as possible. There's no reason to warn the Yankees what we're up to. General Bragg, fill in Pemberton's line as quickly as you can."

Chairs scraped back against the hard ground. Hats and gauntlets were gathered up and good-byes were made.

"General Bragg, before you go," Longstreet called.

Pemberton said his good-byes and exited.

"Tomorrow, stay with General Polk," Longstreet said. "I don't want a repeat of this afternoon's disaster."

"Yes, sir," Bragg agreed.

"If he gives you any trouble, relieve him of his command and place him under arrest. Put General Cleburne in his place."

"General Cleburne has never commanded a corps."

"But he fights," Longstreet said. He returned to the table and poured another cup of coffee. "That's all." He turned his attention to the map and didn't acknowledge Bragg's leaving.

★ ★ ★

"General Grant." The voice didn't belong in his dream. "General Grant." There it was again, more insistent. Someone was shaking his shoulder. He protested this intrusion into his dream of Julia and the children, but the voice wasn't giving up. With a start, Grant sat up.

"Sorry to wake you, sir." The disembodied voice said.

"Mac?" Grant squinted into the blackness.

A match struck and a candle came to life.

Grant shut his eyes against the light. Slowly, he opened them and saw General James McPherson, one of his most trusted subordinates and the closest thing he had to a best friend in this war, standing over him. "What time is it?"

"A little past three. Water?" McPherson held up a canteen.

"Cigar." Grant swung his feet to the ground, but quickly retreated. Rainwater had seeped in under the tent walls and the grass was wet. "Boots." He pointed at his trunk.

McPherson handed over the boots followed by the cigar.

Grant pulled on the boots and lit the cigar. "Now, what's the matter?" He stood and went to the tent door. He gazed south. The sky still glowed orange.

"The Rebs are on the move."

He was disappointed. He expected more of a fight from his old friend. "Are they retreating?"

"No, they're headed north."

Grant blew out a stream of smoke. "Is there any coffee?"

McPherson shook his head. "I can have some made."

Grant made a face. "I'll just take water." He held out his hand. McPherson passed him a canteen. "Is it Bragg on the roads?"

"Stanley reports that it's Pemberton."

Grant puffed on the cigar, deep in concentration. "Are there still Rebs in your front?"

McPherson nodded.

Longstreet must have slid Bragg into Pemberton's line, which could only mean that Longstreet wasn't interested in retreating or moving east to join Lee.

Grant threw the cigar stub on the ground. It hissed when it hit the wet grass. With his toe of his boot, he ground out the ash. "Let's give General Longstreet what he wants. I'll turn Thomas around and have him head north."

McPherson chuckled. "North is pretty vague. Any place in particular."

Grant smiled. "North for right now. In the meantime, pull your men from in front of Bragg and get them on the road as soon as practicable."

"Yes, sir," McPherson said. "Now, go back to sleep."

Grant patted McPherson's on the back. "A little too late for that, my friend." He laughed and pushed McPherson toward the door. "Now, go. I have work to do."

With a laugh, McPherson slipped from the tent.

Longstreet threaded his way through the men tramping through the shallow puddles left by last night's rain. As he did, no soldier raised a cheer at his passing, which took him by surprise. Jackson's Second Corps always produced a shout to wake the dead when the men caught sight of ole Stonewall. The cheers caused Little Sorrel, Jackson's small steed, to hurry Jackson away. Longstreet smiled at the memory, surprised at the feeling of homesickness stabbing his heart.

When he left Virginia, he never thought he would miss his old corps, which was also known to raise a cheer or two whenever he rode by. But he did miss his boys, the calming figure of Lee, and the laughing Jeb Stuart.

General Stewart hailed him. Longstreet drew up and waited for the former college professor to join him. "General Stewart, how are the men?"

"They're in fine spirits," Stewart responded. "The heat's wearing on them though."

Longstreet squinted into the sun. "Heat's wearing on all of us."

"That it is." As if reminded that he was hot, Stewart raised his canteen and drained it. Water ran down his chin and splashed the dust from his jacket.

Longstreet fought the compulsion to drain his own canteen. "I'm looking for General Polk."

Stewart stowed the canteen and wiped the remaining drops of water from his chin. "I haven't seen him this morning, but if I were to guess, I'd say he's riding with General Hardee."

Longstreet thanked Stewart for the guess and headed down the road.

Stewart was correct; Polk was with Hardee. The two corps commanders were sitting under a giant oak, finishing up either a late breakfast or early lunch. Longstreet didn't know for sure because the two generals didn't greet him when he rode up, nor did they invite him to join them.

For an awkward moment, he paced back and forth while the two men finished their coffee. Finally, Hardee excused himself and rode away. Polk's gelding was brought around. He climbed up and waited for Longstreet to do the same.

"What brings you all the way out here?" Polk stifled a yawn.

"We need to clear the air," Longstreet replied.

Polk stifled another yawn. "We do? What about?" He asked innocently.

Longstreet's face began to heat up. "You were ordered to maintain your position yesterday. You didn't and it cost this army a victory."

Polk's cheek tightened in anger. "Am I expected to remain on the line and have my men massacred?"

"There was little chance of that." Longstreet was dismissive.

"The Yankees were advancing en masse," Polk insisted.

"As they were against the entire line, yet the rest of the men held their position and drove the Yankees back. Are you telling me your corps was unable to do its duty?"

"My corps," Polk barked, "is the finest corps in the Confederacy. But it received the bulk of the assault."

"No, it didn't."

Polk drew up sharply.

Longstreet went past him. He wheeled around and saw Polk glaring at him. Never one to be intimidated or out-glared, Longstreet fixed his stare on the obdurate commander.

Polk blinked first. He urged his gelding forward and caught up with Longstreet. He assumed an injured air.

"You were ordered to remain on the line and drive the Yankees back," Longstreet said. "You failed in that mission. That's what's going in my report. The next time I, General Bragg, or any of my aides give you an order, you will obey it."

"If..."

"NO IFS!"

Polk squared his shoulders in defiance "You don't want me as an enemy."

"Oh, I don't?" Longstreet challenged.

Polk turned an icy stare on Longstreet. "No, you don't."

Longstreet pulled up. "General Polk, let's talk as men, shall we?"

Polk nodded and drew up as well.

"I don't know what game you're playing, but if you undercut my command, Richmond will have no choice but to replace me with either General Johnston, if he'll take command again, or General Jackson. General Jackson will be a disaster for this army. His one and only tactic is to hurl his troops against the Yankees and pray that

Providence will grant him victory. You don't want that to happen. We'll lose Tennessee, Atlanta, and the war."

"I can lead this army."

There it was. Polk wanted command.

"You don't want to go to war with me," Longstreet said with a voice of steel. "I'll bury you."

Polk didn't bat an eye. "We'll see."

"Yes, we will." Longstreet leaned forward. "In the meantime, this army belongs to me. You'll obey my orders or be removed from command and court martialed for insubordination. Be thankful Richmond sent me instead of Jackson. Stonewall would have had you shot if you pulled such shenanigans on him. Do you understand me?"

"I do," Polk spat out.

"Good." Longstreet put spurs to Hero's sides and left Polk in the road.

Chapter Eight

Twelve miles south
Of the Ohio River
July 2, 1863

Major General Patrick Cleburne glanced up at the sun. By its position in the sky, he calculated that it had to be about ten in the morning. He eased his watch from his vest pocket and smiled – a quick smile. It was five past ten.

Behind him, hidden from view, his men were forming up, waiting for the artillery to open up and pound the Union position directly in his front. His orders were to storm the stronghold and turn the Union flank.

Cleburne raised his fieldglasses and surveyed the spot General Bragg had designated as the point of attack. It was crawling with blue soldiers, all gripping rifles, all looking his way. The force there had to be corps strength. He lowered the glasses, careful to keep his face averted. He was afraid if his aides saw his expression, they would know that he had serious doubts about what he had been ordered to do.

Last night, after midnight, he had been called from his tent to receive a visitor. Expecting it to be General Hardee's adjutant with orders, he was surprised to see General Bragg waiting for him in the common area. Surprising still, Bragg was alone.

"General Cleburne!" Bragg hailed. He extended his hand.

Stunned by the familiarity, Cleburne shook the offered hand.

"Is there a place where we can speak? Alone?"

Cleburne ushered Bragg into his tent. "Can I get you some coffee?"

Bragg shook his head. "No."

In the lantern light, Cleburne observed Bragg's weariness. But there was something more in his face. Was it dread? Remorse?

C.L. Gray

Bragg collapsed in the chair next to the desk, a defeated slump to his shoulders. Cleburne sat down, his eyes never leaving the commanding general. Bragg must have seen the alarm in Cleburne's face for he suddenly smiled, which did little to ease Cleburne's unease. For the smile foreshadowed tragedy. Even though the night was hot and muggy, Cleburne shivered.

"What can I do for you, General?" Cleburne asked.

"I just came from General Longstreet. He has orders." Bragg stopped speaking. He tugged at his nose and cleared his throat. Cleburne shivered again. "Your division has been ordered to turn the Yankees' flank."

Cleburne's stomach dropped. "My division?" He asked to clarify.

Bragg nodded. "Under the cover of artillery, your division, in columns of regiments, will march from the woods and punch a hole in the Yankees' line. Once you're through, the rest of the army will join you and roll up the Union flank into Pemberton's waiting arms."

Cleburne was stunned. He cast around for something to say besides "oh!" He picked up a pencil and rolled it between his palms. Bragg seemed content to wait until Cleburne found his voice. "Sir, you know my men will do whatever is asked of them. They always have." Cleburne dropped the pencil on the desk. It rolled toward Bragg, who stopped it with a finger. "My division is at least two hundred yards from the Union line. Any advance will be made in plain sight of the Yankees."

"General Longstreet believes that a heavy artillery barrage will keep the Yankees pinned down."

Cleburne didn't believe that and he was certain Bragg didn't either. "But columns of regiments will be susceptible to return artillery. A few well placed shots of canister will decimate my lines before I get anywhere near the Yankees' fortifications."

Bragg rolled the pencil back toward Cleburne. "General Longstreet is certain that our artillery will keep the Yankees quiet."

62

It was suicide mission. No wonder it was Bragg and not Hardee's adjutant sitting across from him. Perhaps Longstreet hadn't ridden the line today. Perhaps he didn't know just how vulnerable the men would be in the open field, marching up hill to reach the Yankees. Perhaps he needed to explain the situation to Longstreet. He said so to Bragg.

"He knows," Bragg said. With his right hand, he rubbed the knuckles of his left hand.

Cleburne slumped back in his chair. He didn't understand why Longstreet would recklessly risk his division.

"General Longstreet believes you can punch through the line," Bragg continued. "You won't be alone long. As soon as you're through, the rest of the army will get up there on the double quick."

Cleburne was disheartened. Bragg wasn't even looking at him but speaking to the desk. "Sir, do you believe my men can succeed?"

Bragg looked up from the desk. His eyes were shiny with tears. "I hope so."

Cleburne's throat tightened. "Hope is not a strategy."

"No, it's not," Bragg concurred. "But those are our orders. I've spent the last hour arguing against this move." He shrugged in defeat. "I was unsuccessful."

"Well, I guess tomorrow is as fine a day to die as any," Cleburne said, his voice flat and low.

The blood drained from Bragg's face. "I want you to lead from the back."

Cleburne shook his head. "I can't ask my men to risk themselves while I remain safe in the rear."

"This war has a long way to go yet. I can't afford to lose you." Bragg's voice wavered. "You're the best I have." He patted Cleburne on the arm.

Bragg's admission brought a lump to Cleburne's throat. He swallowed hard. "What if we advance with horse artillery on either side of us? The sharp sting of horse artillery, coming ever closer, might keep the Yankees pinned down."

Bragg's eyes flew open. He smiled. "I think I could prod General Forrest into volunteering his artillery."

"Good." Cleburne felt much better, but the feeling evaporated. "Will General Longstreet approve it?"

"We won't ask him."

This time it was Cleburne's eyes that flew open. "You're not going to tell him?"

"No."

And Bragg was good to his word. Fifteen minutes ago, two batteries from Forrest arrived and took their place at the front of the line. All that was needed was for the artillery to do its work then he would lead his men forward.

Cleburne glanced up at the sky. Yes, today was as good as any to die.

★★★

"Come in, General," Longstreet called.

Bragg entered the tent and observed Longstreet sitting at a table, a plate of half-eaten food pushed to the side. Papers were scattered around the table. Bragg wasn't sure if the papers had been thrown in a fit of rage or dropped in frustration. His eyes left the papers and came to rest on Longstreet. It looked as if the weight of the world had been shackled to the Georgian's shoulders.

"You just missed General Pemberton," Longstreet remarked. He picked up the fork and poked at the cold food. He poked and poked but never ate. He dropped the fork on the table.

"I'm sorry I did," Bragg said. He gestured toward a chair. Longstreet nodded in permission.

"General Cleburne's charge was a beautiful thing to behold," Longstreet remarked.

"It was," Bragg said. It was also deadly. The division had suffered over thirty percent casualty.

Longstreet picked up the fork. "General Cleburne has a bright future."

Bragg smiled. "Yes, he does."

Longstreet stabbed the fork in a piece of beef shiny with congealed grease. "Not at all happy with him leading the charge, though."

"I talked to him about that," Bragg chuckled, "but you know Irishmen."

"I'm more familiar with stubborn Scotch Presbyterians if you want to know the truth."

Bragg didn't know to whom Longstreet was referring. His confusion must have been written on his face, for Longstreet volunteered, "Jackson! His reckless use of his corps risked the army on more than one occasion."

"Sir, what's next?" Bragg asked, steering the conversation back to practical matters.

"Next?" Longstreet asked, perplexed at the question. He jerked the fork from the beef.

"Yes, sir."

"We attack!" He flourished the fork.

Bragg grimaced. "Sir, I don't know what General Pemberton told you, but my men were firmly rebuffed at great cost."

"Cleburne broke through."

"He did, but was unable to hold his gains. I doubt we can use the same strategy tomorrow."

The fork banged to the table. "Well, perhaps we should entrench and wait for Grant to attack us."

Bragg stared at Longstreet in disbelief. Was the Georgian serious?

"Lincoln can't have us in Kentucky, any more than he can have Lee in Pennsylvania," Longstreet said. "That's why he sent a decimated Army of the Potomac to turn Lee back. He'll order Grant to attack us. The only other option is to retreat."

"That's not our only option," Bragg said. "We can swing east and unite with Lee."

Longstreet frowned. "Lee would never agree to serve under my command."

If Bragg's heart had been tied to a blacksmith's anvil, it couldn't have dropped to the ground any faster than it did. Why in the name of all that was good would Longstreet expect Lee to serve under him? Bragg hoped his face did not give away his disbelief.

"What do you suggest we do?" Longstreet asked.

"Go east."

"Not an option!" Longstreet barked. He yanked the fork from the table and forcefully re-stabbed the meat.

"Then we retreat."

Longstreet glared at Bragg. "You don't think this army can beat the Yankees."

Bragg choked back the angry words he wanted to fling at the man seated opposite him. "Tomorrow?" He snapped. "Do we attack?"

"No. We wait."

Bragg stood. "If there's nothing else."

"No, you're dismissed.

Angry strides took Bragg from the tent.

Chapter Nine

Grant's Headquarters
Florence, Kentucky
July 5, 1863

There was no breeze. The white lace curtains in the wide windows stood motionless. Grant sat at his desk, trying to ignore the heat. A large pile of overdue paperwork demanded his attention, but it was too hot to concentrate on paperwork. It was too hot to do anything but to drink cold lemonade and smoke cigars in the shade.

Footsteps in the hall; voices; a sharp rap on the door. Before Grant could acknowledge the knock, the door flew open and bounced hard against the wall. The curtains swayed briefly. Major General William Tecumseh Sherman stood in the doorway.

"Grant!" Sherman hailed.

"It's about time you got here," Grant rebuked with a laugh.

Sherman threw his hat on the couch and collapsed in a chair in front of the desk. Sweat plastered red hair on his forehead. "You weren't waiting on me before driving the Rebs from Kentucky, were you?"

"Oh, it's too hot for that sort of nonsense," Grant said with a straight face, though his eyes gave away the jest.

Sherman leaned forward, his elbows on his knees. "Seriously Grant, what's going on? Why are you just sitting here?"

Grant turned somber. "The Army of the Potomac has been defeated in Pennsylvania."

"So? Lee has made a fine career out of defeating the Army of the Potomac. The war will be won here in the West. So, let's get about winning it." He made a sweeping gesture toward the door.

Grant refused the invitation. Instead, he reached into the desk's drawer and withdrew a telegram. He passed it over to Sherman. "It's from Lincoln. He has ordered me east to take command of the armies."

Sherman read the slip of paper and handed it back. "Why would you want to do a fool thing like that? Nothing in Washington but politicians. They won't let you win the war. It gets in the way of their power. And I know of which I speak. My brother's the distinguished senator from Ohio."

"Didn't your brother get you your commission?" Grant teased.

Sherman folded his arm across his chest. "You're just making my point for me. Now wire the president and tell him that you can better serve the war effort here."

Grant reached into the ever present humidor and plucked out a cigar. "You're right when you say that the war will be won here. But as long as Lincoln is unable to find a general that can lick Lee, our victories will slowly be stolen from us. I can't let that happen."

Sherman rose and crossed to the window. "The older I get, the more I suffer from the heat. What I wouldn't give to be back on the river. At least there was a cool breeze." He turned and faced the desk. "My advice is for you to stay put."

Grant pointed to the telegram. "I don't think I have that option."

"I'll miss you." Sherman choked on his words.

"Well, don't get all sentimental on me," Grant said, surprised by Sherman's confession.

Sherman waved his hand. "I'm over it." He smiled.

"If you had command of the Western Theater, what would you do?" Grant asked.

"I'd take Atlanta by summer's end."

"That's exactly what I want you to do."

Sherman returned to his chair. "Are you sure? About giving me command? I do have a reputation for being crazy."

Grant tapped his cigar against the edge of a crystal ashtray. The gray ash tumbled in. "And I have a reputation for being a drunk. We make quite the pair." Grant smiled. "But we'll win this war. And a grateful nation will erect statues to us." He paused and waited for a reaction, but Sherman just looked stricken. "Big ones." He raised his arm over his head.

Sherman finally laughed. "When are you leaving?"

"Now that you're here, tonight."

"So soon!" Sherman exclaimed. "I thought you'd want to do something about the Rebs first."

"Consider them a parting gift from me." Grant snubbed out the cigar in the ashtray. "I'm sure you'll know what to do."

Sherman put his fingertips together. "What are your feelings about General Thomas? Is he the right man for the Army of the Cumberland?"

"I believe so." Grant picked up the telegram and fanned himself. "I would put General McPherson in command of the Army of the Tennessee."

Sherman's handkerchief made an appearance. He wiped his forehead. "I was thinking of keeping command."

Grant dropped the telegram on the desk. He raided the humidor and grabbed another cigar. "You can do what you want, of course."

Sherman gave him a sharp look. "But... finish your thought, Grant."

"Commanding the department will be stressful enough without having to command the army as well." Grant lit the cigar.

"You did it."

"For less than a month." He shook the match until it went out. "Besides I just was waiting for you to arrive so I could give you the army." Grant puffed on the cigar. "McPherson is a good man. I wish I could take him with me, but I think you need him more than me. Don't be afraid to use him as a sounding board. His advice and friendship is solid. So is his loyalty."

Sherman's answer was quick. "You're right. McPherson will be fine."

"Only if you're sure," Grant said, feeling as if he influenced Sherman's decision.

"I'm sure."

The door opened. Colonel Rawlins stuck his head into the room. "Good Afternoon, General Sherman."

Sherman gave the adjutant a wave of greeting.

"Cook wanted me to tell you that lunch is ready," Rawlins said to Grant.

"Are you hungry?" Grant asked Sherman.

"You know I can't eat on the transports," Sherman laughed.

Grant stood. "Good. Let's get out of this oven."

Longstreet's Extreme Left Flank
Near Big Bone Creek
July 7, 1863 – Morning

Colonel Isham Garrott stood in the shade of a huge elm. He was grateful for the shade. The sun had just come up, but the morning already held the promise of unbearable heat and humidity. Just like yesterday and the day before that.

For five days the two armies had stared at each other across the expanse that separated them. Stared and stared and stared until the men were tired of staring and began a litany of complaints all stemming from boredom. Garrott had sent word to General Tracy, who then sent word to General Stevenson. Stevenson passed the message up the chain of command to General Stephen D. Lee. Nothing came of it. The order remained the same. Be watchful! Be ready!

Be ready for what? More staring? More waiting? What was wrong with this Longstreet? Why didn't he attack, or if he wasn't going to attack, why wasn't the army marching to Pennsylvania? It made no sense. But what did he know? He just commanded the 20th Alabama in the Third Brigade of Stevenson's Division in the Army of Mississippi.

The men were slowly waking. Soon, the breeze would carry the aroma of coffee and bacon. At the thought of food, Garrott's stomach growled. Every morning and evening, he was always surprised how hungry he got staring.

He could hear the pickets returning from their post, which was about fifty yards from his position. In the thick underbrush, those fifty yards might as well have been five hundred for all he could see. Sergeant Wilson peeled off from the group of men and headed his way.

"Well?" Garrott asked.

"Can't really see anything." Wilson rubbed his hand over his bearded face. "But I think the noise has picked up."

Garrott fixed a reproving stare upon the sergeant. "You think?"

Wilson shifted from foot to foot. "Well, Colonel, it's hard to tell through all them trees and with the sound bouncin' around the woods. All I know is that the Yankees are gettin' louder."

Garrott dismissed the sergeant. He raised his glasses and peered into the woods in front of him. He saw nothing but elm and pine saplings. There was movement to his right. He lowered the glasses. It was Lieutenant Gentry.

"Gentry," he snapped, "shouldn't your men be on the line?"

Gentry took out his watch. "Still got five minutes."

"Wilson's already back. Get your men in position."

Gentry nodded and shouted to a clump of men standing around a fire. Tin cups were drained and rifles picked up. With a nod at Gentry, the men disappeared into the underbrush.

"Wilson reports that the Yankees are getting louder," Garrott informed the lieutenant.

"Louder?"

"Just be on guard. I doubt this staring contest will continue much longer. If we don't make a move soon, the Yankees will."

"Yes, sir." Gentry followed his men into the underbrush.

Garrott fished a small notebook from his pocket, along with an accompanying pencil. He opened the notebook to a blank page and stared at it until he could think of words to convey the fact that the Yankees were getting louder.

The woods crackled with gunfire. The days of stand-off had come to an end. Garrott raised his glasses and peered into the woods. He saw nothing. His men scrambled toward the fortifications of brush and logs.

The gunfire ceased. For a brief moment all was quiet, like the calm before the storm. Then the woods were filled with the sounds of jangling swords and marching boots. Gentry and a dozen men emerged from the woods. They sprinted toward the breastworks and gladly accepted hands that hauled them to safety.

Gentry reported to Garrott. He leaned over, his sides heaving. Garrott waited impatiently while the lieutenant caught his breath.

Gentry stood and wiped sweat from his upper lip. "Sir, Yankees..."

Garrott knew that much. "How many?"

"Corps strength."

Garrott raised his glasses. He couldn't see anything but the same elm and pine saplings. "Are you sure?"

"We didn't stick around to get an exact count, but yeah, I'm sure."

"Okay." Garrott dismissed the lieutenant and called for a courier. His message to General Tracy was succinct. "Come quickly. We're being turned."

★ ★ ★

Forrest jumped from the saddle and stumbled forward. He fell behind a split wood fence. Three bullets slammed into the wood plank above his head. A bullet hit the ground next to his knee. He rolled to the right. Beside him, a trooper fell wounded into the dust. Forrest called for a medic then returned fire into the Yankee trooper running toward him. Forrest reloaded. Right now his men faced Yankee cavalry, but he expected Union infantry to arrive any time.

In this morning's attack, the Yankees had pushed aside Pemberton's left flank as easily as one swats away a fly. Forrest and his men had been on their way to the damaged flank when Bragg had stopped him.

Bragg gestured toward a cloud of dust rapidly moving south. "See that."

"I'd have to blind not to," Forrest snapped.

"General Lee has reported that Yankee cavalry is headed toward Lexington. I need you to stop them."

"General Longstreet ordered me to the left flank."

"Let me take care of that," Bragg replied. "Just get south as fast as possible."

"General Longstreet…"

Bragg interrupted with an angry wave of his hand. "General Longstreet isn't aware of this threat. By time we get new orders, the race will be lost and our retreat will be cut off. So, go!"

"We're retreatin'?" Forrest huffed in exasperation.

"Our flank is broken and the men routed. So, yes we're retreating," Bragg barked.

Disappointment slashed at Forrest's heart. He had expected Longstreet to put some fight his generals, but Bragg was the same old coward. Forrest jammed his spurs in his horse's rib and raced off.

He sent Major Kelley to fetch Morgan, which turned out to be fortuitous because one of Morgan's men had grown up in the area and knew a short-cut. Forrest's men poured out onto the main road to Lexington in front of the Yankees.

For three hours, in the heat and dust, Forrest battled for control of the road, but in the late afternoon, a brigade of Union infantry arrived and took its place on the line.

Morgan dropped down beside him. "Forrest, we can't stay here," he declared over the raging battle. "We're being flanked."

"Is the way east still open?" Forrest asked.

"It won't be open much longer. We've got to go or we'll be cutoff."

Forrest hated running away. Despised it more than anything. But if he stayed pinned behind this fence, he and his men would be slaughtered. "Bring up the horses. Let's get out of here."

★ ★ ★

In the last twelve hours, Sherman had experienced both the highs and lows of command. The highs began when the Seventeenth Corps burst upon the Rebs' left flank. Though his men had surprised the Rebs, the Confederates had fought tenaciously, which stalled his assault. McPherson threw Logan's division into the fray and finally brushed the Rebs aside.

The rest of the Confederate left rolled up like a window shade. The Fifteenth Corps, under the temporary command of Frank Blair, forced its way through and chased the Rebs for more than a mile. Sherman had two corps in the rear of the Reb army. Blair put Thayer's Ohioans on the road to help Stanley hold Lexington until more men could be freed up and sent south.

But success had come at a great price. Men were out of division, out of brigade, and out of position. The loss of cohesion stopped the army's forward momentum. On the verge of victory, everything had come to a screeching halt. Sherman could only fume at his corps commander as they worked to untangle the lines. The Confederates, no more than 100 yards away when the attack began, vanished into thin air.

Sherman sent orders for Stanley to return, but in the hours it took the message to reach the cavalry leader and for Stanley to return, Forrest had set an impenetrable screen that Stanley couldn't pierce. Sherman's victory had been nullified. All that was left was the nagging fear that Longstreet had escaped due to some inadequacy in his plan.

Exasperated, Sherman wadded up his notes and threw them on a small pile of wadded up paper at his feet. He took a deep breath and cleared his mind. He leafed through the stack of maps on his desk until he found the one he wanted. He sketched out the Rebs' last known position then began to plot their most likely routes of retreat.

"May I sit?'

Sherman glanced up and saw McPherson standing in front of him. He gestured to a near-by chair.

"We finally got the men sorted out. We're ready to go," McPherson said.

"Forrest is keeping Stanley at bay so I can't get any information." Sherman slid the maps away from him in anger.

McPherson caught the maps before they fell to the ground. "Do you think the Rebs are trying to cross the river?" McPherson straightened the maps and placed them on the desk.

"I don't know," Sherman barked out, his voice high and reedy. He stood up so fast that his chair fell backward on the ground. He began to pace.

"What does Thomas report?

Sherman rooted through the maps until he found a slip of paper. He thrust it at McPherson, who read it quickly.

"Okay," McPherson said slowly. "Thomas says the roads north are empty. Isn't that good news?"

McPherson's calm demeanor angered Sherman. He snatched the paper from McPherson's hand. "I don't know where the Rebs are!" He angrily waved Thomas' message. "So how is this good news?"

"I don't think it's important where the Rebs are. What's important is where you want to go."

Sherman picked up his chair and sat down. He took a deep breath and waited until his anger subsided. "I promised Grant that I would be in Atlanta by the end of summer."

"Then let's go to Atlanta."

"But…"

McPherson held up his hand. "Can I give you some advice?"

Sherman was about to bark no, but he bit his tongue. Grant had counseled him to trust McPherson. He nodded in permission.

"You can fret and worry about where the Rebs are, or you can move this army south and make Longstreet chase you for a while."

McPherson's counsel was sound. All of Sherman's pent-up anxiety flowed away. "Thank you," he whispered.

McPherson grinned. "Now, General, what should I tell the men."

Sherman folded the top map on the pile. "Get them on the road. South."

Chapter Ten

Knoxville, Tennessee
August, 1863

General Frank Blair paced anxiously behind his lines waiting for the signal that would launch the assault against the Confederate center. All around him was the frantic yet orchestrated actions of an army preparing for imminent battle. He took it all in from the rarified air of command. As Sherman had chased the Rebs from Kentucky, Blair had received word that he had been promoted to major general and given permanent command of the Fifteenth Corps.

He knew his enemies in Washington and Jefferson City would snipe that he had earned this promotion, not by his performance in the field, but because of politics. After all, he was a Missouri congressman commissioned by Lincoln in hopes of entreating Missouri to remain in the Union.

Those same critics also railed against Lincoln's decision to include a Blair, his brother Montgomery, in the Cabinet. Monty was the Postmaster General, an insignificant post when compared to William Seward who was Secretary of State or Edwin Stanton who served as Secretary of War. But from that insignificant post, Blair influenced war policy, a fact that did not sit well with enemies of the Blair family.

Politics had been like mother's milk to Blair. His father, Francis, the patriarch of the boisterous and bellicose family, had played his role before the war, serving as Lincoln's emissary to Colonel Robert E. Lee. In Lincoln's name, Blair, Sr. had offered Lee command of the Union forces, which Lee declined. With his home, Arlington House, visible from the Capital and his family scattered throughout the Virginia countryside, Lee stated that he couldn't command an invading army against his loved ones or his state.

Despite the patriotic passions boiling in his blood, the pacing Blair didn't blame Lee for his decision. For many soldiers on the opposite side of the battlefield, the decision to fight was based on the same premise. Whether it was Virginia, Tennessee, Pennsylvania, where Lee's army was now, or Missouri, for the soldier, the defense of home was at the heart of the matter. This momentary empathy didn't lessen Blair's conviction to see the Confederacy reduced to dust.

When Sherman arrived at Knoxville less than a month ago, he found the Rebs entrenched in a loose semi-circle about five miles in front of the city. He wasted little time in throwing his army at Longstreet's right flank. The Rebs dusted back the blue troops with ease. Sherman shifted his army and attacked Longstreet's left, but Pemberton was waiting. A half-hour after the blue lines surged forward, the battle was over. A week passed before Sherman decided to attack both flanks simultaneously. Again, the entrenched Confederates held. The smell of blood overwhelmed the Union camps and the cries of the wounded rose to Heaven in a pitiful wail. In three assaults, Sherman had lost close to twenty percent of his fighting force.

Sherman switched tactics and sent Stanley across the Tennessee River to establish a beach head. Forrest's troopers met Stanley in a pitch battle that lasted from sun-up to sun-down. The result was the same. Under the cover of darkness, Stanley's whipped forces retreated across the river.

Now Sherman was determined to break the Confederate center. This morning, Blair had reconnoitered the Confederate line. The Rebs stood shoulder-to-shoulder, three deep behind thick fortifications, bristling with artillery.

Memories of Longstreet on Marye's Heights came to mind. Of course, Blair had only read accounts of the massacre in the newspapers, but Burnside had learned to his detriment not to attack Longstreet once he was dug in. Like now.

"General Blair!"

Blair turned toward the voice. In the light of the rising sun, he saw Sherman, or at least Sherman's silhouette, peering down at him from horseback. The mare moved restlessly. Sherman soothed her with a gentle pat on the neck. "General Sherman," Blair returned.

The soldiers gave a cheer. Sherman raised his hand and the men quieted. "Are you men going to take the battle to the Rebs?" Sherman asked. His high-pitched voice could only be described as squeaky.

Blair smiled. Sherman had always been a nervous fellow. Even when he was a banker in St. Louis. It was just his way. But in assuming Grant's command, Sherman's nervousness had seemed to multiply tenfold. It was in his voice, in the restless way his hands moved along the reins, the expression in his face.

Where it wasn't was in his orders. He might have been turned back four times, but he still believed he could lick the Rebs. And because he believed it, the men did to. Sherman was headed to Atlanta, and the army would follow him there barefoot and blindfolded.

"Just let us at them!" The men replied.

Sherman laughed. A high-pitch laugh. "You'll get your chance. Now, I want you boys to obey General Blair as quick as you obeyed me. He's a good man."

"Yes, sir." They saluted sloppily. "When will we be going?"

"Soon enough." With a quick gesture of his hand, he dismissed them. They melted away like butter in a hot frying pan.

"General Blair, I expect the signal to be sounded within the next hour. I'm just waiting for General Schofield to get his men into place."

"Do you think it's wise to place such green men in the center of the line?" Blair asked. "General Schofield's men only arrived from the recruiting camps last week."

Sherman gave him a piercing stare. "What are you saying?"

It would take more than Sherman's stare to rattle him. "This is their first battle. We don't know if they'll turn tail and run back to Ohio."

Sherman didn't care for the response. "Schofield says they're ready. I trust his judgment."

"Sir, I think General Schofield has impeccable judgment," Blair parried.

"So, what's the problem?" Sherman's voice began to rise.

"It's not a problem, but I would be re-missed if I didn't bring my concerns to your attention," Blair said with the same voice he used on the floor of the House of Representatives to woe opponents to his point of view.

"Don't you politic me," Sherman snapped, pointing his finger at Blair. "I've got a brother who's a senator. So I know when I being politicked."

Blair smothered a smile. "I'm not trying to politic you," he declared, even though he was.

"Good!" Sherman declared. "I hate politicians. Except for my brother. And the president. I like the president. He's a good, decent fellow."

"How do you feel about the postmaster general?" Blair quizzed.

The question stymied Sherman for a moment. Then suddenly he burst into laughter. "I'll make an exception for the postmaster general."

"So as politicians go, we like one senator from Ohio, the president, and the postmaster general."

The piercing glare returned. "You forgot a certain congressman from Missouri!"

"Sir, I'm a major general in the United States Army and in command of the finest corps this nation has ever produced."

"You've got that right!" A particularly dirty private shot back.

This time Sherman's glare was fixed on the private, who stood nearby. "Are you eavesdropping on a conversation between generals?"

The private refused to be intimidated. "No, sir. Not eavesdropping. But my ears can't help it if the generals' voices fill them, can they?"

With a laugh, Sherman waved his hand in dismissal.

The private walked away, but Blair watched as he joined a small group of men and recounted the exchange. The men burst into laugher and showered Sherman with affectionate glances.

Sherman never saw them. He had returned to the business of war. "When the signal is given, just get up their fast, okay, Frank. We need to overwhelm and drive the Rebs back before they can react. Keep pushing until they break."

"Schofield?" Blair queried.

Another glare. "You just worry about your assignment." Sherman wheeled his mare and headed into the sunlight.

The morning's quiet was broken by the sharp bark of a ten pound parrot gun. Blair gave the order and watched his corps quickly recede from view. Confederate artillery rained down on his troops like fire and brimstone. Blair hated the devastation shells wrecked upon the men. In an instance, soldiers were cut to pieces. Men with bloody stumps stood bewildered on the battlefield unable to process their sudden reversal of fortune. Blood poured from wounds like water from a spigot. In the dirt below streams of blood began to form.

Union artillery opened up, drowning out the cries of the wounded, the sound of battle, even his own thoughts. The cannon kept up their thundering until Blair thought he was going to go mad.

The barrage stopped. His ears rang in protest. Up ahead, his men continued to advance over a carpet of the dead.

His men hit the Confederate line like a tidal wave. Flabbergasted, Blair could only watch as the wave crashed helplessly against the gray lines. The Rebs didn't budge. The Confederate line belched fire and lead, obscuring the fight in a shroud of gun smoke. Only the regimental flags were visible, but they wouldn't remain so much longer. All Blair could do now was wait.

"Here they come!" Cleburne shouted.

Tin cups hit the ground like rain drops. The men grabbed their rifles and sprinted to the line. Artillery shook the ground. The cups bounced up and down.

A Union shell crashed into the brick factory directly behind Cleburne. He hit the ground as brick splinters and glass shards showered him. A few cut through his uniform jacket. He was preparing to stand when another shell slammed into the factory's remains. Cleburne covered his head with his arms and waited for the dust to clear.

He stood and watched the factory burn. It had stood for seventy-five years and, according to the sign that now lay at his feet, had represented the hard work of at least three generations of the Cole family. But it only took seconds for all that hard work to be obliterated.

When Cleburne first entered Knoxville, the town's citizens greeted the dusty, ragged army that followed in his wake with cheers and buckets of cold water. But not everyone. The next morning, in a heavy downpour, the first wave of refugees departed the city; all their worldly possessions jammed in covered wagons. But it was only a trickle.

The trickle increased when the Yankees arrived, but for the most part, the townsfolk stayed put, safe behind the miles of earthworks thrown up the by the army. Then came the shelling. The Yankees unlimbered their heavy guns and unleashed volley after volley. Shot slammed into homes, churches, and stores. Within hours, the streets were filled with panic.

People fled, hurly-burly, without thought and certainly without plan. Stores sold out of dry-goods and other stock within minutes. Owners boarded up their stores and followed the human torrent escaping south to Chattanooga. The few hearty souls who stayed only remained until Union cavalry raided across the river. Forrest beat them like a rug on a line, but it was enough to seal the fate of the city. By sunset, the city was empty.

The factory's roof caved in with a loud crash and scattered burning embers everywhere. Cleburne's heart panged him. It was only a matter of hours before the surrounding area would be on fire: stately mansions with broad porches and towering shade trees all destroyed by the fires of war. Cleburne was glad the citizens could not see their beloved city, smoldering, burning, dying.

Hardee rode up, trailed by a long line of staff. He dismounted and joined Cleburne. "How are the men, General Cleburne?" He raised his fieldglasses and made a careful survey of the line.

Cleburne didn't know why Hardee bothered. The line was shrouded in smoke. "They'll hold."

Hardee lowered the glasses and gave him a hash look. "What's wrong?"

"Nothing."

"Then why do you sound displeased?"

"Do I?" Cleburne asked, surprised that Hardee so accurately discerned his mood.

"Yes, you do!" Hardee rebuked.

Cleburne waved his hand toward the line. "My men cannot be moved from this position. This is nothing more than a slaughter; a waste of life." He waved his hand toward the burning factory. "And property."

The gun fire was slacking. The Yankees must be retreating for Cleburne knew his men had enough ammunition to last the morning.

Hardee put his hand on his hips. "We didn't ask to be invaded," he barked.

"I know." Cleburne was conciliatory.

"And if we kill every last one of them, then perhaps they will finally let us go." Hardee stowed his glasses, remounted, and rode away, his aides trailing after him.

Chapter Eleven

Longstreet's Headquarters
August 15, 1863

"**A**re you sure?" Longstreet asked sharply.

John Hunt Morgan nodded. "Yes, sir. My scouts returned an hour ago from the Yankees' right flank. It's empty. Only thing left were empty cracker boxes."

"Do you know where they went?" Longstreet barked. He shouldn't have had to ask the question.

"No, sir," Morgan informed him. "I've men behind the enemy's line searching for them now."

Longstreet could only stare dumfounded at the cavalry leader. Somewhere in Tennessee, the Army of the Cumberland was on the move, and Morgan didn't have a clue where.

"Major Sorrel!" He thundered.

The office door swung open and Moxley Sorrel stood in the doorway. He was in his shirt sleeves and munching an apple. "Yes, sir."

"I need to see General Bragg right now."

Sorrel nodded. Before the door closed shut, Longstreet saw his chief-of-staff throw the half-eaten apple in the waste can and grab his jacket.

"Now, General Morgan," Longstreet said with more patience than he felt, "how is it that you lost the Yankees?"

Morgan swelled up like bullfrog. "I didn't lose anyone, sir. And I resent you saying so. This morning, General Cumming sent word that the trenches in front of his brigade were empty. I sent my men to check it out. They were empty and had been so for a while judging by the state of the campfires."

Longstreet reached down, plucked up a piece of paper, and folded it in half. What were the Yankees up to? He folded the paper

85

in half again. Where had they gone? The paper received another fold. Where they getting ready to hit his left? How long would it take to get Pemberton on the move? He forced the paper into another fold.

Morgan shifted impatiently.

"Where's General Forrest?" Longstreet asked.

"Yankee cavalry crossed the river early this morning. He's giving chase."

Longstreet wadded up the paper. He didn't like the sound of that. "General Morgan, I need to hear the moment you find the Yankees."

Morgan nodded and left the room. He slammed the door shut in a not so subtle protest of his rough treatment.

Longstreet crossed to the window and looked out. An ambulance rumbled down the street, creating a small dust storm, but Bragg was nowhere in sight.

He returned to his desk and scratched out an order to Pemberton to be prepared to move the moment Morgan found the Yankees. "Captain Goree!" He shouted.

The door opened and the Texan stuck his head into the room. "You called for me?"

"Take this to General Pemberton." He held out the order.

Goree slipped into the office, took the paper, and left as quickly as he entered.

Longstreet unfolded a map of a Knoxville and the surrounding area. Where were the Yankees headed?

Information came quickly, most of it jumbled and contradictory. Bragg was the first to arrive. He informed Longstreet that the Yankees were still in his front and, no, they didn't appear to be going anywhere. Word came from Forrest that he was skirmishing with

Stanley near Kingsley Station. The fighting was fierce, but he was holding his own.

A dusty courier arrived from Morgan with mixed news. His men had finally run into the enemy but were unable to probe any further due to stiff resistance from the Yankees. Longstreet ordered Morgan to Kinglsey Station to reinforce Forrest.

Around sundown, Hardee informed Bragg that the Yankees were beginning to move out. Did Hardee know where? Hardee's reply was less than helpful. He couldn't tell in the gathering darkness.

"Well?" Longstreet asked Bragg. "Do you think the Yankees are retreating?"

Bragg had a bad habit of snorting through his nose whenever he thought a comment was especially obtuse. He did so now and it drove Longstreet mad with anger. "You don't think the Yankees would retreat?"

"Why don't we bring in General Pemberton and quiz him on General Grant's penchant for retreating."

Longstreet exhaled in anger. "In case you haven't noticed, we aren't facing Grant.

"Yes, General, I am well aware that." Bragg pushed his water glass across the desk with such force that water sloshed out the top and soaked a pile of maps. "Sherman is Grant's protégé, and he's as pugnacious and stubborn as Grant. Pemberton will be able to tell you that as well. Sherman's hatred of us is well documented throughout Mississippi. He isn't retreating."

The door banged open. Forrest barged into the room. "The Yankees are crossin' the Tennessee River near Louden. Wheeler found 'em about two hours ago."

Longstreet's breath left in a rush. The Yankees had stolen a march on him! He should have realized the truth this morning when Morgan brought word of the empty trenches. More proof came in Stanley's sudden desire to fight. He had dithered and hesitated and now he had most of the Union Army in his rear and thirty miles down the road to Chattanooga. If Sherman should arrive at the mountain passes in northern Georgia before him…

Bragg interrupted his musing. "Pemberton should get underway."

Since his throat was in vise, Longstreet wrote up the order and sent it to Pemberton via Sorrel.

"General Forrest, can your men ride tonight?" Again it was Bragg asking the right question.

With great reluctance, Forrest shook his head. "We've been fightin' all day. The horses are jaded and the men are exhausted."

Longstreet found his voice. "When will you be able to do so?"

"Tomorrow mornin'. I'll get under way as soon as practicable."

Bragg gave Longstreet a pointed look. "We need to slow the Yankees down. Wouldn't it be prudent to send Forrest behind the Union lines and cut the railroad? Make Sherman waste time protecting his supply line."

Even though he was exhausted, Forrest's eyes gleamed at the promise of battle.

"Can you do it with just your brigade and Morgan's?" Longstreet questioned. "I'll need Wheeler out in the front of the main body."

"Of course I can," Forrest snapped.

"When I left my lines this afternoon, both Polk and Hardee had a considerable force before them. There's no way the Yankees will clear the river before dawn. We need to attack the remaining troops. The Yankees will have to re-cross the river to stop us from getting in their rear," Bragg volunteered.

Longstreet leaned back and stroked his beard. "Get Hardee underway as well. Let Polk roll up the flank."

"Who's gonna make sure Polk obeys his orders?" Forrest demanded.

"General Bragg will," Longstreet assured Forest, who made an unpleasant face. "Don't worry. I've had a conversation with General Polk. We've come to an understanding."

The unpleasant face remained.

Longstreet turned to Bragg. "If General Polk refuses any order, relieve him of command and place him under arrest."

"Yes, sir," Bragg said.

"General Forrest, go get some rest," Longstreet said.

Without another word, Forrest departed the room.

Bragg stood. "Do you need anything else from me?"

"No. Don't take any unnecessary chances. We're only trying to slow the Yankees down, not defeat them. I'll be with Pemberton if you need me."

25 Miles North of
Cleveland, Tennessee

Sherman rode down the dusty road alone, his aides trailing a good twenty yards behind him. He thought them a cowardly bunch. They would rather choke on the dust kicked up by his mare then risk his bad temper.

The march had been easy to steal. The bulk of the Union army had already been on the move for hours before word came from his pickets that they had been spotted by Reb cavalry. By then, most of the army was already across the river, and Thomas had been on the road to Philadelphia for the better part of a day. Only Washburn's division was left in the trenches to guard the rear of the advancing column.

Then yesterday morning, Polk's Corps launched a surprise attack and quickly overran Washburn's position. Washburn ran back toward the pontoon bridges with Polk in hot pursuit. Sherman had no choice but to order Blair to re-cross the river and drive the Rebs back. As Blair's troops poured over the pontoon bridges, the Rebs retreated. But the damage was done. Sherman's quick march had been effectively slowed.

His scouts reported Pemberton's army was practically galloping down the road to Maryville. The race was on. The finish line was Chattanooga and Sherman wasn't about to lose. Last night, just when he thought the worse was behind him, more bad news arrived. Forrest had cut the Union supply line to the west.

The army tramped down roads packed with refugees. Eastern Tennessee might be pro-Union, but the sight of long blue columns sent people fleeing from farms and cities. The roads were crammed with wagons, buggies, and other vehicles, a virtual blockade that dammed up his army. Sherman sent troops to clear a path, but his men could only keep the roads clear for about a mile before the refugees reclaimed them. Sherman passed miles of broken down wagons, desperate women cowering at the sight of his men, and hundreds of children dressed in rags, begging for a scrap of food.

The few soldiers and exhausted refugees sharing the road suddenly scattered. Sherman saw Stanley and his aides riding toward him. The cavalry leader drew up and saluted.

"Well?" Sherman barked.

"Wheeler holds Cleveland," Stanley reported.

"Just cavalry?" Sherman asked impatiently. If it was just cavalry, he could send a brigade of infantry to chase them out.

Stanley nodded. Relief washed over Sherman. He started to smile when the look on Stanley's face stopped him. "What now?" He barked.

"We pressed on to Chattanooga. Lee's there and digging in."

Stanley's word made it official. He had lost the race. If he wanted Chattanooga, he would have to lay siege to it. And if siege is what the fates had in store for him, then the first thing he needed to do was drive Forrest from the railroad. Without supplies, Sherman couldn't besiege a village let alone a major city.

"General Stanley, Forrest is a thorn in our side. We can't let him keep cutting our supply lines with impunity," Sherman said.

Stanley reached over and patted his mare on the neck. "I'll keep our supply lines secure," he said with quiet conviction.

"You won't have to do it alone. I'll give you help."

Stanley nodded.

"Go get some rest. Tomorrow, chase Forrest out of Tennessee."

"Yes, sir." Stanley saluted again and rode past Sherman toward the rear and sleep.

"Captain Dayton," Sherman called. The captain rode forward. "Order a halt and send the wagons out. Tell them not to come back until they have food."

"Yes, sir," Dayton replied. He spurred his horse and rode off after Stanley.

Siege! Sherman shoved the thought from his mind. Instead, he focused on more positive thoughts. On the other side of Chattanooga was the mountain passes leading to Atlanta. And he would ride through those passes, capture Atlanta, and win this war.

Chapter Twelve

Union trenches
October 28, 1863

T he last time Sheridan saw blue skies, white clouds, and sunshine had been four long days ago. Since then, it had been one steady downpour. His boots were rotting from the constant soaking, and every pair of socks he owned was wet. His India rubber coat no longer kept the rain out. His wool jacket was heavy with water. There were no cook fires, so that meant no coffee or hot food. He was eating hardtack, but without coffee to soak the hardtack in – to soften it and to force out the weevils that made their homes in the government's idea of food – he was eating less and less as the days dragged by. Even his tent didn't bring respite. The tent floor was a sea of mud, the sides leaked, and his bedding was wet.

His men had been forced to eat the disgusting hardtack because Forrest had conducted yet another raid on the railroad at their back, stealing supplies and ammunition. Sheridan's anger rapidly kindled toward Stanley, who chased Forrest all through Tennessee without ever catching him. Sherman ordered ninety-day recruits to guard the railroad and protect it from the marauding Rebels.

But if Stanley knew only how to give hopeless chase, the new recruits knew only how to march aimlessly up and down the iron tracks, always arriving a day after the trains had been spoiled. Such incompetency! Sheridan desired nothing more than to take command of the cavalry. He would certainly make quick work of Forrest.

Then Stanley stole a page from Forrest's book, rode through Alabama, and attacked the railroad at Rome. But he was thrown back by Morgan and Wheeler. Stanley reported to Sherman that he was surprised to find the Rebs waiting for him.

Sheridan sniffed in derision. Of course, Wheeler and Morgan were waiting. How could it be any other way? The countryside was a veritable hotbed of spies who reported Stanley's every move to the Rebs. Sheridan wondered if he was the only man in the army with any sense.

He brushed impatiently at the water dripping from his kepi's bill. Deep within Chattanooga, he heard a train's whistle, which made him angrier at the rain, at the commanders who refused to fight, and at the Rebs for eating so well when he was left with nothing but pest-ridden bits of rock.

He raised his face turned the heavens. The rain pelted his cheeks, stinging them. "Get me out of here!" He silently screamed to the Providence who seemed to be laughing at his fate.

Rain got in his eyes. With a curse, he removed his water soaked glove and rubbed at his eyes. He blinked and blinked until he could see again. When he could, he saw Sherman ride by with McPherson and Thomas; all with serious expressions on their faces. Something was up!

Sheridan forgot about the rain, the cold, the mud, his hunger, and his misery. Finally, something might be happening. He whipped out his fieldglasses and spied on the generals, who had dismounted and were now in a deep conversation that grew more serious with each passing moment.

Now they were gesturing! Sheridan followed the direction of the gesture. They were pointing across the river, toward Chattanooga, the Confederate line, and Atlanta.

General McCook joined the group then Schofield, McClernand, and Blair. Sheridan wished he could read lips, but if he had to guess, the generals were planning an assault. A thrill danced down his spine. As soon as the rain let up and the ground dried, they would be hitting the Rebs.

★★★

The battlefield was quiet. The cries of the wounded had died away. The sun was sinking in the west, ready to render this day of death to history. For eight hours, Sherman watched his men hit the Confederate breastworks erected in the shadow of the mountains and ridges. Never had he seen a finer assault done by a group of men. The artillery thundered, the ground shook, the rifles barked, and the lead flew.

Sherman walked the ground, littered with the remains of the valiant attack: bullets, bloody bandages, bits of blue uniforms, hats lost in the mad scramble, canteens, haversacks, a gold frame with a likeness of a woman holding a child, and a torn letter to Samuel from his wife Delia. These remnants told individual stories of valor and the greater story of men fighting to put down a rebellion and restore the Union. Selfless men, who fought and died for something greater than themselves.

Sherman reached down and picked up the gold frame. The woman didn't know it yet, but her husband wasn't coming home. He pocketed the frame. War was all hell and by his order, he had unleashed hell and killed many good men, many good husbands, and many good fathers here today.

He knew one day that he would stand before God and answer for those deaths. Would the Lord, known to be merciful, have mercy on him, who first ordered the men to assault the Confederate breastwork for country, but as the battle continued, the reasons became less about country and more about anger and frustration.

Altogether, he had ordered five assaults on the enemy's fortifications and had been amazed at the ease in which the gray troops had beaten back his men. The Rebs weren't even breaking a sweat, while his men were dying by the thousands. That had gotten his blood up. The dead in those last two assaults were on him. And whatever punishment the Lord meted out, he knew he deserved it.

Through the fading light a figure approached. It was McPherson. Sherman was glad to see a friendly face.

"Hard day," McPherson said.

"Hard day indeed," Sherman mumbled.

"The men were heroic."

Sherman touched the frame in his pocket. "They're always heroic. They make us look good."

They fell silent. In his mind's eye, Sherman saw the blue lines sweep forward, bayonets glimmering in the sunlight, flags whipping in the crisp autumn breeze, and the drums pounding the long, long roll.

Four corpsmen passed them, laboring with a stretcher. The wounded soldier clutched his stomach and moaned in agony. Sherman wanted to speak kindly to the injured man, but to stop the stretcher might consign the man to death. The corpsmen passed by and the moaning faded away.

"I received a letter from Grant on the last train," McPherson said.

Bless McPherson! Here was a topic that didn't have death and loss in it. Sherman smiled in gratitude. "How is he?"

McPherson chuckled. "Oh, he's full of the usual complaints. Washington is too crowded and the politicians are buzzing around him like mosquitoes. The president pressures him every day to march on Harrisburg. He is resistant to the idea. Doesn't think the Army of the Potomac is ready. He thinks highly of John Reynolds, though."

"Anything else?" Sherman quizzed. The last letter he received from Grant listed the same litany of complaints.

"Julia and the children have arrived. Sam says having Julia nearby is worth the hassle of having to deal with those pesky politicians. And he's invited me to Washington to spend Christmas with his family," McPherson added as an afterthought.

Sherman's practical mind thought instantly of the advantages of having politicians buzzing around McPherson like mosquitoes and asking what could they do to help the war effort in the West. "You should go."

"I'd like to, but Christmas is a long way off. We could be in Atlanta by then, and you'll need me." McPherson gave him look. "We're still going to Atlanta, right?

"Not by frontal assault that much is clear. If we're going to Atlanta, we're going to have to flank the Rebs out of position like we did at Knoxville. But those ridges," Sherman pointed at the high ridges to the south, looming up as impenetrable fortresses in the setting sun, "are going to present a major obstacle. And with winter coming on..."

"We could attack before winter," McPherson said.

Sherman shook his head. Tomorrow would be the first of November. Indian summer was fading; winter would arrive any day. The rains would turn the roads to mud and slush. Cold fronts would freeze the roads and rising temperatures would thaw them out. You couldn't move artillery and troops through half a foot of mud and sludge. He would have to wait until late April or early May before he attacked.

Six months was an eternity in this war. What would happen during that time with Lee's formidable army wintering in Harrisburg or Philadelphia? With the coal cut off? Would the cowardly politicians be satisfied with their war profits and force Lincoln to sue for peace?

His brother had written that the pressure on the president was increasing – and his failure to beat the Rebs to Chattanooga had only increased that pressure. The fate of the Union was now tied to Lincoln's determination to see the war through to the bitter end.

He reached into his pocket and produced the gold frame. "Can you get this to General McClernand? Find out which soldier it belongs to? I want to return it to his wife with a letter."

McPherson took the frame. "I'll see General McClernand tomorrow."

Chapter Thirteen

A small dusting of snow still blanketed the ground, and the sun looked like a faded seal on a graying parchment. The pine tree next to Longstreet's tent swayed in the winter wind. A puff of wind twisted the tree to the left before it spun back to the right. It was a graceful dance, and if the wind wasn't biting his cheeks and nose, Bragg would have been glad to stand and watch the pine swirl in the wind for hours. But the wind cut through his great coat like a knife, and his toes were numbing in his boots. Bragg gave a knock on the tent flap and was ordered to enter.

Inside, the tent was warm and welcoming. Bragg quickly divested of his coat and hat and handed them to a corpsman.

"Happy New Year!" Longstreet said in greeting.

"The same to you," Bragg returned. "And to you, General Pemberton."

"Come, stand next to the fire and get warm before dinner." Longstreet grabbed Bragg's elbow and guided him to the stove in the corner of the tent. "You must be frozen after that long ride."

Bragg followed meekly. When he reached the stove, he held out his hands and let the warmth thaw his fingers.

"Glass of port?" Pemberton asked. He held up a bottle.

"Port!" Bragg exclaimed. Pemberton poured tawny liquid into a glass. "Where did you get port? And the wine glasses?"

"They came in yesterday's train from Atlanta," Longstreet said. He took a cigar from a worn leather case. "That bottle is just one of many that made it past the failing Yankee blockade."

The wine became distasteful to Bragg. Medicine, bandages, rifles, ammunition, shoes, and a million other things vital to the survival of the Confederacy should be the ships' priority, not port

98

wine, silk dresses, and other luxuries that made blockade runners wealthy.

Pemberton handed the glass to Bragg, who hesitated.

"Something wrong?" Pemberton questioned.

Bragg took the glass. "I guess I'm feeling guilty. This army is in need of so many things. I hate to think that the ship holds were filled with frou-frous."

"Relax, General," Longstreet laughed, "and drink your port with a clear conscience." He lit a match and put it to the cigar. He puffed and puffed until the cigar caught fire. "Those same ships unloaded over 5,000 rifles, 10,000 pairs of shoes, and hundreds of cases of medicine. It's the first of many shipments to come. If the blockade runners want to earn some money by providing luxuries, I don't think we should begrudge them their profit."

"Five thousand rifles!"

"Made for us by the best English factories," Longstreet said.

Bragg whistled in appreciation. "And the blockade has fallen?" He sipped the port. It was a fine wine. He held out his glass for more.

Longstreet crossed to his desk and rummaged through a drawer. He pulled out a newspaper and opened it. He quickly skimmed the pages. "Here it is." He folded the paper and began to read. "The blockade, though it has not fallen as of this date, has been severely compromised by a lack of coal. The Army of Northern Virginia's campaign to damage the coal fields is beginning to reap great benefits. Two nights ago, six ships slipped into Savannah's harbor unmolested."

Bragg raised his glass. "To the Army of Northern Virginia."

Pemberton raised his. "To the Army of Northern Virginia."

Longstreet returned the paper to the drawer. "Gentlemen, if you'd like to have a seat, I believe dinner is ready."

Bragg glanced at the small table. It was set for four. "Aren't we going to wait for General Forrest?"

Longstreet shook his head and gestured to a corpsman, who quickly stripped one place setting from the table. "General Forrest decided today was a perfect day for raiding. His men lit out before sunup. By now, he should be well behind Union lines."

Pemberton took the seat to the left of Longstreet, leaving Bragg the chair closest to the door. Every time a corpsman brought in a new platter of food, the wind's tendrils gripped him.

"I think Forrest has the right idea." Longstreet plucked a biscuit from a plate and scooted the plate toward Pemberton. "He isn't giving the Yankees any relief. Plus he's only filling our coffers with blankets, uniforms, and ammunition."

Pemberton slit open a biscuit and slathered it with butter.

"May I have a biscuit, General?" Bragg asked Pemberton.

"Of course." Pemberton wiped his hands on his napkin and passed the plate to Bragg. "I'm surprised the Yankees have been so quiet of late."

With his hands free, Pemberton snatched up a bowl of potatoes. He scraped a third of them onto his plate then passed the bowl to Longstreet. In despair, Bragg watched Longstreet empty the bowl.

"Don't take silence for inactivity," Longstreet said. He stabbed his fork into a pile of meat and transferred a hearty serving to his plate. "I'm sure Sherman and his lieutenants are sitting around their tables plotting how to get at us. And what they're plotting is what we must anticipate, gentlemen."

Bragg put down his fork. The food had lost its savor. He should have known this was going to be a working dinner. He had hoped, for just one day, not to have to think about the war. He poured another glass of port.

"After the licking we gave them in October, I'm not surprised that the Yankees don't want to tangle with us again," Pemberton crowed.

Longstreet laughed with delight.

"The Yankees won't attack us again like they did in October. That smacked of desperation," Bragg said

Anger flashed in Longstreet's eyes. "Are you a soothsayer, General?"

"No, I'm not." Bragg poured a final glass of port. "But as I've said before, Sherman learned from Grant, and Grant was a master of maneuver. Sherman will try to break our flank and push by us."

"I invite them to try," Pemberton said defiantly.

Longstreet cut a piece of beef; the knife scraped on the plate. "But if they should roll up your flank, General...

"NEVER!" Pemberton insisted with a fist bang on the table.

The port in the glasses danced perilously close to the top. Bragg hurriedly picked up his wine glass just in case a precious drop should spill.

"General Pemberton, I appreciate your confidence," Longstreet said, "but we need to prepare for every contingency. I'm confident we'll beat the Yankees back. And we'll give chase when they retreat. That means pontoon bridges at the ready. Three day rations in haversacks. We leave our wagons behind and march thirty miles a day if we have to."

Bragg thought Longstreet too... what was the word he wanted... casual in his assessment of the upcoming spring campaign. There were a million things that could go wrong in a battle, not the least of them Polk and Hardee.

"No, General Lee can't win this war," Longstreet continued. "No matter how many victories he and that dour Presbyterian manage to win in Pennsylvania. No matter how many coalfields they shut down. The problem is that General Lee really doesn't understand how to successfully execute this war. I tried repeatedly to get him to adopt my strategies, but he stubbornly refused to listen."

Bragg couldn't believe that Longstreet would talk about the South's venerable general with such disrespect. Pemberton must not have believed it either because he just stared, slack-jawed, at Longstreet. "You must not like General Lee very much," Bragg said.

"I like General Lee just fine. He's a good and gracious man. It's just that both he and Jackson receive credit for victories and strategies that are not theirs."

Pemberton's jaw snapped closed. "I know General Lee, sir. He would never take credit if it rightfully belonged to another."

Longstreet pushed back his empty plate. "I didn't say he did. I said he received credit for strategies that were not his. And so has Jackson. In the government, in the newspapers, in the parlors, they are hailed as victors. Do you know who is responsible for Jackson's famous Valley campaign?"

"You?" Pemberton asked, not hiding his disbelief.

"We have dessert coming," Longstreet told the men. "I believe it is a chocolate cake, so I hope you saved room."

Pemberton stared at Bragg in amazement. Bragg could only stare back.

"Yes, me," Longstreet said, returning to the subject of Jackson's Valley campaign. "I had assumed temporary command of the Army of the Potomac, and I wrote Jackson that I would bring him reinforcements and take command of the Army of the Valley. I also informed him that only I could bring the necessary vigor to conduct such an operation. He declined, of course. He didn't want to give up his command. But he did adopt most of my strategy."

A corpsman opened the tent flap and the wind swept in.

Bragg gasped when the cold blast hit him. "Hurry up, corpsman, and shut that flap!" He hollered. The flap closed but the chill lingered. He walked over to the stove to warm up.

"I think we need some coffee," Longstreet said. He was jovial, but he was the only one.

The corpsman nodded and headed outdoors. Another burst of frigid air sent Bragg retreating closer to the stove.

"Much of Lee's success can be attributed to me. I don't say that arrogantly. It's a simple fact. My corps was instrumental for the win at Second Manassas, even though I had to practically disobey Lee's order that I take the field in order to save Jackson. At Sharpsburg, I warned Lee not to split his forces, but he did anyway. We almost lost the day, but my corps preserved our victory. The credit for Fredericksburg belongs to me alone. General Bragg, come have some cake."

Bragg had no appetite. He returned to his seat and stared at the huge piece Longstreet had plopped on his plate. His head was spinning from Longstreet's confession. Here was a general who believed all the army's success belonged solely to him. Bragg knew the danger of such thoughts. There were heroics that he, as commanding general, would never hear of but were responsible for the holding of a line or the securing of victory. Those heroics were due to the brotherhood of the men, born from the march and shared deprivation. To take credit for those things! Bragg shivered but this time not from the cold.

"I need coffee," Longstreet announced. He glared at the tent door in hopes that his declaration would produce a corpsman. It didn't. With a sigh of exasperation, he excused himself and left the tent.

"Can you believe that?" Pemberton gasped.

Bragg couldn't but he wasn't about to get in to it at Longstreet's table. Besides, he would probably get two sentences out before Longstreet returned.

Pemberton was looking at him, waiting for an answer. Bragg took a bite of cake. "General Longstreet is right. This is very good cake."

★ ★ ★

Sheridan stood outside General Thomas' tent waiting for the general, aide, or corpsman to realize he had arrived. He shivered as the wind cut through his great coat. He would wait five more minutes then he was going to barge into Thomas' tent.

An officer crossed the common area at a run. Sheridan recognized him as one of Thomas' aides. "Excuse me!" He barked. The aide came to a halt. "I'm General Sheridan. General Thomas sent for me."

The aide smiled. "Yes, General Sheridan. I'm Colonel Flynt, General Thomas' adjutant."

Sheridan frowned. "What happened to General Garfield?"

"He's a congressman now."

Well, some fellows have all the luck, Sheridan thought jealously. Instead of sitting in the frozen mud, Garfield was probably sitting in some Washington parlor being plied hot drinks by a pretty hostess. "Can General Thomas see me now?"

"Give me a moment." Flynt disappeared into the tent.

A gust a wind blew with such force that it almost knocked Sheridan over. He turned his back against the wind and swung his arms to keep warm. After a long moment, Flynt beckoned from the tent door. "General Sheridan."

Sheridan hurried into tent.

Thomas was sitting behind his desk. "Come, have a seat." Sheridan slid into a chair. "Thank you, Colonel Flynt." The adjutant exited the tent. "Cold enough for you, General?"

"I've lived through colder."

Thomas didn't reply. He searched a pile of papers until he found what he was looking for. He extracted a piece and laid it before him. "The Army of the Potomac has lost a valuable member. General Buford has passed away."

Thomas seemed to be waiting for a response, so Sherman mustered up a hasty "oh."

"His contributions to the cavalry will be missed."

It was hot in the tent. Sheridan jerked the buttons from their holes. "What's that got to do with me?"

"General Reynolds needs a new cavalry commander."

Sheridan wriggled free from his coat. "Have Sherman send him Stanley. He isn't doing us any good."

"I don't think you and I are qualified to instruct General Sherman on matters of personnel." Sheridan scowled at the rebuke. "General Halleck has recommended that you replace General Buford. Here are your orders." Thomas slid the paper over.

Sheridan smiled at the news. General Garfield wasn't the only one who would no longer be sitting in the mud. "When can I leave?"

"As soon as practicable," Thomas said.

Sheridan stood and donned his coat. "It's been a pleasure serving under your command, General Thomas."

"Thank you, General Sheridan," Thomas said with a smile. "Give General Grant my regards."

"I will." Sheridan saluted and exited the tent.

Chapter Fourteen

Chattanooga, Tennessee
Middle of May
1864

Sherman stood at the river's edge and watched his men lay pontoon bridges. A total of five slowly stretched across the gray water. The bridges were the prelude to an attack that should conclude with the Union army occupying the trenches the Rebs had called home since last summer.

He glanced up at the sky, half-believing that the brilliant blue sky would suddenly fill with menacing thunder clouds. Rain had been his personal nemesis since the end of April. That is when Mother Nature took it upon herself to thwart his plans.

On the day the attack was originally planned, he had been awakened by a loud clap of thunder. He rushed to his tent door and beheld black clouds emptying themselves of water. Sherman wasn't a believing man, but how he had prayed that the rain would end before the river rose. The more he prayed, the harder it rained. The rain kept falling until the river overflowed its banks. The flooding wasn't severe, but it delayed his attack.

Sherman didn't have time to stand around and wait until Mother Nature turned cooperative. The Union was falling apart at the seams. The riots along the Eastern Seaboard had politicians running for cover. His brother had written imploring him to push Longstreet out of the way and seize Atlanta as quickly as possible. If Lincoln was going to survive the political storm about to crash over his head, he needed victories on all fronts.

But Sherman couldn't strike, push, or chase any Reb any where because he was stuck in the mud on the wrong side of the Tennessee River. And when the rain finally stopped, he would still have a devil of a fight on his hands to dislodge Longstreet.

He took advantage of a break in the rain to ride his line. As he approached the left flank, he saw Frank Blair sitting under a fly tent, reading a book. Perhaps Frank had heard from his father or brother about the state of affairs in Washington City.

"General Blair!" Sherman dismounted and joined Frank under the canopy. Blair stood. "Sit! Sit!" Sherman insisted. Blair retook his seat. Sherman slumped in the chair next to him. "What do you hear from you brother?"

"Probably the same thing you're hearing from yours."

"John is very pessimistic about the future," he confessed.

"So is Monty. He wrote the other day that the mood in Washington is grim. Stanton's afraid Lincoln may lose the election to George McClellan in November. Since Little Mac quieted the riots, he is very popular."

Interested, Sherman bolted upright. "Has McClellan declared?"

"No."

Disappointed, Sherman slouched back in his chair. "Then what makes Stanton think he'll run."

"To be honest, Stanton sees any new arrival on the political landscape as a potential threat to his power. But my father agrees with him. McClellan's sudden appearance was calculated to embarrass Lincoln and to position himself for a presidential run."

The rain started up. They sat and listened to raindrops plink the ground and splash the many puddles in the common area.

"Will McClellan win?" Sherman asked.

"If the election was held today, yes, he would. The people are tired of the depravation of war. And if Lee manages to beat Grant..."

"Won't happen!" Sherman declared.

Frank waved his hand. "Well, let's just say for argument's sake that it does. Any loss will only increase McClellan's popularity."

The people knew nothing of depravation, Sherman thought. Let them sit in the mud for weeks on end eating hardtack and drinking bitter coffee without cream or sugar.

"Father says McClellan will sign a peace treaty with the South."

Sherman jumped to his feet and began to pace.

"But Grant won't lose to Lee," Blair declared.

Sherman whirled around and pointed a finger at Blair. "No, sir, he will not!"

But Grant did lose. The Army of the Potomac suffered a huge loss along the banks of the Susquehanna. Grant immediately marched south believing Lee would follow in order to protect his supply line, which ran through the Shenandoah Valley.

Lee broke all conventions and headed east instead. Grant had been caught out of position and had been forced to gallop across Pennsylvania to the shores of Shippack Creek near Philadelphia. Two days of hard fighting had resulted in heavy Union losses and another Confederate victory. The newspaper editors and politicians howled for Lincoln to make peace with Richmond.

Four days after Sherman's visit to Blair, the rain finally ended and the long absent sun finally shone. The blue skies were the most beautiful sight Sherman had ever beheld. There was not a cloud in the sky. The river fell rapidly. The ground hardened. Blair led his Fifteenth Corps across the pontoon bridge and against the Rebs' left flank.

Missionary Ridge
Polk's Line

Polk peered through his fieldglasses and observed blue troops amassing on his right. He had a very real fear that the Yankees were going to slide through the valley to the south of Tunnel Hill and attack him from the rear. With Forrest at the end of the valley, guarding the junction of the Nashville and Chattanooga Railroad and the Western and Atlantic Railroad, Polk should have felt safe, but he didn't.

A week ago Tuesday, the Yankees had poured over the pontoon bridges and drove the Confederates from the trenches they had held since last autumn. Since then, Polk had watched as the blue lines snaked their way toward the flanks, looking for a weakness to exploit. On Lookout Mountain, Pemberton had suffered most of the blows. It looked like today would be Bragg's turn.

Polk sent his adjutant, Major Richmond, to Longstreet for help. A careful sweep of the Confederate line revealed no reinforcements marching toward his position. He hurried a message to General Stewart to keep a sharp eye. Stewart sent back word that his skirmishers on the lower ridges of Tunnel Hill reported no Yankees in sight.

His artillery let loose a barrage at the Yankees ascending toward his center. The shells sailed over the head of the enemy and crashed somewhere below. Polk could hear his chief artillery officer hollering instructions, trying to get the cannon situated in order to stop the blue uniformed soldiers scrambling up the side of the hill.

Down below Cheatham's division fired a volley. Polk smiled as the Yankees ran back down the hill. At the bottom, they reformed and began the climb again.

Bragg rode up. Major Richmond was with him. "Where are my reinforcements?" Polk demanded the moment Bragg dismounted.

"General Longstreet's denying them for now. Pemberton is being pushed hard on Lookout Mountain. Longstreet says for you to hold on."

Polk shook his head in disgust. He whipped his fieldglasses from around his neck and thrust them into Bragg's unexpecting hands. "Look there!" He barked and pointed toward Tunnel Hill.

Bragg gave Polk a nasty stare. Without a word he handed the glasses back to the impatient Bishop. "Colonel Brent, bring me my glasses."

Brent jumped from his horse and retrieved the glasses. He bounded over and handed them to Bragg. "Thank you, Colonel." With that Brent retreated. Bragg raised the glasses and surveyed Polk's line.

Polk huffed in irritation as he waited. Cheatham's men fired again. Bragg swung his glasses toward the sound of gunfire.

"The Yankees are climbing the ridge in force. I must be allowed to pull Cheatham back to the ridge top. I need to pull Stewart back too," Polk insisted. It was ridiculous that he had to beg permission before he could do what was best for his men.

"A regiment or two hardly qualifies as in force," Bragg stated. He threaded the glasses' leather strap over his head and around his neck.

"I want..."

"We're not having this discussion," Bragg thundered. "If you withdraw at your whim..."

"Whim!" Polk was equally angry.

Bragg raised his hand. "The only one who doesn't understand what is at stake is you. Ask any private if they most hold this ground and they will say yes. You withdraw and the battle is lost."

Polk started to speak, but Bragg seized his arm. "Lay aside your ambition and do what's right for the country. Just this once."

Polk jerked Bragg's hand away. "I don't like what you're insinuating, General!"

"I am not insinuating anything. I'm saying it straight out." Bragg's face was purple with rage. "You're not to withdraw unless you have orders from General Longstreet or me to do so."

"General, is there a problem?" An alarmed Brent was staring at the two generals.

Polk glared at the aide.

"No, Colonel," Bragg said. "General Polk understands his duty." He dismissed the adjutant with a wave of his hand. "I'll have General

Forrest reinforce your line." Polk shook his head in disagreement. "It's Forrest or it's no one," Bragg snapped.

Polk seethed with hatred for the man standing before him. "Fine!" He spat out.

"I'll be with General Hardee," Bragg said. He strode back toward the gaggle of aides, covering the ground in long, angry strides. He remounted and rode away, clumps of mud flying out from horse hooves.

With a wrathful heart, Polk watched him go. He was suddenly aware of Major Richmond staring at him. Too mortified to glance in the adjutant's direction, he raised his glasses and used them to shield himself from Richmond's continued stares. The Yankees were advancing again. He saw his men fire. Dead Yankees tumbled down the mountain.

Forrest carefully threaded his way along the steep path. He pushed King Philip as fast as he dared, but roots, branches, and stones cluttered the path. His men were stretched out behind him. He heard stones plinking off the side the ridge as horses slid on the unsteady terrain. He could have chosen a less steep path, but he didn't believe he had the time. Bragg's message was as dull as the man who had authored it, but the messenger was anything but.

"If I hadn't intervened when I did, I believe the argument would have ended in a brawl," Brent had breathlessly reported.

Forrest's opinion of Bragg raised a notch or two. From time-to-time he also felt the urge to take a poke at that stodgy Bishop. He ordered his men to ascend the ridge at the first path that would lead to the top and the battle.

King Philip slipped. Forrest pulled back on the reins. "My fault, my fault," he soothed. The gelding settled down. Forrest was impatient to reach the top but knew that if he hurried the war horse, there was the very real possibility that both of them would be pitched over the side and fall to their death.

Gunshots up ahead. He pressed King Philip forward. Behind him, he could hear the line of horses speed up. Pebbles and rocks dropping down the ridge increased in sound and frequency. The sounds bounced up from the bottom until the whole south side resounded with the noise of falling rocks.

Suddenly, a waterfall of gray, butternut, and brown encased the hillside as soldiers spilled over the ridge in a mad rush to escape some unseen devil. They skidded between the trees, mostly on foot, but a few, here and there, tumbled down the hill.

Without regard for his safety, Forrest urged King Philip on. In front of him, soldiers still slid by – out of reach of his hand, but not his voice. "You, men!" He shouted.

Only a few looked his way. The rest streamed by him. One soldier tumbled sideways and came to rest a few feet in front.

Forrest jumped from the saddle and hugged the side of the hill as he skirted around King Philip. A few quick strides and he reached the fallen soldier's side.

The young man gazed up at Forrest with unfocused eyes. "Where are you men headed?" Forrest asked.

"Orders to retreat, sir." The soldier's voice was as wobbly as his eyes.

"Who gave them!"

"I don't know, sir." He shook his head. "But the whole line was ordered to retreat. So, I skedaddled out of there with the rest of my company."

"Where's your rendezvous point?"

"Rendezvous point?" The soldier warbled back.

Forrest wasn't sure if the young man's confusion came from his fall or from the use of the fancy word. "Where are ya'll are supposed to meet up?"

"Don't know of one." Forrest cursed in exasperation. "Sorry, sir. If you want to know for sure, I'd ask one of the majors or colonels."

Forrest watched the river of humanity flow down the mountain side. A brigade or two must have gone him. Above him another brigade slipped and slid down the hill.

"Can I go, sir?" The private questioned.

Forrest gave permission.

The young man rose on shaking legs. He snatched his hat from the ground, jammed it on his head, and threw himself down the hill after his friends. He went a few yards before he lost his footing. He pitched head forward and somersaulted down the mountain.

Forrest grabbed King Philip's reins. In the tight space he managed to get remounted. He had to find someone who knew what was going on.

A shower of pebbles, twigs, and sticks rained down. He threw up his arms to protect his head. The storm stopped. He opened his eyes. General Stewart stood before him on the path.

"General Forrest!" Stewart gasped in amazement

"Stewart! Turn these men around and re-climb the hill!" Forrest pointed toward the crest.

"The Yankees have taken us from the rear," Stewart answered.

"I've been climbin' this ridge for the past little bit. I ain't seen no Yankees."

Stewart stared at Forrest in shock. "General Polk…"

"Not Bragg! Not Longstreet!" Forrest interrupted.

"My orders came from Polk's aide."

"Turn your men around and git back to the fight."

Stewart rubbed his jaw. "My orders…"

"Damn your orders!" Forrest thundered. "I'm giving you new orders. If you want to keep your command, you'll turn your men around! Now!"

"I'll do my best," Stewart assured him.

"Do better than your best," Forrest snapped. "Now, clear out of the way and let my men pass."

Stewart acknowledged the order with a nod of his head. He grabbed a tree root and hauled himself back up the hillside. Once he was secure, he hollered at the men to turn around.

Forrest continued to climb. The shadows of the trees gave way to the light. A few more feet and warm sunlight bathed him. He took no time to appreciate it. All around him, chaos reigned. To his immediate left, Cleburne's men wrestled against an enemy pouring in from both the front and the flank.

"Major Kelley, have the men report to General Cleburne. Hopefully, Stewart will be able to turn our men around."

"Where are you going?" Kelley questioned

"To find out who's responsible for this catastrophe."

The responsible party was preparing to follow his men down the side of the ridge when Forrest raced up.

"General Forrest, you're too late," Polk informed him calmly. "We had to evacuate the ridge before we were over run."

Forrest threw himself off King Philip. "Who gave you orders to retreat?"

"I don't answer to you!"

Forrest reared back and slugged the Bishop.

Polk fell to the ground in a heap. He didn't stay there long. He came up, spitting blood, his lip already swelling. He wiped at his lip. "I'll have you arrested!"

"Who ordered you to move out?" Forrest asked again.

Polk covered himself with an injured air. For that, Forrest wanted to hit him again. "We're being attacked from the rear," Polk insisted.

"If you was being attacked, it weren't by no more than a regiment!"

Polk laughed. "I believe our danger was far more serious than that."

114

"You're a fool, Polk! Cleburne is tryin' to hold off half the Army of the Cumberland by hisself. I told General Stewart to gather up the men and hi-tail it back here."

"You did what?" Polk bellowed. "You had no authority…"

Forrest hauled back to show Polk some authority.

"GENERAL FORREST!"

Forrest spun around to see Longstreet, Bragg, and a multitude of aides, each looking more thunderous than the next.

"Fisticuffs never solved anything," Longstreet rebuked.

Forrest scoffed. In the right situation, fisticuffs settled many a score.

"General Polk, you're relieved of command," Longstreet said.

Forrest thought him as calm as a summer day.

"You don't have the authority to relieve me," Polk stormed.

For one celebratory moment, Forrest though Longstreet was going to take a poke at Polk. But Longstreet's better angels prevailed and Polk remained untouched.

"Colonel Sorrel, send for the provost and have him take General Polk into custody. General Bragg." Bragg turned attentive eyes on Longstreet. "We need to stop the hemorrhaging. That's our number one priority."

"Forrest, where's Wheeler?" Bragg asked.

"He's down at the bottom of the ridge makin' sure the Yankees don't flank us." Forrest threw Polk a murderous stare.

"Could he join us?" Bragg asked.

"It would take some time for his men to climb the ridge. Besides if I know Wheeler, he's probably corrallin' Polk's men before they run all the way to Atlanta."

"General Morgan?" This came from Longstreet.

"Lookout Mountain."

"So, no help from the cavalry," Bragg lamented.

Ten soldiers climbed over the ridge. A sergeant drew off his hat and cautiously approached the clutch of generals. "General Stewart said we were to return. Where do you want us?"

"How many men has Stewart rounded up?" Forrest asked.

"We're the first. But the general is doing some mighty fine hollering down on that hillside. He should be able to round up a hundred or more."

"Report to General Cleburne," Bragg said.

The small group of men ran off.

"Let's give General Stewart some help," Longstreet said. "Major Goree, you and General Bragg's aides climb down the hill and get those men back up here."

Goree, followed by a small parade of aides, slipped over the side of the mountain.

"General Forrest, how fast can that war horse go?" Longstreet asked.

"Fast enough, I reckon. Why?"

"If we can't repair the damage, you need to warn General Pemberton that he might have company on his flank."

Forrest asked about the signal post, but Longstreet replied that he didn't want to alert the Yankees to the seriousness of the situation. Forrest gathered up the reins and threw himself on King Philip. Before he started down the ridge toward the valley below, he saw Colonel Sorrel returning with the provost guard. The thought of Polk under arrest brought a smile to his face.

★★★

The long afternoon dragged on, minutes as long as hours. The Yankees established a stronghold on the right end of the ridge. Longstreet tried to reinforce Cleburne with brigades from Hardee's corps, but a well-timed assault on Hardee's line made that impossible. Cleburne was on his own. All Longstreet could do was face west and pray that Providence would be ever kind to him and sink the sun behind the ridges that stretched out before his eyes.

Cleburne bent and then bent some more but, thankfully, did not break. Forrest had said that Cleburne was a fighter. And in the heat and dust of the long afternoon, the Irishman earned that reputation. He turned the ridge into a threshing floor of death. Bayonet struck bayonet. Bodies fell pierced through. Soldiers wielded their rifle butts like clubs and beat the Yankees back. When the sun finally did slip from sight, the Confederate dead was in the thousands and the territory they held had been reduced by three-fourths.

"Well?" Longstreet asked Bragg. He raised his canteen to drink. His hand shook from fatigue.

"We need to retreat." Even though Bragg was blunt, his voice registered his disappointment. "Tomorrow morning, the Yankees will re-engage and Hardee will give way. The Yankees will take control of the Ridge and from there turn Pemberton's line."

Longstreet couldn't get the cork back in the canteen. He clutched it in his fist. "This is my fault. I knew what I had in Polk after Kentucky. I should have listened to you, but I foolishly thought the general and I had reached an understanding."

"I have much to say on the subject of Leonidas Polk, but not now." Bragg smiled compassionately. "Give me your canteen."

Longstreet handed it over. Bragg slid the cork into the opening and returned the canteen to its owner.

"General Longstreet. General Bragg." An exhausted Cleburne appeared before them. His face was streaked with sweat and dust.

"You were a lion today," Longstreet praised the Irishman.

Cleburne heaved a weary sigh. "Without reinforcements, I don't think I can hold. Can you give me any help?"

"We're retreating," Bragg informed him.

Cleburne sagged in despair. "Is that our only course of action? The men have fought so hard..." Emotion choked his voice.

"I don't like it any more than you," Longstreet replied. "But Polk's Corps is strewn from here to Ringgold Gap. We don't have the numbers."

"I'm sorry to hear that, sir." Cleburne's voice was no more than a whisper. "What are your orders?"

"I'm afraid your day isn't over," Longstreet said. He watched Cleburne stiffen his spine and his admiration for the division commander increased tenfold. "General Polk has been relieved. I need you to take command of the corps. Get yourself down the hill, help Wheeler gather up your men, and take command at Ringgold Gap. The rest of the army will be along directly."

"My wounded?"

"I'll take care of them," Bragg said.

"Thank you, General."

Longstreet patted Cleburne on the back. "Go on." He watched until Cleburne disappeared in the darkness. "General Bragg, we've suffered a needless defeat here today, but as long this army has men the caliber of General Cleburne, the Cause will not be defeated. And for that I thank God."

Hardee glanced over the edge of the letter. Polk was dabbing a water-soaked towel to his bruised jaw. Their eyes met and Hardee's eyes returned to the letter, which was a strong indictment of Longstreet's leadership. Hardee had read this type of denunciation before, so he wasn't shocked at the harshness of the language or the frankness of the criticism. The sound of water dragged his attention from the letter's angry content. Polk wrung out the towel over a shallow bowl and re-laid it on his jaw.

"Does it hurt?" Hardee asked sympathetically. He gestured at his own jaw.

Polk ignored the question. "Are you finished?"

"Not yet." Hardee returned to the letter. With each word he read, his dread grew. Polk's charges were edging close to defamation of character. Conveniently missing from the narrative were Polk's own actions in suddenly decamping from Missionary Ridge.

Throughout Polk's many battles with Braxton Bragg over control of the army, Hardee had supported the Bishop without question. He knew Polk expected that same blind loyalty now. But this time, he wouldn't receive it. Not without answering a few frank questions first. Hardee lowered the letter.

"I need your backing." It was an order. Polk soaked the towel in the bowl again.

Hardee laid the letter on the desk. His finger tapped it slowly then he slid it across the desk. "No."

Polk threw the towel on the ground. In the candlelight, Hardee observed Forrest's handiwork. Polk's jaw was swollen and black.

"I'm facing a court martial," Polk railed. "That stupid Georgian has put Cleburne in charge of my corps. And we're in Georgia! If we don't do something, we'll lose the war. We owe it to this army to let the president know just how incompetent Longstreet is."

Hardee reached down and picked up the towel. He folded it and placed it over a chair. "If Richmond relieves Longstreet, who will take his place?" Pemberton?" Hardee shook his head. "I don't think he's up to it. Perhaps Beauregard? Kirby-Smith?" Polk's eyes narrowed but he didn't speak. "Do you think Lee would let Jackson go? I don't think so."

"You." Polk said, but his voice lacked conviction.

Hardee laughed. "No, I don't think I would be effective commanding an army."

"I'll take the army."

The declaration didn't surprise Hardee. He was fully aware that the Bishop had been angling for command since Perryville. "I don't think that would be wise. I think we should stick with Longstreet."

Polk's face turned bright red, which caused the bruise on his jaw to stand out even more. "I'd advise you not to oppose me on this!"

"Don't raise your voice at me," Hardee warned.

Polk bowed slightly. "I'm sorry." He sat down and pushed the letter toward Hardee. "Sign it."

"I'm not signing it," Hardee pointed at the letter, "until I get some answers as to why you pulled out yesterday afternoon."

An uncomfortable silence filled the tent.

"I was flanked," Polk finally spat out. "And since Bragg and Longstreet refused to send me reinforcements, I had no choice but to retreat."

Hardee frowned. "I talked to Forrest. He said there may have been a regiment on your flank if that."

"Since when did you start listening to that illiterate slave-trader? Forrest is wrong. I was flanked," Polk insisted.

"You sent no word. You just pulled out."

The blood drained from Polk's face. "I didn't have time…"

Hardee cut him off with an angry sweep of his hand. "I refuse to accept that explanation. You left me totally exposed. If it wasn't for Cleburne's quick thinking, my corps would have been lost, and the Yankees would have swept up Pemberton. It was irresponsible of you to just pull like you did."

Polk lowered his head. "I was wrong not to send word." He raised his head. "But Forrest is wrong too. I was flanked," he said defiantly.

If that was true, then Longstreet wouldn't have had Polk arrested. Hardee certainly didn't want to call Polk a liar to his face. And if the argument continued, he would have to do so. "Okay," he yielded.

Surprisingly, Polk looked chastened and not triumphant. "I need you to sign the letter. I need to get out of this tent and back to my corps."

Hardee suddenly felt sorry for the man. He pointed at the paper. "I don't agree with it."

Polk's anger flashed then receded. "I'll rewrite it."

"Okay, but I'll only sign it if I agree with it." Hardee stood. "Now, if you'll excuse me, I have a staff meeting."

A soft tap on the bedroom door roused Lincoln from a fitful sleep. "Just a minute," he called. He fumbled at the bedside table. His seeking fingers finally struck the base of the lamp and traced upward until they found the switch. He turned it and the room slowly filled with light. He swung his legs from the bed. The wood floor was cool to his feet. Long strides took him to the door. He jerked it open. A blue-uniformed private stood in the hallway. He held a telegram in his hand.

Lincoln paled. No good news ever came after two in the morning. He desired nothing more than to shut the door and return to the safety of his bed, but curiosity took hold. "From Grant or Sherman?"

"Sherman," the young man replied.

Lincoln reached out for the telegram. "Thank you, Private."

He sat down hard on the bed and stared at the envelope. His heart leapt into his throat, choking him. Please, let it be good news.

"I write you from Georgia…"

Lincoln read no further. He flopped back on the bed and raised his hands in victory.

Chapter Fifteen

F orrest watched his men pull another section of the Memphis and Charleston Railroad from the ground. Yesterday, his men had destroyed over three miles of rail line, but before dawn, Union engineers had make repairs. This morning, a long train rumbled east from Nashville filled with new recruits. Corn-fed youths from Iowa, Illinois, and Indiana to replace the men Sherman lost in his futile attempts to dislodge Longstreet from Rocky Face Ridge.

But where would Longstreet go to replace the men he lost? Joe Brown's pets? The Georgia militia that Governor Brown had protected from even Robert E. Lee's grasp. War had finally come to Georgia, but Brown still refused to heed the pleas of Davis, Seddon, and Longstreet and send the militia to the front to help defend the State from invasion. If Longstreet didn't come out from behind his defenses and begin to battle the Yankees, Sherman would win the war by default. Sooner or later, Longstreet just wouldn't have enough men standing on the line.

Yet, Longstreet refused to listen to any other opinion. Any suggestion that this defensive strategy might be a losing proposition quickly escalated into an argument. But Forrest was never one to hold his peace. Before riding out to Alabama, he had paid a visit to Longstreet's headquarters.

"I know you ain't no coward, but if you don't change your tactics, you're gonna lose the war. Tomorrow mornin', you're the one who must attack." Forrest was blunt. He pulled the cinch tight on King Philip.

"I don't have to do any such thing!" Longstreet was madder than Forrest had ever seen him.

Forrest threw his hands up in the air. "Damnation and hellfire, General!"

"That's enough. If you can't lead my cavalry, just say the word. I'll send for Jeb Stuart."

Forrest snapped backed and glared at Longstreet. "You don't need to be askin' for some ostrich-plumed, cape-wearin' dandy to come and take command. I'll obey my orders." He threw himself into the saddle and galloped off in a cloud of dust.

Forrest wasn't the only one pressing Longstreet to leave his defenses, but Longstreet ignored Davis' telegrams as readily as he dismissed Forrest's advice. Time was running out. Sooner or later Longstreet would have to abandon his fortifications and fight it out like a man with the Yankees.

Like Forrest and his men did every day. There was just something satisfying about standing at arm's length from your opponent, trading blow for blow, leaving everything on the field, and knowing that the victory you won, you did so by your wits and prowess. He preferred it over hiding behind a breastwork any day.

A cloud of dust formed in the west.

"Yankees on the way!" He shouted to the men.

Without a word, they put down their shovels and crowbars and picked up their guns. Forrest smiled. Yes, he preferred fighting the enemy face-to-face.

Snake Creek Gap
Near Resaca, Georgia
July, 1864

General Bate lowered his fieldglasses. The gap was empty as it was every day since his division had received orders to guard this insignificant entry way into Sugar Valley. It was an inconsequential assignment, but it was his. He was a good thirteen miles from the main fight at Mill Creek Gap and Dug Gap. The only activity Bate's men had seen was the occasional visit from General Hannon, whose cavalry brigade was posted at the other end of the gap. Hannon was to keep Bate informed of the Yankees' movement, but three days had past since Hannon's last message. Concerned by the lack of communication, Bate sent a courier asking for an update. Hannon's response was less than helpful. He would report when there was something to report.

Longstreet had visited the camp two weeks ago. Bate asked when his men might see some action. Longstreet gave a patient smile that sank Bate's hope of ever leaving this place. Since that visit, his division might as well have been marooned on a desert island. Not even an aide from Hardee had come to check on his men.

"Sir!" It was General Finely. "The valley is full of Yankees."

Bates hurried to the breastworks and peered through his glasses. "What division is that?" He gestured down the valley. "Do you recognize any of the flags?"

Finley raised his glasses and scanned the valley. "Sir, that's no division. Those flags belong to the Army of the Ohio."

"Lieutenant!" Bate called to his nearest aide. The young man stared at him through wide eyes. "Get word to General Hardee at Tilton. Tell him I need immediate help."

The lieutenant ran toward the horses. Bate turned to Finley. "We need to hold them off as long as we can."

The sound of thousands of stamping brogans echoed throughout the valley, growing louder with each step the Yankees took. Bate ordered his artillery to open fire. Great holes were blown in the blue lines, but the Yankees reformed and kept coming. "Hold your fire!" He called out. "Wait for my command!" The distance closed, 200 yards, 100 yards, fifty yards. Closer, the Yankees came. They were close enough. "Fire!"

His line fired as one man. Blue sheets of flame quickly changed to acrid smoke. Ramrods rattled in gun barrels. Before his men could get off a second shot, the Yankees' front line fired. Bullets plunked into the dirt mounds that formed the majority of Bate's breastwork. Dirt wasn't all the bullets pierced. The dead slipped quietly to the ground; the wounded cried out for help. The Yankees' second wave fired. The smoke thickened. Union artillery thundered.

"Where do you want my men?"

Bate turned and saw General Wheeler. He let out his breath in relief. "On the line."

Wheeler barked the order and his men dismounted and ran toward the fortifications. "General Hardee is about an hour away," Wheeler said. "He was loading the cars as I was leaving."

"What happened to Hannon?" Bate asked.

"I don't know," Wheeler responded.

Bate let it go for now. But if he survived the day, he would find out.

Help didn't arrive within the hour. It didn't even come within two. Wheeler hurried scouts to Resaca, but when they returned, they reported the rail lines empty. Unsatisfied with the answer, Wheeler sent the scouts north to find the missing train and inform Hardee of just how desperate the situation had become.

Pushing the Yankees back grew more difficult as morning turned to afternoon. Bate found himself looking south, hoping to see the tell-tale dust cloud that announced soldiers on the march. Finally, he gave up. Even if Hardee and his troops had disembarked the cars and were on their way, they wouldn't arrive before the battle was lost. His fate was sealed. Either this attack or the next would be the fatal blow. His men, exhausted and extremely low on ammunition, would be overrun.

"General Wheeler, you need to round up as many men as you can and clear out of here."

"What do you plan to do?" Wheeler asked.

"I'm going to surrender."

As Wheeler rode into Resaca, he saw the steam from the train's engine rising in the air. Hardee had arrived. Too late to save Bate but not late enough to save Resaca, the railroad, and Longstreet's left flank. He urged his mare on. When he cleared the buildings, he saw a long line of railcars. Soldiers hurried down the ramps and officers quickly shepherded them into column of fours.

"General Wheeler!" Wheeler pulled up and looked about him. "General Wheeler! Over here!

Up by the engine, Wheeler saw Hardee standing with General Walker. He galloped over and threw himself from his exhausted mare.

"What's the news from Snake Creek Gap?" Hardee asked.

"Bate is surrendering."

"What?" Hardee gasped. "His orders were to hold."

Wheeler fired up. "You left him no choice. You said you would be here in an hour. We held out for four without a word from you!" He angrily slapped his hand against his leg and waited for an explanation.

"It took longer to load the trains than I anticipated," Hardee said.

"Obviously."

"You and I can fight about that later. Right now, tell me what General Walker and I are facing."

Despair extinguished Wheeler's anger. Hardee had only brought Walker's division with him. It was a foul up of the worst kind. Bate had sacrificed the better part of his command so that Resaca and the railroad could be saved. Well, Resaca wasn't going to be held nor was the railroad going to be saved. Hardee didn't have enough men. "Sir, the Army of the Ohio should be here within the next two hours."

Wheeler watched the enormity of the situation strike Hardee.

"How many men?" Hardee choked out.

"More than we have," Wheeler replied.

Walker weighed in. "Sir, we can't let the Yankees take Resaca. General Longstreet will be flanked. Send for General Withers."

"Major Roy!" Hardee shouted. The adjutant trotted over. "Send a telegram to Tilton. Tell General Withers to have his men waiting at the station. Take the cars back to Tilton and make sure Withers doesn't waste a minute loading his men on the train."

"How long's that going to take?" Wheeler was flabbergasted at the senselessness of the order. By time Withers arrived, Resaca would be in Union hands.

Hardee glared Wheeler into temporary silence. "Do you understand what's at stake?" Hardee questioned his adjutant. Roy nodded. "Then go." Roy ran toward the telegraph office. "General Wheeler, I need a defensive position. What do you recommend?"

Wheeler didn't hesitate. "You need to cross the river, burn the bridges, and dig in."

"There's no other alternative?" Hardee questioned brusquely

"There are plenty of alternatives," Wheeler said sarcastically. "But I reckon you want to survive the day."

Hardee scowled. "Of course."

"Then cross the river."

"What of Withers?" Walker said.

"Unless Major Roy can work some kind of miracle, Withers will get here sometime after the Yankees do," Wheeler said.

Hardee put his hand on his hips and thought for a long moment. "Let's get the men across the river. Burn the bridges." He retrieved a small notebook from his pocket and hastily scratched a note. He ripped the paper from the notebook and thrust it at Wheeler. "Get this to General Longstreet."

Wheeler glanced at the note. *We are over run and retreating across the Oostanaula.*

Chapter Sixteen

Near Cassville, Georgia
July 12, 1864

Y*ou must retreat no further. You outnumber the Yankees...* Longstreet quit reading and added the telegram to a growing pile of telegrams, all from Davis, all imploring Longstreet to take his superior forces and drive the Yankees from Georgia. At first, Longstreet battled back Davis' misconceptions that he outnumbered the Yankees by sending detailed casualty reports. Davis' reply was to send another telegram.

As for the president's misconception that Longstreet wasn't giving fight, while it may be true that he wasn't on the offensive, he was fighting. Unfortunately, there were no sensational headlines in repelling an assault. No thrilling flank march through the marsh as Jackson had done in Pennsylvania to fire the public imagination. But in the light of his manpower shortage, his strategy was smart. Not to Davis though, who only equated victory with Yankees running pell-mell from Georgia.

Sorrel entered, another telegram in his hand.

"I don't want to see it," Longstreet growled. "I no longer know what to write to make the president understand what we're facing."

"It's not about that," Sorrel replied. He came to the desk and held out the telegram. "Davis wants you to reinstate General Polk."

Longstreet let loose with a long chuckle. "That I know how to respond to. Write back, tell the president no."

"That won't be the final word on the subject." Sorrel laid the telegram on the desk.

"I'm sure it won't," Longstreet said in dismissal.

"Yes, sir." Sorrel exited the tent.

Longstreet heard voices outside. Sorrel returned. "Sir, it's General Bragg. Do you have a moment?"

Longstreet nodded. Sorrel went and Bragg stood in his place. Bragg plopped down in a chair and removed his gauntlets. "I just received word from Cleburne. His corps has cleared Adairsville. Pemberton is twenty miles behind."

Longstreet handed Bragg the president's telegram. Bragg read it and laid it on the table. "I can't retreat over the Etowah without giving battle. If I do, I'll be relieved," Longstreet said.

Bragg stretched his arms over his head and gave a low moan. "I'm sorry, sir. I was in the saddle all night."

"Colonel Sorrel, can we get some coffee in here," Longstreet bellowed.

"Are you going to attack?" Bragg asked.

"Would you?"

Sorrel entered with a steaming pot of coffee. He set it between the two generals then left quietly. Bragg poured a cup and took a long drink. He held the cup in both hands and stared at Longstreet. "No, we can't afford the casualties."

"The best thing for the army is to get across the river and dig in." Bragg gave him a look. "If we drive the Yankees back, I'm sure all will be forgiven in Richmond." He was confident that would be the case. "When does Hardee arrive?"

"Sometime late this afternoon," Bragg replied. A yawn caught him off guard. He threw his hand over his mouth then shook his head. "Sorry."

"Cleburne?"

Bragg poured another cup of coffee. "No later than tomorrow morning."

"Send Cleburne and Hardee across the Etowah to Alltoona. I'll send Pemberton to Dallas."

"What are you planning?"

Longstreet gave a quick grin. He grabbed his hat and gauntlets.

"Are you going somewhere?"

Longstreet tugged on a gauntlet. "Why? Do you want to come?"

Bragg set down the cup and gathered up his gauntlets.

In the gray gloom of dawn, McPherson stood on the southern bank of the Etowah watching his artillery rumble over the pontoon bridges. The infantry had crossed last night and the men were spread out for miles. Most were still sleeping but a few were up and cooking breakfast. It was the last food the men may see for a while. Morgan had cut the railroad again. General Dodge reported that it would take at least a week to get the trains running, provided Morgan didn't undo what Dodge just fixed.

On the opposite bank, curled up like a snake, supply wagons sat, waiting for their turn to cross. The mules brayed impatiently. Once his trains were on the other side, McPherson was to head toward Alltoona where the Confederates were dug in and waiting.

The sun would be up in another fifteen minutes or so. That should speed up the crossing. His aide approached with a cup of scalding hot coffee. McPherson received it with gratitude.

The gray sky slowly gave way to blue hues. It was going to be a beautiful day. Hopefully the heat and humidity of the past few days would be the thing of the past, but without rain or a breeze, the chances of that were slim. He blew on his coffee and ventured a sip. It was tolerable.

A blood curdling Rebel yell punctured the quiet. McPherson looked about in confusion. The sound was almost on top of him. The yell resounded again. He wasn't imagining it. The Rebels were very close. Was it just Forrest? Or maybe Wheeler? A regiment or a division?

He dropped the cup on the ground and didn't feel the hot coffee splatter his pants and burn his legs. With a savage jerk, he pulled his fieldglasses free. He focused on the heights above the river bank. His mouth fell open in surprise. The ground above him was filled with Confederate soldiers.

The Rebs' lowered their guns and fired. Instant pandemonium as his men scrambled from their bedrolls or campfire to retrieve their rifles. Officers sprang into action, trying to form some kind of line, but indecision ruled. There was simply no place to form up, no where to dig in. The river was at their back, the bridges jammed with slow moving artillery, and the opposite shore lined with supply wagons.

It was a slaughter. Every volley from the Confederates dropped men where they stood; hundreds with every volley. *What if the Rebs advanced!*

Horrified at the thought, McPherson ran to the closest bridge. An artillery crew was attempting to back up a 20-pound parrot. The horses protested with loud whinnies. The lead horse reared.

"Don't back them up!" McPherson hollered. He gestured the men onward. "Clear the bridges so the men can cross."

A young private dove into the muddy waters and disappeared. When he resurfaced, he pulled himself onto the bridge. The lead horse reared again. The private grabbed the bridle. He shushed and cajoled. The horse, its sweat glistening in the rising sun, calmed down. Smiling in triumph at McPherson, the private led the team of horses onto the shore.

McPherson patted the young man on the back. "Good job."

A bullet pierced the private's heart. His warm blood splattered McPherson's face and uniform. McPherson reached out a hand, but the lad collapsed to the ground.

The Rebel yell fractured the air again. McPherson glanced up. Waves of screaming soldier rushed down the small hill toward him.

"Hurry up, men!" McPherson yelled. He waved them toward the river. The bridges filled with fleeing soldiers. Men dove into the river and began to swim across. Rifles, canteens, boots, and haversacks littered the river bank.

Frank Blair dashed up.

"How many men are left?" McPherson asked.

"Too many!" Blair said. He pointed down the bank. "Can we get some help from Schofield?"

The Army of the Ohio was crossing five miles down river. Thomas further west. "No," McPherson said.

Confederate artillery resounded. Shells screamed overhead, hit the bank and the river, and threw up dirt, rocks, and geysers of water. A dull thud jerked McPherson off his feet. He grabbed Blair's arm, but Blair's face was streaked with blood. Was Frank wounded?

Blair was shouting, but his voice sounded far away. McPherson strained to hear him. The trees, once brilliant green, now appeared muddy brown. The sky was no longer blue, but gray, turning black. Frank was still shouting. McPherson no longer cared. He slowly sank to the ground.

Grant's office in the new War Department building was an airless sweatbox. He sat with his jacket off, his vest unbuttoned, and his shirt sleeves rolled up above his elbows. The pitcher of water sitting on the desk had long been emptied. Whenever the breeze did blow through the open window, it brought with it the putrid stench of the Washington Channel into the room.

The heat and the stink weren't the only things Grant had to contend with since his return from Pennsylvania. Politicians, every minute of the day, it seemed. The staunch oak office door might as well be a revolving glass door the way senators and congressmen just came on in and made themselves at home. And they always came bearing advice. Each and every one of them knew exactly how to beat the Rebs. He couldn't even escape them when he returned to his rooms at the Willard Hotel. They approached him in the dining room or while he walked across the lobby. Once, a particularly pushy congressman from Indiana pounded on his door well after midnight.

Grant longed to be back in the field. He couldn't get away from the city fast enough. Except the army needed rest and re-supply. Fresh recruits were arriving from the western states at the end of next week. General Reynolds wanted to give them at least a couple of weeks to drill. And the army had lost plenty of good men in Pennsylvania. Generals Sedgwick and Meade had been killed and General Burnside had been captured. Newly promoted officers needed time to acclimate to their positions and grow familiar with the men under their command. Even though an agitated Lincoln sent messages every day imploring Grant to get after Lee, Grant sided with Reynolds. A few weeks rest would do the army a whole lot of good.

There was a soft knock on the door. In despair, Grant dropped his head backwards and stared at the ceiling. He couldn't bear to listen to another fool politician. Maybe if he pretended he wasn't in, the person would go away. Another knock, more insistent than the last. Whoever it was wasn't leaving.

He slowly raised his head. The door came into view. He gathered up his papers. He wasn't about to risk some nosey politician with the ability to read upside down getting a hold of his plans and spreading them all over Washington by dinner time. "Come in!" He called.

The door opened revealing Colonel Rawlins. The adjutant looked like death. His eyes were enormous in his bloodless face.

The adjutant held up a telegram. "Sherman was turned back at the Etowah."

The news was bad but it certainly didn't warrant Rawlins' deathly pallor. "Sherman will figure out a way to get across the river."

Rawlins didn't respond. He just slid the telegram through his fingers. Grant pointed at the paper. "May I see it?"

Rawlins slid it across the desk. "If you'll excuse me."

Before Grant could dismiss him, the adjutant fled.

Grant picked up the telegram. Above Sherman's name were three earth-shattering words: *McPherson is dead.*

His breath left in a rush. Never in a hundred years could he imagine that a telegram could bear such horrifying news: the sudden and irrevocable loss of his best friend. His body convulsed in sobs. He put his head down on the desk and wept. *McPherson is dead.*

The door opened. "Go away!" The door closed, but the person remained. Grant raised his head to bark angry words at the intruder, but through his tears he saw John Reynolds.

Glad to see a friendly face, he shoved the telegram, now a wad of paper, over to Reynolds. "I can't believe..." Sobs cut off his words.

Reynolds put down the telegram, withdrew a handkerchief from his jacket pocket, and handed it to Grant. "I only knew General McPherson by reputation. But he must have been a good man to garner such a reaction from Colonel Rawlins and yourself."

"You didn't meet him when he came to visit at Christmas?" Grant wiped his eyes with the handkerchief.

"No, I spent Christmas in Pennsylvania." Reynolds took a seat.

"Oh, that's right. It's too bad, really. You'd have liked him."

"I'm sure," Reynolds agreed.

"I've seen a lot of good men die, but never has the war hit this close to home." Grant's tears began anew. "How do I go on?"

"When Hancock was killed at Duncannon, I stood in his tent packing his papers and his billet all the while my heart was breaking." Tears filled Reynolds' eyes. "He was a brilliant general and one of my dearest friends. I have to admit that I thought those first few days of the retreat, when I expected Jackson to fall on us at any moment, would be the most difficult of my life, but I was wrong." He rubbed his nose. "The hardest days came when I accompanied Win's body back home for his funeral and burial." He shook his head to clear the memories and looked Grant in the eyes.

"You need to go to McPherson's funeral. You need to say a proper good-bye. That's how you go on."

Grant demurred. "The funeral will probably be in held in northern Ohio. I can't…"

"You can. Even though saying good-bye to Win was difficult, I'm glad I had that moment. He was my friend and I did my duty as only a friend could."

"But Lee…"

"Lee will be here when you come back." Reynolds gave a small smile.

"The politicians…"

"Leave the politicians to me."

This caused Grant to smile. "You aren't any good at handling politicians."

"I'm better at it than you. At least I know how to hide." Grant laughed. "Go to the funeral, Sam."

Another tear traced its way down Grant's cheek. "Okay."

Chapter Seventeen

Sherman's Headquarters
Kingston, Georgia
August 3, 1863

B lair dismounted and waited until one of the corpsmen relaxing under the shade of a large tree dragged himself out into the blinding sunlight and took the horse's reins.

"Give him something to drink," Blair said. The corpsman mumbled something, but Blair didn't catch it. He patted the gelding on the rump as the huge black animal walked past him.

Blair glanced at the other corpsmen, but they carefully avoided his eyes. No one wanted to be exposed to the sun's furnace blast. "Where can I find General Sherman?"

"I'm over here!" Blair heard Sherman's high-pitched voice. He looked about and saw Sherman sitting beneath a giant oak. Blair waved in acknowledgement. He reached the embrace of the oak's limbs and felt the temperature lower by several degrees. He ducked under a low hanging branch and observed a table covered with maps. A small breeze caught the top map and sent it sailing. It hit the ground and skipped along until it wrapped itself around Blair's ankles. Blair reached down, peeled the map from his boots, and returned it to the table, securing it with a paperweight.

"Have a seat, General," Sherman said.

Blair dragged a camp stool over to the table and sat down.

"Frank, let's get straight to business. First of all, I want to offer my thanks for extracting the army from the Rebs' ambush after McPherson died." Sherman paused, grief briefly marring his face. "I wrote to General Grant about your heroics..." Blair blushed in embarrassment. It was hardly heroics that influenced his actions, but self-preservation. "...and he shared the telegram with the president."

At that, Blair flushed to his hairline. "That was very kind of General Grant."

"I also told Grant that I wanted you to take McPherson's place." Blair laughed. "Did I say something amusing, General?"

"Sir, let's be honest." Blair started to laugh again, "I have more enemies in Washington than I do in the Reb army. The Senate won't confirm my promotion."

"That's why I want you." Sherman was brusque. "You aren't afraid to make enemies."

Blair gave Sherman a boyish grin. "That's true."

"General Grant approves. So does the president. And John promises to shepherd your appointment through the Senate."

Blair absorbed the news. "I'm honored."

"Of course you are," Sherman barked. "The Army of the Tennessee is the best army this county has ever assembled."

"You better not let General Thomas hear you speak like that." Blair was playful.

Sherman narrowed his eyes and for a brief moment, Blair was afraid that Sherman wouldn't get his jest. Then Sherman started to laugh, noiseless, his body shaking with mirth. His laughter slowly abated and he gestured toward the map Blair had just rescued from his boots. "Now I know that you've only been in command for a couple of minutes, but I need your advice. Feel free to share your opinions. That is something I especially valued from Mac."

Blair made a fearful face. "I don't know about that, General. I'm afraid we Blairs usually make our blunt opinions known at the top of our lungs."

Sherman pondered Blair's words. "I can handle blunt."

"Then I'll do my best not to deliver them at the top of my lungs."

"That would be much appreciated." Sherman smiled. "I spoke to General Thomas earlier today. He wants to cross the river further west and drive toward the railroad."

"How far west?"

"Rome."

"He wants to retreat?"

"He wants to get across the river," Sherman said severely. "Once across, he'll head toward Van Wert. That should loosen the Rebs' left flank. They'll have to retreat to protect the railroad."

Blair turned one of the maps around and studied it intensely. "And me?"

"You'll cross at Canton and march toward Roswell."

Blair noted the route on the map. He sat back in surprise. "That leaves us extremely vulnerable. We'd be a two-day hard march from each other with Pemberton and Bragg in between us."

"It has its risks," Sherman conceded.

It has its risks! The plan could very well end in disaster. Blair quickly swallowed the blunt words he desired to shout at the top of his lung. Instead, he settled for a diplomatic, "Sir, it may be too risky."

"We've tried to force a crossing and have been met with nothing but slaughter."

Blair began to pace, careful to stay in the shade. In Thomas' plan, every thing had to go right, but if just one thing went wrong, it would be the death of them all. A week ago, Morgan had destroyed the bridge at Bridgeport, Alabama, which was crucial to the re-supply of the army. That meant his men only had four days worth of rations left, and they couldn't live off the land. The Rebs had picked it clean. The surrounding roads were rough, which made it difficult to move artillery and supply wagons. What if it rained? The roads would turn into sludge, hampering their march. It had been two weeks since the last rain fell. That would not last. Georgia was due soon for some wet weather.

Blair stopped pacing. "Schofield?"

"I'm going to have him hold his position. To keep the Rebs in place."

Blair shook his head in disagreement. "Once we cross the Etowah, it won't take long for Forrest or Wheeler to discover our march."

Sherman exhaled in exasperation. "General, the most important element of command is to offer suggestions and not just criticism."

Blair angered. Sherman had presented this strategy as a *fait accompli*. It was dangerous and reckless and now Sherman was resentful because he dare point out the plan's weaknesses. Well, welcome to command, Francis Preston Blair. He leaned against the oak tree. "Give me your orders, and I'll carry them out."

"Now, now, Frank, don't pout," Sherman scolded.

"I'm not pouting," Blair insisted, his voice rising in anger. He pushed off from the tree and returned to the camp stool. "I just have reservations."

Sherman drummed his fingers on the table. "Frank…"

Blair interrupted. "Forrest and Wheeler will discover our march."

Sherman scowled. His fingers increased their drumming.

"So, we need to be on Longstreet's flanks by time we're discovered."

Sherman's fingers went still. "A night march?"

"It's the only way. We cross the river at dusk. A forced march until we reach our goal." Blair saw Sherman's interest. "But General, Stanley's screen must be tight." He gave a disappointed sigh. "I just don't know if Stanley is up to the task."

"I'll stress the importance of a tight screen to Stanley," Sherman said.

Blair knew that even this gambit, marching through hostile land in the dark, with enemy eyes reporting their every move to the Rebs, was a long shot. But Sherman was correct. They couldn't stay where they were. The Confederates maintained a solid hold on the river. "When do we march?" He asked in resignation.

"Day after tomorrow soon enough."

Blair nodded.

Sherman stood and the interview came to an end. Blair found his feet. "Congratulations, Blair on your new command."

Blair gave a small smile. He was tempted to give the command back, but didn't. After all, he was a Blair and Blairs never backed down from a challenge.

Kennesaw Mountain
25 miles from Atlanta

Longstreet looked down at the tents of the Union army spread out in the valley below Kennesaw Mountain. The tents looked more like sheep, lots and lots of sheep, than they did tents. So pastoral and peaceful. Since the Yankees' arrival at the bottom of the mountain, the tents had remained in place, the soldiers had rested, and Longstreet had waited for the flanking move that would cause him to abandon these heights and retreat to Atlanta.

After three bloody and deadly assaults along the Etowah, the Yankees had decided to flank him again. When Forrest sent word that the head of Thomas' column was entering Van Wert, Longstreet prepared orders for Pemberton to shift his men back into the fortifications at Dallas, but a courier from Wheeler made the order superfluous. Wheeler reported another Union column approaching Roswell.

Longstreet gave the order. His men forsook the positions they had valiantly held and high-tailed it toward Atlanta. Longstreet sent Bragg ahead to lay out a new line. Longstreet looked about him. Bragg had a good eye for ground.

"Sir, General Polk is here."

Longstreet turned and saw Goree. Behind the Texan stood Leonidas Polk. When Polk saw Longstreet's stare, he waved.

"In a moment, Major." Longstreet turned back around and gazed again at the tents and the activity of the soldiers beneath him.

The Etowah had indeed been Longstreet's Rubicon. Angry telegrams arrived from Seddon and Davis demanding Longstreet quit his retreats and push the Yankees back across the Tennessee River once and for all. To ensure Atlanta didn't fall, Davis pried the Homeguard from Governor Brown. Yesterday, a long column of old men and teenagers marched into camp. Bragg and Pemberton divided them up and the division commanders fought over them. The Homeguard also had its share of able-bodied young men who had never heard the sounds of battle. Those men, in spotless uniforms and shiny swords, received well deserved catcalls from veterans who had fought the Yankees in Tennessee, Mississippi, Kentucky, and, now, Georgia.

Next, Davis ordered Longstreet to return Polk to command. Longstreet balked but Davis refused to listen to any more objections. Longstreet thoroughly resented Davis' interference in his command. Lee didn't have to put up with this sort of nonsense, why should he? Davis' last telegram was an ultimatum. Either Polk was returned to his corps or Longstreet would be removed from command. Checkmated, Longstreet had sent for Polk.

Longstreet breathed deeply, stowed his temper, and summoned his patience. "Okay, Major."

Goree mumbled to Polk. Longstreet gave the Bishop a cursory glance then stared down into the valley below.

"General Longstreet," Polk said. He extended his hand.

Longstreet ignored the hand and tried to ignore the triumph in Polk's voice. He gave the Bishop a hard stare. "I don't want you to think you've won."

"I warned you that I had powerful allies."

"Yes, you did." Longstreet reached into his pocked and withdrew a cigar. "For some reason, President Davis has proven to be a most loyal friend." Longstreet rolled the cigar between his thumb and forefinger. "He refuses to hear any criticism regarding the deficiencies in your performance during this campaign."

Polk folded his arms across his chest. "Am I to be returned to my corps?"

"Yes." Longstreet clamped the cigar between his teeth.

Polk gave a big smile. "Thank you, sir."

Longstreet held up his hand. "Not so fast."

Polk reeled back as if he had been struck. "I believe President Davis has ordered you to reinstate me."

"He has. But I've been very impressed with General Cleburne. He's handled his corps..."

"My corps," Polk interrupted heatedly.

Longstreet narrowed his eyes. "Don't interrupt me again." Polk seethed in silence. "Therefore, I'll be dividing your corps into two. You'll be returned to the First Corps and Cleburne will command the Third Corps."

"My division commanders will not stand for this," Polk insisted.

Longstreet laughed, loud and hard. Polk stalked away. He turned and stood with his hands on his hips. Longstreet's laughter faded. "Oh, they did. They fought to be in Cleburne's corps."

"I don't believe it."

By the shocked expression on Polk's face, Longstreet knew this was the truth. "Let me disabuse you of your notion that the men hold you in high regards. They don't. Every last soldier knows you turned tail and ran on Missionary Ridge."

Polk exploded in anger. "I was flanked."

"Forrest..."

"That black-hearted varmint! You're taking his word over mine!" Polk shouted so loudly that Longstreet was sure the Yankees in the valley below could hear him.

"There is only one man who buys your outraged act. And I'm sure if Davis was here and had to put up with your back-stabbing and naked ambition, he would personally order your court-martial."

Longstreet shrugged. "Unfortunately, he isn't here, and you have done an excellent job in deceiving him."

Polk fixed a cold stare on Longstreet. "Sir, you slander me."

"Do I? Answer me this, Bishop. I've had the privilege of knowing some fine Christian men. Both General Jackson and General Lee are sterling examples of how a Christian should behave. You on the other hand…" Longstreet shook his head in disgust.

"How did you get command, General?" There was an unspoken accusation in the Bishop's voice.

"I earned it," Longstreet shot back.

"Really?" Polk fell silent.

"Don't leave it there." Longstreet could feel his anger rising. "Say what you have to say."

"That your ambition is just as naked as mine."

"That's enough," Longstreet warned.

"What's the matter, General?" Polk asked innocently. "Did my words hit too close to home."

They did, but Longstreet wasn't about to admit it to Polk. He thought he was careful to keep his face neutral, but Polk must have read something there, for his eyes danced maliciously.

"Where can I find my men?" Polk questioned.

"Major Goree!" Longstreet summoned the aide. "The Major will show you the way. But, General, if you disobey even the tiniest order, I will have you cashiered. And I don't care how many telegrams I get from Richmond, I will not reinstate you."

Polk didn't reply. He turned to Goree. "If you're ready, Major."

Goree glanced at Longstreet for permission. Longstreet nodded and turned his attention back to the valley.

Chapter Eighteen

Colonel William Wallace, commanding the 15th Ohio Volunteer Infantry, stood at the bottom of the ridge called Little Kennesaw. He squinted into the rising sun. The mountain, hill really, rose 200 feet into the air. At the top, he could see the Rebs' battle flags floating in the early morning breeze. There was movement behind the fortifications. The Rebs were awake.

A train whistle pierced the quiet. His men gave a little cheer. Trains meant food, something in short supply lately. Reb cavalry was still playing havoc with the railroads. He sent his men repeatedly into the countryside for grub, but they only brought back one chicken and a hog. Most of the farms his men visited had been abandoned, but every once in a while, his men would come upon a small cabin occupied by a woman and her barefooted children. The little beggars bravely surrounded the blue-uniformed men and clamored for food. His men had nothing to give.

The train whistled again. He hoped the commissary would get the rations divided and distributed throughout the brigades quickly. It would be nice to have a hot meal waiting when they returned from battle. And they would return. The Rebs were dug in too deep for his men to dislodge them, especially at the end of a tired run up the side of a mountain.

The bugle called his men to the line. It was a melancholy sound, for the shrill notes did more than call men to the fight. They also called men to eternity. Wallace sighed. Today might be such a day for him. Was he ready to meet his Lord? He believed so.

The breeze picked up the regiment's battle flag. The Stars and Stripes were faded from weather and marred with bullet holes. Wallace could still read the regiment's name in the fourth stripe. *15th*

Regiment O.V.I. The regiment had answered the call at Shiloh and every battle since.

The drums began to roll. The hill echoed with the steady beats. Wallace walked his line, nodding at the men as he passed. He took a moment to smile at his friends and relatives. "Men of Ohio!" He hollered to be heard. "If we break the Rebs here, their retreat will take them across the Chattahoochee and into Atlanta. So, let's climb that hill and show those Rebs that Ohio was here!"

The men lifted their caps and raised a spirited huzzah. Down the line came the order: "Forward!"

Wallace drew his sword from its scabbard and raised it high the in air. "Forward!" He shouted. He pointed the sword up the hill.

The drums continued to sound the advance. His men followed behind – in tight formation, shoulder-to-shoulder. The climb grew steeper. Wallace scrambled over a log and around some scrub brushes. Confederate shot raked through the regiment. He glanced behind. His men were closing up ranks.

The drums increased their cadence. "Men, on the double-quick!" He began to run. Up and over a small rise. Wallace saw the head logs of the Confederate trenches. He recognized the flags floating over his head. He had fought the Tennesseans from A.P. Stewart's Brigade before. Stubborn men who fought like wildcats. But then so did his Buckeyes.

The Confederates rose as one and fired: blue flame, white smoke, and a hail of minie balls. Men dropped on Wallace's left and right. Blue flame, white smoke, and another hail of minie balls. His men reformed and lowered their guns.

"Fire!" Wallace ordered.

Bullets thudded into the logs and dirt of the ramparts. A few Rebs disappeared, but not enough. Through the gun smoke he could see the defenses still jammed with butternut uniformed soldiers. The Tennesseans lowered their guns and fired. A bullet whizzed by

Wallace's ear and hit the young private behind him. The back of Wallace's neck was soaked with blood.

Over the din of battle, Wallace heard a bugle sound the retreat.

"Retreat!" Wallace called out. He didn't need to tell his men twice. They poured one more volley into the Rebs then backed swiftly down the hill. When Wallace reached the bottom of the hill, a courier from McCook was waiting. There would be a second assault.

"How are the men, Captain?" Wallace asked a visibly fatigued Captain Cope.

Cope gestured up the hill. "We left a lot of them up there."

"There's nothing we can do about that now. Just get me a headcount."

Cope added a column of figures on a small slip of paper. "If I did the math right, a little less than fifty men."

Wallace sent the number to McCook.

"Get the men to the supply trains," he told Cope. "Make sure they have sixty rounds and full canteens."

"Yes, sir."

Wallace walked over to a small tree and took a seat. He fished his handkerchief from his pocket and wiped at the blood trickling down his neck. A few of the men gathered around. They sat silently, not wishing to waste strength on needless conversation. Canteens made trip after trip to thirsty mouths. "Save some water for the fight, boys," Wallace said. There were some grumbles but the men secured their canteens.

Wallace dropped his head back against the tree trunk and closed his eyes. The ground shook beneath him. He jerked awake. The mountain was exploding in dirt and rock. Again and again, shells pummeled the top of the hill. Then silence. In the quiet, the drums called the men to the line.

"Let's go, men," Wallace said.

The drums quickened. As soon as the men were ready, Wallace began the ascent. The artillery had set the woods on fire. To his right a large evergreen burned.

The way became harder to navigate. Wallace slowly picked his way over the wounded. Hands reached up toward him, not to impede him, but to beg for help. Men with bloody stumps and limbs without owners. Sickening sights that turned his stomach. He tried to look ahead, but he tripped over a body. It was the young private. Wallace caught a glimpse of open eyes staring into the air but seeing nothing.

Canister whipped through his line. Wallace had ascended into hell. He wanted to drop to the ground and wait out the storm, but he knew if he did, his men would be trapped on the side of the hill. He motioned the blue lines onward but could sense the men's reluctance to follow him. "Come on!"

The Rebs opened fire, stealing courage from the men. They hesitated.

"Fire!" Wallace cried.

The volley did little damage. It was time to go. Wallace turned to signal his men to retreat. A bullet hit him in the back. All feeling left his legs. He crumpled to the ground. He dug his fingers in the ground and pulled himself down the hill, his strength oozing away with every inch he covered. He reached the young private, still staring, still seeing nothing. Depleted of energy, he quit crawling. He wished he could see the blue skies and the white clouds one more time before the darkness overtook him, but he didn't have the strength to turn over. Wallace gasped one long breath… then he was still.

Chapter Nineteen

Forrest pushed King Philip hard down the small, shaded bridle path. Up ahead, he heard angry gunfire. He rounded a corner and was thumped hard by a tree branch. King Philip stumbled and almost went down. Forrest drew up and hopped off.

"Major Kelley! Get word to Pemberton. Tell him that the Yankees are flankin' us on Old Sandtown Road."

Kelley disappeared in a cloud of dust. Forrest rubbed the gelding's forelegs. He sighed in relief. The war horse didn't appear to be hurt.

He mounted up and spurred King Philip onward. He broke out of the shade and into the bright sunlight. He saw Wheeler's men engaged in a heated battle. He dismounted and threaded his way through the wounded as they made their way back to rear.

"Soldier!" Forrest called to a private who was limping back from the line. Forrest grimaced at the ugly gash in the soldier's thigh. "Where's General Wheeler?"

"I can't rightly say," the soldier panted. He pivoted on his crutch, which was his rifle. "Last I saw him, he was over yonder by that large tree." He straightened up, gasped in pain, and pointed quickly to his left. He collapsed back on the crutch.

"Thank you," Forrest said.

"Go get 'em, General," the private responded before limping on.

Forrest headed in the direction of the tree. He saw the dark-haired Wheeler surrounded by aides. "Wheeler!"

Wheeler whirled about. "Forrest, thank God you're here!" He exclaimed in relief.

"Whatcha facing?"

"Division strength from what I can tell," Wheeler said. "I tried to get scouts down the road, but the Yankees are everywhere."

"My men'll be on the line in the next half hour or so."

Wheeler's face revealed his dismay. "My word, Forrest, that's not near enough."

"I sent word to Pemberton."

Wheeler's dismay now turned to anguish. "Pemberton doesn't have men to spare. The Yankees are pressing him hard."

Forrest didn't reply but watched as his troopers hurried to the breastwork of saplings and scrub Wheeler's men had hastily thrown together.

Wheeler wasn't exaggerating when he said that the Yankees were everywhere. The road was blue with them. Forrest looked back the way he came, hoping to spy Kelley arriving with good news. He waited, but there was no Kelley, just a steady stream of wounded troopers heading away from the line.

Forrest surveyed the landscape. He needed a stronger position to hold off the surging Yankees until Pemberton arrived...if Pemberton arrived. He cast the worrisome thought from his mind. Pemberton would come. He knew what was at stake.

Forrest paced away from the tree about 100 feet, his eyes constantly raking the ground. He stopped. The road narrowed about forty yards from where he was standing. On the right side of the road was a rocky formation. The left side was flanked by scrub and evergreens, which could be protected with horse artillery.

He trotted back to Wheeler and explained what he wanted to do.

"How are we going to keep the Yankees off us while we retreat?" Wheeler questioned.

"It don't need to be elegant, Joe," Forrest fumed. "I'll get my men workin' on the new defenses now. When it's ready, we fire all we got into the Yankees and set 'em back on their heels. While they regroup, we hi-tail it back to the new line and wait for Pemberton."

Wheeler wasn't convinced. He was winding up for an argument, which Forrest didn't have the patience to participate in. "Wheeler, look around. The men you see is all the men comin' 'til Pemberton sends help. If the Yankees get down this road, Atlanta will be lost.

You have your orders. I suggest you find some way of carryin' 'em out."

Wheeler barked commands to his aides and ordered the horses moved behind the new defenses.

"General Forrest!" Forrest recognized Major Kelley's voice. He whirled about and saw Kelley throw himself from his lathered mare. Once free from her burden, the mare stumbled in fatigue. A young corpsman with a string of horses following after him caught her reins and led her away.

"What's the news from Pemberton?" Forrest asked Kelley.

Kelley removed his hat and wiped his forehead with the sleeve of his jacket. "On my way…"

If Kelley hadn't found Pemberton, Forrest was going to throttle him. "Did you speak to Pemberton or not?"

"Not."

Forrest's face contorted with rage.

"I found Lee," Kelley spat out. Forrest smiled. Lee was better than Pemberton. "He's being pressed hard, but he'll send us what he can spare. But General…"

Forrest didn't care for the *but*. He glared at his adjutant. "But what?"

"Lee's line is at least a two hour march from here. Even on the double-quick."

Two hours! It might as well be two years. Forrest whirled around and stared hard at the line. The exhausted men wouldn't be able to defend it much longer.

"Major, I want you to ride back to Lee. Stress to him that we're barely hangin' on. If he don't come now, the Yankees will beat us to Atlanta. Then find General Longstreet and give him the same message."

Kelley nodded. "I need a fresh horse."

"Wheeler!" Forrest hollered. "Fresh horse!" He pointed at the half dozen or so horses tethered to a line.

Wheeler barked instructions to an aide. The captain untied a bay and hurried the horse over. Kelley swung up on the saddle, spurred the horse hard, and bolted toward the rear.

Forrest grabbed the captain's arm. "You go back to the hospitals and gather up all the men who can hold a rifle and send them to the new defenses. If the docs give you lip, tell 'em I said so. Kick the slackers in the rear if you gotta, but get 'em to the line."

The captain nodded and raced off toward the makeshift hospitals. Forrest heard someone calling his name. A young soldier ran up, came to sudden stop, and whipped his hat from his head.

"General Forrest, sir. Major Hurd says the defenses are ready." He plopped his hat back on his head and ran away before Forrest could reply.

A shout of anguish! The men staggered back from the defenses. Yankees were pouring through the fortifications. Wheeler stood in the middle of a flood of men, urging them toward the new defenses. Yankees quickly surrounded the artillery.

An aide jerked Forrest by the arm. "Let's go, General." The aide started running. Forrest did too. It wouldn't serve any purpose to be captured.

Forrest fell behind the defenses, made from rocks, logs, and scrub brushes. It wasn't as sturdy as he'd like it, but considering Major Hurd only had twenty minutes to construct it, the breastworks were a masterpiece. But masterpiece or not, it wouldn't hold the Yankees back. They were rushing forward now, rounding up all gray uniformed troopers in their path. There must be at least 300 of his men marching to the rear and, eventually, to prisoner of war camps in the North.

Wheeler appeared by his side. "General, how soon will Lee arrive?"

Forrest sized Wheeler up. He looked like a man who already knew the truth. "I sent Major Kelley to hurry him up, but he's at least two hours away. We hold to the last man."

Wheeler didn't flinch. "To the last man."

Sherman peered through his fieldglasses and saw church spires close enough to touch. His heart fluttered. He panned to the left and observed a network of trenches and breastworks encircling Atlanta. After the breakthrough on Old Sandtown Road, he had hurried Thomas east to encircle and capture the city before Longstreet could organize a defense. If his men could seize both the Western and the Atlanta Railroad and the Georgia Railroad, he could force Longstreet to evacuate the city. Thomas charged over Peachtree Creek, but Pemberton was there to stubbornly contest the small stream.

As the sun set on Kennesaw Mountain, Bragg retreated, marching swiftly in the dark. Blair got his men on the road, leaving his wagons behind in an effort to outrace Bragg to the city. As the sun came up, Blair's lead elements were within three miles of the city's center, but found Bragg waiting in the trenches. The fighting was as fierce and bloody as the battle along Peachtree Creek yesterday. Sherman threw in Schofield, hoping to overwhelm Bragg by sheer mass. From sunup to sundown, the cannons roared, the rifles unleashed blue flame and death, the ground shook, and the dead mounted. But Bragg stubbornly held.

The next morning, Sherman ordered Thomas to re-cross Peachtree Creek. The fighting quickly descended into a slugfest – bayonets slashed and tore, churning up whole regiments. Foot-by-foot Thomas pushed Pemberton back, but Pemberton made Thomas pay for each foot in blood. The Army of the Cumberland's quartermaster could barely keep up with the demands for ammunition. The hospitals were overwhelmed. Thomas requested doctors from Blair and Schofield, but the two generals didn't have any doctors to spare. Instead, Thomas put his wounded on the trains and sent them up the rails to Chattanooga. It was Thomas' only choice, but in doing so, he sentenced many soldiers to an excruciating death.

About 3:00 in the afternoon, the guns fell silent. Sherman sent Major Dayton to find out if Thomas had managed to break Pemberton. Dayton's report ended Sherman's hope of wrestling the city and the railroads from Longstreet. Thomas' army had waded across Peachtree Creek but had been unable to catch the Rebs before they occupied the trenches along the Decatur Road.

Sherman drew a deep breath and prepared himself for what lie ahead.

Chapter Twenty

September 30, 1864
10:00 A.M.

General Grant,
*   I cannot stress my displeasure at the orders given to General Thomas. To withdraw the Army of the Cumberland at this point gives the Rebs the opportunity to go on the offensive and drive me across the Chattahoochee. I implore you to reconsider your order.*

> *W.T. Sherman*
> *Major General Commanding*

September 30, 1864
5:00 P.M.

General Sherman,
*   The Army of the Cumberland instrumental to my defeat of Lee. Please convey orders to Thomas immediately.*

> *U.S. Grant*
> *Lt. General*

October 1, 1864
Noon

General Grant,
*   Atlanta is instrumental to defeat of the Rebellion. The loss of Thomas puts this in jeopardy. I cannot take Atlanta with just the Army of the Tennessee.*

C.L. Gray

W.T. Sherman
Major General Commanding

October 1, 1864
11:00 P.M.

General Sherman,
    I realize importance of Atlanta. Your current numbers should be sufficient. Convey order to Thomas. Need him on road as soon as possible.

U.S. Grant
Lt. General

October 2, 1864
2:00 P.M.

General Grant,
    Current numbers are not sufficient to take Atlanta. Without Thomas, the enterprise is doomed.

W.T. Sherman
Major General Commanding

October 2, 1864
10:30 p.m.

General Sherman,
    20,000 reinforcements on way to Atlanta. Should arrive in 3 weeks. Send Thomas now.

U.S. Grant
Lt. General

October 3, 1864
6:00 A.M.

General Grant,
Can order to Thomas be delayed until reinforcements arrive? Cannot hold position with present strength.

W.T. Sherman
Major General Commanding

October 3, 1864
4:30 P.M.

General Sherman,
Forward order to Thomas today.

U.S. Grant
Lt. General

October 3, 1864
11:30 P.M.

General Grant,
Will send Right Wing tomorrow morning. Hold Left Wing until reinforcements come.

W.T. Sherman
Major General Commanding

October 4, 1864
6:00 A.M.

General Sherman,
Put Thomas on road today. That's an order.

U.S. Grant
Lt. General

"General Sherman." Sherman turned from searching his trunk and saw Major Dayton framed in the tent door. "General Thomas is here."

"Show him in." Sherman closed the trunk's lid. He swept his jacket off the bed and put it on. Thomas entered and stood at attention. "Sit down, General." Thomas took a seat. "Has the fighting restarted?"

"About noon. It's sporadic. I think the Rebs are as tired as we are," Thomas chuckled.

"I have new orders for you. General Grant has ordered you to Virginia."

Thomas fiddled with the gauntlets lying on the table. "Has my performance displeased you?"

"No," Sherman said quickly. "Let me disabuse you of that notion right now. It's not just you who is going. General Grant has ordered your army to Virginia."

Thomas' face revealed his disbelief. "Sir, what will happen... how can..." He held up his hand. "Can you take Atlanta without my men?"

"No." Sherman was blunt. "I can't."

"Did you explain that to General Grant?" Thomas asked.

Sherman reached behind him and snatched up a small pile of telegrams from his desk. He dealt them, one by one, across the table. Thomas gathered them up. "I've explained it to General Grant," Sherman said tightly. "He wants your army on the road as soon as possible."

Thomas' shoulders slumped. "I know my men would have liked nothing more than to march victoriously into Atlanta."

"Your men have proven they are worthy the accolades poured out on them."

Thomas stood. He extended his hand. "Sir, it's been an honor serving under your command."

Sherman took his hand. "Your dedication to the Union won't be forgotten."

Thomas gathered up his gauntlets and exited the tent.

"Sir."

Longstreet motioned the nervous aide forward. The aide thrust forward his hand. Longstreet saw a slip of paper between the thumb and forefinger. He pointed to it. "Is that for me?"

The aide gulped. Longstreet hid a smile. The lad couldn't be any older than sixteen. "Yes, sir," he squeaked nervously. He still didn't turn loose the paper.

"Can I have it?" Longstreet questioned.

"Oh yes, sir," he squeaked again. He gently laid the slip of paper into Longstreet's outstretched hand.

"Thank you. What's your name?"

"Morris, sir." He stood at attention. "I'm to wait for an answer."

Longstreet read the poorly spelled letter. "Major Goree, let's go visit General Forrest." Longstreet turned to the young man. "Will you take me?"

"Yes, sir." He ran to his horse and was in the saddle before Goree could bring Hero forward.

"What's the matter, sir?" Goree asked.

Longstreet swung up in the saddle. "Seems the Yankees are retreating." With that, Longstreet motioned to Morris. The young man turned his horse and trotted out of camp.

★ ★ ★

Forrest was waiting when Longstreet rode up. Without a word of greeting or explanation, Forrest stalked away. Longstreet hurried to catch up. Forrest stopped, pulled his fieldglasses from their case, and handed them to Longstreet. "The Yankees are pullin' out. Started about two hours ago. Artillery's gone already. Troops leavin' now. We need to hit them." Forrest looked up in the sky. "Two hours of daylight left. Plenty of time."

"You don't mind if I take a look," Longstreet rebuked, but his laugh softened the reprimand.

"If you must," Forrest sighed in irritation.

Longstreet scanned the blue troops moving out of their trenches. "Do you know where they're going?"

"Of course," Forrest huffed. "They're boardin' trains, which are chuggin' north." At the word train, Longstreet lowered the glasses and stared at Forrest. "I've spies in Marietta. They'll verify my thinkin' when the trains pass through."

"You mean if," Longstreet corrected.

"If I meant if, I woulda said if," Forrest snapped. "Union artillery is cloggin' the road to Marietta. That's been verified, just so you know."

"You have been your usual thorough self," Longstreet praised, but it was wasted on Forrest. Longstreet peered through the glasses again. The Yankees were obviously heading somewhere, but he wasn't ready to take Forrest's word that they were heading north. It made no sense for Sherman to send half his army away.

Beside him, Forrest shifted impatiently. Longstreet ignored it and the loud sigh of exasperation that followed. What if Thomas was shifting his troops to slip behind Bragg and seize the Western and Atlanta Railroad from the west? He had to make sure. "Major Goree, check with General Bragg. Tell him to watch out for his left flank."

Forrest fixed a dagger stare on him. "We attackin'?"

"Not until I know for sure where those Yankees are headed?" He cut off Forrest's protests. "I don't doubt your system of spies, but Forrest, it doesn't make any sense. Why would Sherman open himself up like that? All we have to do is cross Peachtree Creek and roll him up. No, there is something else going on. There has to be!"

"Who you tryin' to convince?" Forrest asked.

That was a good question. Longstreet knew Jackson wouldn't hesitate if presented with such an opportunity. He'd already had his corps up and across Peachtree Creek. Longstreet gazed west at the sinking sun. There wasn't enough time to mount a true offensive. "I'll speak with General Pemberton tonight. Get his thoughts," Longstreet announced. Forrest deflated. "We'll hit them at dawn."

Forrest had been correct. The trains that chugged through Marietta were filled with the Army of the Cumberland. Artillery and supply wagons rumbled through the city during the night and long into the next day. Pemberton's corps dashed across Peachtree Creek in hopes of rolling up the Yankees' left flank. But Sherman was gone. During the night, he had crossed the Chattahoochee and put his army out of reach.

Chapter Twenty One

West of Atlanta
December 25, 1864

"**B**illie, see 'em yet?"

"Nope," Billie replied. He swiped at his runny nose with his jacket sleeve. "They've never been late before." He glanced at a third soldier, who was leaning against a pecan tree. "Whatcha think, Johnny, do ya think them Yankees are coming?"

Them Yankees were entrepreneurs who braved the cold waters of the Chattahoochee and the long walk to the Confederate line to trade coffee for tobacco. The Confederates were happy to make the trade since they got the better of the deal: two cups of coffee for one pipe full of tobacco.

Johnny didn't move a muscle. "They'll be coming."

"I hope so," Luke said, worried. "We'se got eggs and bacon this morning, it bein' Christmas and all. Plus, Ma sent a cake. Coffee sure would be good to wash it down with."

"I wonder what the Yankees are fixin' for breakfast. General Morgan cut the railroad again. That's why we ain't heard train whistles for the longest time." Billie said.

"And the trains keep coming from Floreeda bringin' us all kinds of treats. Colonel Carter said just yesterday that we might even have a chicken for Christmas dinner!" Luke licked his lips in anticipation of such feasting. The usual fare was stale bread, a taste of bacon, and whatever else could be scrounged in the countryside.

"I'll believe it when I see it," Johnny said.

"I believe…"

Johnny held up his hand. Luke fell silent. Billie joined the two brothers under the tree.

"What's wrong?" Billie whispered.

"Too much noise comin' from yonder." Johnny pointed toward the river.

"Maybe it's a cow!" Luke was careful to keep his voice soft.

"A cow? Don't be silly, Luke!" Johnny scolded.

"Cows escape the Yankee pens all the time. Colonel Savage's men found one stumblin' through the underbrush just last week. They ate beef for two days."

"It ain't a cow," Billie said. He reached down and grabbed up his rifle.

"What is it?" Luke questioned, his voice rising.

"Ssshhhhh!" Johnny hissed.

Luke clamped his lips shut and gathered up his rifle.

"I'm goin' to check it out." Johnny picked up the remaining rifle and slipped out of the stand of trees. He crossed the clearing and disappeared into the evergreen bushes.

Rifle shots shattered the quiet. Billie raised his rifle. Luke followed suit.

Yankees poured through the bushes.

"Let's go," Billie ordered.

"We need to wait for Johnny," Luke insisted. "We cain't leave him."

Billie grabbed Luke's arm. "Johnny ain't coming back."

Realization dawn. The gunshots! The Yankees had killed his brother! Luke fought Billie's grasp. "Let me go!"

"We gotta warn Colonel Carter that the Yankees are comin'," Billie insisted. "It's what Johnny woulda done."

Luke saw the Yankees advancing across the clearing. Hot anger boiled his blood. One of them blue bellies had killed his brother. He wanted to murder them all, but he only had one shot. He raised his rifle, slowed his breathing, and squeezed the trigger. The ball bore into the chest of a soldier. The Yankee spit up blood then collapsed on the ground. Luke turned and followed Billie.

He made it back to the line only a couple of steps in front of the Yankees. He dove over the breastworks to find the defenses lightly manned. Billie somersaulted next to him. The aroma of bacon and eggs filled the air.

"Yankees!" Billie shouted at the top of his lungs.

No one paid him any mind, so Luke added his voice to Billie's warnings. They were both ignored. Luke turned and looked back the way he had just come. The Yankees were spreading out in line of battle, two waves with bayonets glistening in the rising sun.

Luke reloaded his rifle. The ramrod was clumsy in his hand. He tried to breathe normally but couldn't. Finally, the ramrod slid down the barrel. He drew it out and returned it to its resting place. He raised the rifle to his shoulder and fired. His shot missed. The Yankees kept approaching.

The rifle shot pulled the rest of the men's attention from the breakfast to the fast approaching danger. With a shout, they threw down their mess kits. Skillets overturned in the cook fire and breakfast fell in the flames. They quickly surrounded Luke. Rifles were leveled, triggers cocked, and a volley delivered, but it didn't slow the Yankees down. Three quick strides brought them to the breastworks. Then they were over and within the Confederate line.

Fists flew as gray and blue struggled for supremacy.

"Retreat!" Colonel Carter shouted. "Retreat!"

Luke threw one more fist, which connected with the smooth cheek of the Yankee in front of him. The solider collapsed. Luke fell on top of him, driving his fist repeatedly into the Yankee's face.

Arms grabbed him and hauled him off the unconscious Yankee. Luke whirled about to confront this new threat. He found himself staring into Billie's face. "We gotta go," Billie said.

Luke grabbed his rifle and scrambled after Billie, past the camp fires, now filled with scorched and blackened breakfast. Hot wrath gave him strength and speed. Up ahead, he could see Colonel Carter forming a new battle line. He hurried to the end of the line. One volley and they were running again. Not only was his regiment running, but it seemed all of Donelson's brigade was fleeing as well.

On they ran. After a sprint of a half-mile Luke's lungs burned and a sharp pain stabbed his side. He wanted to stop, but bullets whizzed over head. The Yankees were right behind, closing the gap with every stride. Luke commanded his feet to keep running, but he knew that if he wasn't ordered to stop soon, he would collapse in exhaustion.

Confederate artillery rumbled. Luke glanced behind. The Yankees were ducking for cover. Their pursuit slackened. So did Luke's steps. "You can rest, but only for a moment," he told himself. He began to walk, gulping air into his oxygen-starved lungs. Tears flowed down his cheeks. Johnny had always been his protector in a house filled with violence. When Johnny enlisted in the army, Luke followed so he wouldn't have to stay at home. In the camps, on the march, or on the line, Johnny had watched over him and told him what to do. Now, he was alone. The pain in his side eased, but not the pain in his heart. He tripped over an exposed root and fell hard on the ground. He began to weep.

"Luke." A gentle voice called from overhead.

Luke looked up. It was Billie. "We gotta go."

"Why did you come back for me?"

Billie jerked Luke to his feet. "I promised Johnny that I'd look after you if he was kilt." Billie gave a small smile. "But if I'm to keep that promise, you gotta run."

Luke nodded. Billie turned and trotted off. Luke mirrored his movement. Before he knew it, he was running again.

They quit running when they reached a small church. Ezra Church, this little village was called. Waiting up ahead were a series of trenches and breastworks. Billie jumped into the trench; Luke was second only by a few minutes. Colonel Carter walked behind – calm, cool. His unruffled demeanor did much to settle Luke's fears. Now, here came General Donelson. He conferred with Colonel Carter.

Luke strained to hear what the two men were saying, but another burst of artillery drowned out their conversation.

General Polk was preparing to enter the pulpit when a courier dashed up the center aisle. Between gasps, he announced that the Yankees had cross the Chattahoochee in force. Polk threw off his priestly vestments and headed toward the back of the large tent. Adjutant, aides, and division commanders followed him. They untied their horses and departed Polk's headquarters in all directions.

"Major Richmond," Polk called to his adjutant. "Please inform General Bragg that I have gone to see General Cheatham to ascertain the damage. Ask him to join me as soon as possible."

Major Richmond swung up on his mare and rode off. Polk headed toward the cook tent. He needed some coffee. A quick cup and then he would be off.

The damage was extensive. Cheatham had been pushed off Proctor Creek and back toward the Atlanta and West Point Railroad. A gap then developed between Cheatham's and Withers' divisions. If the Yankees pushed through, Cheatham's would be isolated and surrounded. Polk knew he had no choice but to order his entire corps back into the fortifications protecting the railroad, but he hesitated. He had no desire to face an angry Longstreet accusing him of disobeying orders again. If such a decision had to be made, let it be made by Bragg, who should be here shortly if Major Richmond was true to his orders.

The Yankees began to circle toward the gap between the two divisions. Polk knew he couldn't wait any longer. He sent an aide scurrying to Cheatham with orders to retreat.

Wheeler's brigade came from the direction of the railroad. The troopers dismounted and took their places next to Donelson's exhausted men. Wheeler ordered his battery of horse artillery advanced. Against tremendous fire, the artillery men fired round after round into the blue lines. It was David versus Goliath, but this time the ending would be different. Goliath's strength obliterated horses, men, and limbers. Finally Wheeler ordered the remaining cannons abandoned and the men to safety. Precious time had been gained. The first of Cheatham's men could be seen emerging from the trees. Polk galloped over to greet them.

"Merry Christmas!" They exclaimed when he approached. Despite their cheerful greeting, Polk could see exhaustion in the tired slump of their shoulders.

Drive them back, men," Polk said.

"Will do, General!"

Polk watched as officers corralled them toward the defenses.

"General Polk!" Cheatham pulled up his horse. The gelding's black eyes were rolling and his ears were pinned back in fear. "General Donelson is pulling back also."

"Any word from General Maney?" Polk asked.

A shell exploded. Cheatham's horse reared, blood flowing from a deep gash in its neck. The poor beast staggered wildly. Cheatham jumped off. The horse pitched forward then crashed to the ground. Hooves tore into the dead grass, tearing large grooves in the red clay. Cheatham jerked his pistol from his holster and fired. The great steed's agony ended. Another shell exploded. "General, let's get out of here!" Cheatham shouted. He dashed toward the defenses.

Polk knew good advice when he heard it. He spurred his horse and headed down the line to make sure Maney was falling back as well.

★ ★ ★

Bragg arrived within the hour. He brought news that Hardee was in the process of falling back but Cleburne was holding.

"How are the men?" Bragg asked.

"They have fought to a frazzle," Polk said frankly. "The Yankees keep stretching my line to the left. Can't I get some help from Pemberton?"

"I've sent word to General Longstreet asking for reinforcements, but I don't know what's happening with Pemberton. You need to be prepared to hold with the men you have."

"You make it sound so simple!" Polk spat out. "I'll just multiply men like the Good Lord did with the loaves and the fishes!"

Bragg laughed freely.

"What's so funny?" Polk demanded, his face turning crimson in anger.

"I thought you were a believing man," Bragg said between guffaws. "Surely, you, of all men, can believe for a Christmas miracle."

Polk didn't find the humor in Bragg's statement. He glared at the man but Bragg continued to laugh. Polk couldn't stand it any longer. He stalked away to find Cheatham and figure out a way to extend the line.

★ ★ ★

Polk jerked his watch from his pocket. Three o'clock! Darkness was still two hours away. A half-hour ago the Yankees had punched a hole in his line and wasted no time in flooding the gap with soldiers. Wheeler and Cheatham pushed and shoved and forced the Yankees back. In the respite that followed, Wheeler reported shortages of ammunition, men, and strength. Polk mounted up and rode off to find Bragg.

"General Bragg," Polk called as he leapt off his horse. "My men can't hold any longer. We need to retreat."

"No, you must hold," Bragg informed him.

Find a way to hold! How! Polk thought in frustration.

A shout went up along the line. A long column of men, battle flags waving in the air and drums pounding out a steady rhythm, came from the direction of Pemberton's line.

"It's Pemberton!" Polk shouted, so relieved that he wanted to hug Bragg.

It wasn't Pemberton but Stephen D. Lee. He raised his hand and the column came to a halt. "General Bragg, General Longstreet sends his compliments. Where do you want my men?"

Polk was busy counting the flags. "A division!" He exclaimed in horror. "Pemberton only sent a division."

"It's all he could spare," Lee said.

"Why? Is he under attack?" Polk demanded. He had not heard one angry shot from the east all day.

"No, but the Yankees have been demonstrating all along his line since dawn," Lee replied.

"Demonstrating! I have men dying and Pemberton's afraid of a little demonstration!"

"That's enough, General!" Bragg barked.

Lee ignored Polk and directed a tired eye at Bragg. "Where do you want my men?"

Bragg directed Lee toward the flank. Lee saluted and gave the order. The long column marched by. Polk watched with rising ire. Pemberton was a scoundrel; Longstreet a complete idiot. Why hadn't Longstreet come to see the battle for himself? Or at least sent one of his aides – the ubiquitous Sorrel or the infuriating Goree.

Bragg was staring at him. "Do you expect General Lee to take command of your corps?" Bragg asked.

With a sneer, Polk went to see to his flank.

★ ★ ★

The sun refused to set. Again and again Polk glanced skyward only to observe the sun in the exact same spot in the sky.

"General Polk!" It was Captain Baxter. With a trembling hand, the artillery man wiped a handkerchief across his cheeks and nose, leaving a swathe of pink skin in his soot-covered face. "We're nearly out of ammunition. I've sent two couriers to General Hardee, but I haven't heard back."

Polk's heart sank. Canister and shot were all that was keeping the Yankees off the breastworks. "How many rounds remain?"

"Twenty per battery."

Polk glanced up the sky again. The sun must be glued to that portion of the sky. "Major Richmond!" The adjutant trotted over. "Find General Hardee. Ask him for half his ammunition. Don't take no for an answer. Once the ammunition is on its way, go see General Cleburne and ask for half his."

Richmond nodded and hurried toward his horse.

"What should I do in the meantime?" Baxter asked.

"Fire when the Yankees are close enough to do maximum damage," Polk said. "When they are on top of us," he emphasized.

"Yes, sir," Baxter said. He ran off.

Polk watched him go. All around him the Confederate army lay shipwrecked. Cannon had been blown apart and abandoned. Dead horses lay everywhere. Haversacks, canteens, bayonets, cartridge boxes, and blood-stained bandages cluttered the area. Polk eyes found the sun. No movement! Twenty rounds per battery and then what?

"Here they come!" The shout went up from the line.

Chapter Twenty Two

Sherman leaned against a tree and listened to a soldier singing a Christmas carol. As the voice soared higher, each note pure and perfect, Sherman forgot about the battle just concluded. The song ended and the low rumble of supply trains crossing the pontoon bridges jolted him back to reality.

"Private!" He called to one of the corpsmen packing up his headquarters in preparation of moving it across the Chattahoochee. "Go find that soldier and tell him to sing another carol." The private trotted from the camp.

Sherman smiled. How different this moment felt from those days of despair after the Army of the Cumberland had marched away. He honestly believed then that he would never take Atlanta. Especially after Grant's idea of reinforcements marched into camp. They were conscripts from Washington City, New Orleans, and further points west. Before Sherman could even mount an attack, he had to make soldiers out of the lot of them. He interspersed them through both armies, growing the Army of the Ohio by almost half, and ordered Blair and Schofield to whip the raw recruits into soldiers.

Sherman attended a review of General Osterhaus' Fifteenth Corps. As the soldiers drilled, Sherman couldn't tell the conscripts from the veterans. It was good enough. He ordered the attack for Christmas morning. When the battle came to an end, Sherman watched Osterhaus' men return from battle. All were equally exhausted, equally filthy, and equally satisfied with the efforts of the day.

Music overtook his thoughts. The young soldier had chosen to sing *Silent Night* – his wife's favorite. Tonight, it was the most beautiful song he had ever heard. Was it the song's sentiments or the relief from today's victory that washed over him now? Probably a little bit of both.

Silent night, holy night
Son of God, love's pure light
Radiant beams from Thy holy face
With the dawn of redeeming grace
Jesus, Lord at Thy birth
Jesus, Lord at Thy birth

Major Dayton appeared out of the darkness. "That boy can sing!"

Sherman agreed. The last note faded away. He cleared his throat. "Are the siege guns in place?"

"They will be in about an hour," the adjutant reported.

Christmas wasn't over. Sherman still had one more gift to give to the Rebs.

★ ★ ★

Longstreet threw his hat and gauntlets on a low table. He plopped down on the brocade couch and wrestled his boots from his feet. With a groan he stretched out. His hand sought and found the wool blanket that rested on the couch back. He covered himself and closed his eyes. Even though his body screamed for sleep, his mind refused to obey. The Yankees had caught his army completely off-guard. Once routed the men never recovered their equilibrium. By time the sun had set, the Yankees were firmly entrenched on this side of the Chattahoochee.

With a groan, Longstreet gave up trying to sleep and sat up. From the dining room, he could hear the corpsmen setting the table for dinner. The sound of clinking silver and china stirred up memories of his wife and children during happier times. He allowed the memories to survive until they brought the inevitable sadness, then he searched for something else to fill his mind. The memory that replaced the smiling faces of his children wasn't a happy one either. It was of Forrest accusing him of squandering any chance of winning the war by not attacking Sherman after the Army of the Cumberland had marched away.

While Longstreet believed he had good reason for not giving into Forrest's demands, those reasons grew harder and harder to justify as the days passed. Even though the Confederates had gained a numerical supremacy over Sherman's troops, Sherman held a stronger advantage than numbers. Any attack initiated by the Confederates would include crossing the Chattahoochee, effectively eliminating any surprise. Longstreet couldn't march his men into the waiting guns of the Yankees. He would not be Burnside at Fredericksburg. Those horrible, cold days of December had schooled him in the futility of a direct assault on an entrenched army.

His refusal to advance drew criticism not only from Forrest and Pemberton, but Bragg as well. He could withstand Forrest's criticism as easily as he could dismiss Pemberton's. But Bragg's reproach bothered him.

"I don't understand your reticent," Bragg said over breakfast. "Every day the trains bring more and more soldiers. It won't be long until Sherman returns to full strength. Why are you content just to dig trenches?"

Longstreet scraped eggs from a bowl onto his plate. "I'm preparing for a siege."

"We can't survive a siege."

"As long as we control the railroads from the south, we can," Longstreet replied testily. He was tired of having this argument. "I can't, in good conscience, order an assault. Assaults are costly in supplies, but more importantly in men. These men are all that we have. Lee was severely damaged along the Potomac. He will receive any new recruits Richmond can scrape together."

"Lee was strong enough to repel the Yankees at Manassas," Bragg replied. He poured coffee in his cup. "But if we can drive the Yankees from Georgia..."

"Then what?" Longstreet questioned harshly. "Lincoln has suspended the election. He has proved that he will see this war through to the end. So, we must hold on."

"Hold on? For how long? Until Sherman is strong enough to flank us out of position again? Then what? We retreat to Savannah?" Bragg didn't disguise his frustration. "I know how you feel about frontal assaults. I've heard your all your theories and arguments. But you're letting a golden opportunity pass you by. Attack now, and we could win the war."

"Or lose it!"

Bragg jerked back into his chair. "Pete, you can't let that fear dictate your strategy."

"I'm not," Longstreet insisted.

"Are you sure?" Bragg turned compassionate. "I understand what your legacy means to you."

"I don't know what you mean." Longstreet's answer was icy cold.

Bragg didn't back down. "I'm sure you do. You've spoken of it often."

Longstreet's mind raced. Had he slipped up and given voice to his ambition: his desire to prove himself a greater general than Lee. He didn't think so. "You have me at a loss." His voice shook. He cleared his throat "I honestly don't know what you mean."

Bragg held up his hand. "Perhaps I was mistaken."

Of course Bragg was mistaken. His decision not to attack had nothing to do with protecting his legacy. Jackson's bold gamble to invade Pennsylvania had failed. The losses suffered along the Potomac had reduced the great Army of Northern Virginia to nothing more than a guerilla band. In the spring, Grant would lead the Army of the Potomac from Washington, join up with the Army of the Cumberland, and crush Lee.

That left him. He alone held the hope of Southern Independence in his hands. With Lincoln's suspension of the election, there would be no surrender of Northern resolve and purpose. And when Lee surrendered, Grant would head toward Georgia to join up with Sherman. Then Longstreet would need every last man he could get his hands on. How dare he use up that precious resource to deflect the criticism now coming his way?

He did what he had to do. He constructed three distinct sets of defenses in and around Atlanta. He erected breastworks to defend the railroads coming from the south. He ordered the town emptied of its citizens so they would not be a hindrance to him. He sent them south to Macon and Savannah. Only those men working in the munitions factory were given permission to stay.

He brought in slaves from the surrounding plantations and set them to work turning Atlanta into a fortress. He stockpiled ammunition, food, and water. He took the majority of supplies that came in from Europe and what he sent to Lee, he did so with reluctance. Lee was lost. He was not.

He ordered Morgan to return from Tennessee. The Kentuckian had annoyed the Yankees all he could. When Morgan arrived at headquarters, Longstreet congratulated him on a job well done and gave him a new order. His men were to travel into southern Georgia and northern Florida and strip it bare of livestock.

Morgan was appalled. "We can't steal from our women and children."

"The Yankees will do it," Longstreet replied.

"Yes, but we aren't Yankees," Morgan shot back. "We just can't do that to our people. They've have sacrificed enough."

"I'll leave it up to you as to how much you take from each family," Longstreet conceded.

Longstreet watched his corrals, barns, and warehouses fill. The wounded were shipped to Savannah as soon as they could travel. The solid walls of Fortress Atlanta rose in the streets; the trenches were dug deep and secured by wood and brick.

Then this morning, while he still slept, the Yankees had attacked.

Too tired to think anymore, Longstreet laid back down. He was all thought out. He just wanted to sleep.

Thunder interrupted Longstreet's dream of a summer picnic with Louise. Longstreet frowned. The afternoon had been perfect up until now. The day was warm, the food delicious, and Louise never prettier. He crossed his fingers and prayed that the rain would hold off until they finished their lunch. Now, something was burning. The dream began to fade. The cook must have burned the Christmas goose. He opened his eyes. It wasn't thunder; it was artillery. It wasn't the goose; Atlanta was burning.

The door opened slowly. Colonel Sorrel stood in the doorway, holding a candle. "General Longstreet?" He questioned softly.

"I'm awake," Longstreet replied.

Sorrel opened wide the door. "Sir..."

"When did the shelling start?" Longstreet wrestled on his boots.

"It just did," Sorrel replied. He lit a match and applied it to a lamp.

The house shook. The lamp's flame danced on the wall.

The last vestiges of sleep slipped away. Longstreet was fully alert. This wasn't ordinary artillery. The Yankees had brought up the big siege guns.

"Should we answer them, sir?" Sorrel asked.

Another round of artillery exploded in the city. In three long strides Longstreet reached the window. He threw it open and stuck his head out. A fire engine raced down the street. Soldiers chased after it. Across the street, a house was on fire, but the fire engine and soldiers raced past it. They turned the corner and disappeared. Longstreet could see flames in the direction of the warehouses.

Longstreet withdrew his head from the window. "Colonel Sorrel, round up all the soldiers you can. Get them to the warehouses. If the fires can't be put out, remove the ammunition and supplies. Don't wait too long before you make that decision."

Sorrel nodded. He exited the parlor. Longstreet stuck his head back out of the window. His concern was now for the hospitals. "Major Goree!" Longstreet hollered.

Hurried footsteps came down the hall. Goree burst through the door.

"T.J., go the hospitals. If the wounded are threatened in any way, and I mean in any way, evacuate them."

"Yes, sir." As Sorrel did before him, Goree pivoted and raced from the room. Longstreet heard him run down the hall. The front door slammed against the wall before bouncing shut with a loud bang.

Longstreet closed the window. A shell hit near-by and the house rocked back and forward. He struck the window sill with a fist. How many raids had Forrest and Morgan conducted against the railroad? How many miles of tracks had the two cavalry leaders torn up? How many bridges had they burned?

Longstreet laughed bitterly. After Chancellorsville, when he, Lee, Jackson, and Stuart had met with Davis to discuss strategy, Longstreet believed Jackson's foolish strategy of shutting down the coal mines focused too much on economics and not enough on warfare. It had enraged him when Lee and Davis had agreed with Jackson. Now he knew the truth. Jackson had been right and he had been wrong. The Union war machine was the true enemy. Sherman had lost an entire army, and within six weeks, Washington had practically sent a new one via the railroads. Sherman replaced men, rifles, food, medicine, uniforms, horses, cannon, and anything else his army needed, like siege guns, as quickly as it took the train to rumble down the tracks from Chattanooga.

The house shook again and drew Longstreet from that long ago morning in May. But he still held the railroad to the south and to the east. As long as he held those, he could survive any siege the Yankees threw at him. Even if they burned Atlanta to the ground around him.

Chapter Twenty Three

For the past ten days two things remained constant. The Yankees shelled Atlanta from sundown to sunup and from sunup to sundown they stretched Longstreet's lines to the east and to the south. When the fighting came to a merciful end with the approaching night, soldiers dropped where they stood in the red Georgia clay and slept dreamlessly until the boom of artillery woke them.

Then disaster struck along the Decatur Road. Schofield's constant march to the right stretched Pemberton's line taut. The tipping point arrived at noon when Pemberton finally snapped. Stevenson's Division received the brunt of the Federal attack. General Alfred Cumming's Second Brigade was decimated. Cumming fell rallying his men. The Georgia brigade followed their commander's last request and stood and died for Dixie.

With Cumming's brigade destroyed, the task fell on Isham Garrott's Alabamians to hold the Yankees back. Garrott fell wounded. His men dragged him toward the defenses a mile south of the Decatur Road, but he was dead before they reached safety. Stephen D. Lee steadied his corps and held the fortifications, but Lee couldn't undo the deepest cut. The Georgia Railroad, the Confederate's lifeline to Augusta and the east, was in Union hands.

The stretch of Bragg's line began in earnest south of White Hall. Bragg shifted Polk south to dig in along Utoy Creek. Hardee held the line from White Hall to Five Points. Cleburne was responsible for keeping Bragg linked with Pemberton. But Cleburne's line was paper thin. So intent was Sherman on capturing the railroad that he didn't even notice that Longstreet had left the front door to Atlanta wide open. One push, as Schofield had done on the Decatur Road, and Atlanta would fall.

★ ★ ★

Longstreet found Bragg placing a battery of artillery near the center of his defenses. Like Jackson, Bragg was once an artillery man, so from time-to-time he liked to see to such things himself. Longstreet watched as Bragg sighted the guns.

Sorrel approached. "Sir, General Forrest reports his men are at East Point." At East Point, the railroad from Atlanta split into two. One line ran west into Alabama; the other south to Savannah. "He says Morgan will be joining him there shortly."

"Okay," Longstreet said. He gazed up at the rain swollen clouds. "How much longer 'til it rains?"

Sorrel examined the sky. "I don't know, sir. But not much longer, I should think."

A raised voice drew Longstreet's attention from the storm clouds. Bragg was expressing his intense displeasure about something. With a wave of his hand, Bragg moved the men out of the way and began to push the cannon into place. The cannon refused to move. He yelled again. The men snapped to and added their weight to the wheels. The cannon slid into place.

Longstreet gave Sorrel a pat on the shoulder. "If General Bragg is satisfied with his artillery placement, tell him to open fire."

★ ★ ★

Bragg was satisfied and the artillery unleashed a deafening barrage. Union artillery answered immediately. Shells pounded the Confederate defenses. Polk's men hunkered down behind their fortifications to wait out the storm. The shelling ceased. In the quiet, the skies had their say. Torrents of rain began to fall.

Shouts – pure terror in them. Longstreet looked in the direction of the commotion. Through sheets of rain, he saw a clump of men standing near one of the cannons. The shouts now had words. The men were frantically calling for a doctor. More soldiers ran over. Colonel Brent burst from the group.

"I need a doctor!" Bragg's adjutant hollered at the top of his lungs.

Longstreet's world went spinning. Brent's panic could only mean one thing. The wounded man was Bragg. Brent took off running down the line. He was still shouting at the top of his lungs for a doctor.

Brent wasn't the only running. Longstreet sprinted toward the group of men. He pushed his way through the gaping soldiers and stared down at the wounded, correction, dying man. A large piece of shrapnel stuck out of Bragg's chest. Blood pooled around his body. The rain mixed with the blood and the pool became a puddle that lapped at Longstreet's boots. He fell heavily to his knees, splashing water from the red-tinged puddle onto his pants.

"General Bragg," Longstreet gasped. "What can I do for you?"

Bragg didn't respond. His eyes were closed; his face chalky white. His hands were clenched in fists, which shook uncontrollably.

"Braxton," Longstreet whispered.

Bragg's eyes opened only for a moment. He mumbled something and turned his head.

"Colonel Sorrel, fetch me a blanket or a poncho. Let's keep the rain out of his face." Longstreet's voice trembled with emotion.

Sorrel grabbed a blanket off the nearest artillery man. He gave one end to Goree and together they stretched the blanket out over Bragg. Under the blanket's cover, Longstreet was alone with the dying man.

Longstreet felt hot tears tracing their way down his face. Bragg opened his eyes. Longstreet shuddered in fear. Bragg's eyes had a far away look in them. He was already transitioning from this world to the world to come. Longstreet reached down and took Bragg's hand in his own. The dying man no longer had the strength to keep his hands in fist.

"Tell my wife..." Bragg fought for words and breath. "...that I love her."

"I will."

Bragg closed his eyes and was quiet.

"Braxton!" Longstreet whispered. "Stay with me."

Bragg opened his eyes. "I can't." He closed his eyes. Longstreet felt Bragg's hand go limp. He was in Heaven, leaving Longstreet all alone in war ravaged Georgia.

The blanket must be gone, for Longstreet felt the cold rain on his face, mixing with his tears. He was grateful for that. He didn't want his emotions on display for the men to see. He heaved himself to his feet. Corpsmen stood nearby, a stretcher at the ready. He motioned to them. "Take him to his headquarters."

Longstreet backed out of the way and allowed the corpsmen to do their work. They loaded Bragg's body into an ambulance.

Longstreet sat at his desk, gazing out the window, and remembering the first time he had met Bragg. It had been in Bragg's tent when Longstreet had arrived from Virginia to lay out his ambitious plan to invade the North and win for himself much deserved accolades. And for a brief time, he had succeeded wildly. But since that high water mark just shy of the Ohio River, his army had been pushed back. Now they had been pushed back into the last of the Atlanta defenses and barely hanging on. When Sherman finally pushed at White Hall or East Point, or any where in between, the Yankees would win the prize. Where would the Confederates go then? To Macon, perhaps? But that was for future and he couldn't think of that right now.

A knock on the door roused him from his thoughts. "Come."

It was the cook carrying a tray. The aroma of food filled the study, turning Longstreet's stomach. He waved his hand. "Take it away."

"Colonel Sorrel said you have to eat something."

This time Longstreet waved the cook to put the tray on the desk. There was a stew and some freshly baked bread on the tray, but even his favorite foods couldn't stir his appetite. "Thank Colonel Sorrel for me."

The cook exited, leaving Longstreet alone with his thoughts. Something he didn't really want to be left alone with. Soldiers moved down the street, singularly, in pairs, and in small groups. He watched until the setting sun turned them into shadows and night swallowed them up altogether.

The door opened. Colonel Sorrel stood in the doorway. He entered and lit a small lamp on a table. The room filled with light. Longstreet blinked and blinked until his eyes grew accustomed.

"You didn't eat," Sorrel admonished.

"Not hungry."

"Can I bring you anything else? Some soup?"

"I said I wasn't hungry!" Longstreet barked. He held up his hand. "I'm sorry."

"It's okay," Sorrel said.

"Rudeness is never acceptable."

"Yes, sir. I'll get this out of the way." He took the tray and exited the room.

Longstreet wished his adjutant had turned off the light as well. He was more comfortable with his ghosts in the dark.

Sorrel was back. "Sir, General Polk is here. He says it's important."

Longstreet groaned. The last thing he wanted to do was verbally spar with the Fighting Bishop. "No."

Sorrel said something to Polk. Longstreet could hear the tones escalating. Polk wasn't leaving.

"Moxley, tell General Polk to come in," Longstreet ordered. The argument ceased. Polk came into the room and stood at attention. "What can I do for you, General?"

Polk relaxed his rigid stand. "May I?" He pointed toward a chair.

Longstreet shook his head. "You won't be staying that long."

Polk's eyes tightened and his smile faded. "I'm sorry about General Bragg." Longstreet's silence forced Polk to speak. "Sir, what are you going to do about the army?"

At least Polk didn't waste any time getting to the point. "General Hardee turned down command."

"I know," Polk informed him. A quizzical lift of Longstreet's brow brought forth more truth. "I stopped by his headquarters on the way here."

"Hhmmm."

"Who will replace General Bragg?" This time it was a glare that caused Polk to continue to speak. "I know my timing could be better. I'm mean with General Bragg barely cold. But we are in extremis, sir. And the men need to know…"

"Know what?" Longstreet interrupted. Polk said nothing. "If General Cleburne turns down command, I'll write General Lee and request he send me General Hood."

"You would bring in a stranger?" Polk was aghast.

"General Hood is no stranger."

Polk's chest swelled with indignation. "To this army, he is."

"I trust General Hood." Longstreet sucked in his breath and exhaled slowly to dispel his anger. "And I don't trust you. That's why I would rather bring in a stranger then give you the army. That's why you're here, isn't it? To ask for it?"

"To insist, actually." Polk's tone was cold.

"So you can stab me in the back like you've done in the past?" Longstreet shook his head. "No, thank you."

"I believe I've proven…"

Longstreet pointed a finger at Polk. "This army will be pressed in the next couple of weeks. Pressed like it has never been pressed before. I can't have you in command. I can't be worrying every minute whether *this* is the minute you decide orders are irrelevant. I need a man I can count on. General Cleburne has proven that I can count on him. General Hood has proven the same. If General Lee turns down my request, then General Forrest has proven he will obey orders even when he disagrees with them."

"You would place that slave trader over me?" Polk questioned harshly.

"Yes, I would." Longstreet's answer was frank. "And I would let him decide on his command structure."

Polk rubbed his jaw. "He hates me."

"Yes, he tends to hate cowards."

Polk's face burned with anger. "Be careful what you say, sir."

Longstreet gave him level glance. "Or what? You'll write another letter to President Davis, this time protesting my choice of phrase?"

Polk paced back and forth as if marshalling his arguments for one more go. "The men know me."

Longstreet leaned back in his chair. "You don't incite loyalty in the men. They won't march for you like they do Jackson. They won't die for you like they do Lee."

"I believe you're wrong," Polk replied coldly.

"I don't care what you believe. I lost a good man and a friend this afternoon. If you had any decency, you would have respected that."

Polk's body jerked at the rebuke. "Are you saying that you resent my timing?"

"I resent you," Longstreet said, tired of entertaining this fool. "You have your answer."

Polk strode to the door. "Is there anything I can do to change your mind?"

Longstreet stared at the man. He needed to pull back on some of his sharp words. Polk still led a corps, and Longstreet couldn't afford to have Polk sabotaging the army's effort in the field. He sighed in resignation. "I'll take command of the army myself for the next week or two. Prove to me that you are right for command and I may reconsider. May."

Triumph blazed in Polk's eyes. "You won't regret it, sir." He exited the room.

Rain fell non-stop for five days and Longstreet was thankful. The rain gave his men the rest they desperately needed. Only pickets remained in the trenches. The rest of the men were billeted in houses, barns, slave quarters – anywhere they could find shelter. Extra rations were distributed. Longstreet evacuated all the wounded to Savannah and from Savannah to points south. A quick count showed that his army had lost nearly 10,000 men in the fight for Georgia. Men he could ill afford to lose, for there was no one left to take their place. Georgia, Florida, Alabama, and South Carolina had sent all the men they had. North Carolina's home guard was protecting the state from the Army of the Cumberland. Tennessee and Mississippi had given all they had a long time ago. Virginia's men were spoken for. Those who had managed to avoid the draft or their conscience were not going to enlist now. The dire straits of their nation would not be enough to bring them to the fight. They were cowards and a desperate fight never hardened a coward's spine. Pemberton's army was under 30,000 and Bragg's, dear Bragg, army could bring 32,000 rifles to the line. Sixty-two thousand men were all that were left.

Longstreet re-shifted his strength, drawing Pemberton and Wheeler toward the city's center. From the east, his defenses spread out like a lopsided question mark. Hardee took Cleburne's place at the curve of the question mark. Longstreet was depending on Sherman's tunnel vision to keep Hardee's men safe.

Cleburne and Polk were dug in from the White Hall to Red Oak. Longstreet drew men and cannon from both Hardee and Pemberton and sent them south to East Point. If the Yankees managed to break through at East Point, the only option would be to retreat across the Flint River to the high ground near Jonesboro.

On the sixth day, Longstreet woke to blue skies. The waiting game began: for the roads to dry and for the Yankees to attack. He had done everything humanly possible to guarantee success. It was now up to Jackson's ever kind Providence to grant him victory.

★★★

Longstreet threw back his blanket, sat up, reached beneath his camp bed, and located his boots. He shivered. The morning was cold and the fire in the iron stove had gone out. He gathered up his great coat from off his trunk and slipped it on. Another shiver. He needed coffee. He stepped from the tent.

"Good morning, General," Sorrel hailed.

"Moxley," Longstreet returned. Long strides took him to the fire. He warmed his hands over the flames.

"Cup of coffee?" Sorrel asked.

Longstreet nodded. "Please."

Goree stumbled from his tent, more asleep than awake. He sat at the common table, yawned, and stared into space.

"T.J.," Longstreet greeted.

Goree didn't answer but continued to stare into space. Sorrel chuckled and handed Longstreet a tin cup.

Cannon fire pierced the quiet, jolting Goree awake. He stood and glanced from Longstreet to Sorrel.

"Get the horses, T.J.," Longstreet ordered. Goree ran toward the corral. Longstreet drank his coffee as fast the hot liquid would allow.

His stomach growled in protest. Well, it would have to make due with coffee. There was no time for anything more. Goree was coming with the horses.

✷ ✷ ✷

The battlefield was in chaos. Gray troops rushed by Longstreet, running east toward the Flint River. Longstreet drew up and glanced about him, trying to find someone in charge. Confederate artillery was quiet and over half the guns were already limbered up, preparing to move out. Damaged guns or those lacking horses and mules to move them had already been spiked.

Longstreet saw Cleburne sitting calmly on his horse, directing the retreat. Longstreet urged Hero over. "General Cleburne!"

Cleburne turned. Longstreet saw a bloody gash on the Irishman's cheek. "The Yankees hit us before dawn. They broke through our lines in about a half-dozen places. General Govan is trying to hold them off, but I'm going to have to extract him or his division will be lost to us." Cleburne stopped speaking long enough to wipe the blood off his face with the back of his hand. Longstreet reached into his pocket and jerked out a large bandana. He handed it to Cleburne, who smiled his thanks. This time Cleburne took his time and cleaned the blood from his cheek. "My men are crossing the Flint. I have engineers standing by to burn the bridges once Govan is across."

"Any word from Polk?" Longstreet asked.

"Last I heard, he was fighting, sir," Cleburne responded.

"When was that?"

"About a half hour after the Yankees opened up."

"Do you need anything from me?"

"No, sir," Cleburne said. As an after thought, he offered Longstreet his bandana back.

"Keep it," Longstreet said with a smile.

"Yes, sir. Excuse me, sir." Cleburne spurred his horse and galloped off.

The scene repeated itself once Longstreet reached Polk's line. He knew Polk gave the order reluctantly. Since their confrontation on the night of Bragg's death, Polk had turned into a tenacious warrior bent on proving he was fit for command. He fought his men hard, led from the front, and demanded that they hold against overwhelming odds. He had earned both Longstreet's grudging respect and anger. Where was this Polk in Kentucky or on Missionary Ridge? Why had Polk decided on subterfuge and back-biting as the way to secure promotion? Why hadn't he realized courage and loyalty would have served him better?

"General Longstreet." It was the object of his conflicted emotions. "I had no choice." Polk's explanation was halting.

Longstreet could sense fear in the man. "I know."

"My men are preparing to follow General Cleburne across the Flint."

Longstreet dismounted, took his fieldglasses from their case, and surveyed the field. What he saw depressed him. The dead and wounded filled the field. Dead, swollen horses lay intermixed.

"General Polk, get your corps across the river," Longstreet said.

Polk was replaced by Goree. He handed Longstreet Hero's reins. Longstreet threw himself into the saddle. He was the last one over the Flint. As soon as he reached the eastern shore, the engineers set fire to the bridges.

Chapter Twenty Four

The sun had set on this particularly cold day in January, set on Longstreet's ambition, and set on the hope for Southern independence. For the army was routed and Atlanta was lost. Sherman had attacked on all fronts at dawn and by mid-morning, the Confederates were in full flight south to Lovejoy Station. There was no desperate fight through the countryside, just a mad dash to safety.

Sherman hadn't followed Polk and Cleburne across the Flint. Longstreet watched the Yankees arrive at the river and go into bivouac. He lowered his fieldglasses. "Tomorrow morning, then," he thought. He had that long to dig in at Jonesboro and bring up reinforcements. Throughout the long afternoon men dug in the red clay, burrowing deeper into the ground and reinforcing the breastworks with whatever they could lay their hands on.

Longstreet ordered Hardee south. When the roads were clear, Pemberton was to follow. The first of Hardee's men arrived at Jonesboro in the wee hours of the morning – a trickle at first, then a constant stream. The stream suddenly dried up. The roads from Atlanta were empty. Longstreet questioned General Preston as he followed his brigade to the line, but the Kentuckian didn't know anything. Longstreet sent an aide to Atlanta to find out what was happening, but the ground seemed to have swallowed him up.

A harried courier from Pemberton rode into camp. He handed Longstreet a hastily written message. *We are cut off.* Longstreet turned the message over. The back side was blank. "What happened?" He quizzed the courier.

"The Yankees attacked before the sun was up. We were over run within the hour. Sir, there were Yankees everywhere. On our flank, behind us. Every where we turned."

Longstreet patted him on the back. "Go get yourself a cup of coffee. Major Goree." Longstreet watched Goree lead the courier to the rear.

At mid-morning, the battle opened up at Jonesboro. The thrust of the Union attack targeted Polk's left flank. Sherman stretched the Confederate line and without Hardee and Pemberton, Polk lacked the men to match the constant march to the left. An hour, two hours...never relenting, the Yankees attacked, regrouped, and attacked again.

The next assault brought the Union Fifteenth Corps crashing into Cleburne's right. Not strong enough to hold against the weight of thousands of soldiers, the flank crumpled. The men began to retreat. With good order, they marched south. But when the Yankees gave chase, that good order evaporated. Cleburne's corps dissolved into chaos. The rest of the line collapsed like dominos. The Army of Tennessee was fleeing down the roads to Lovejoy Station.

And just when disaster seemed about to overtake them, Forrest and Morgan were there. Forrest threw himself at the Yankees, giving the routed army time to escape and regroup. The men slid into the defenses and waited. The attack didn't come. No one cared why. They just thanked God that the Yankees had stopped.

Midnight found Longstreet under a tree, wrapped in two blankets, trying to sleep. A small fire blazed but it offered very little warmth against the winter night. He heard another blanket go down. He opened his eyes and saw Forrest collapse on the blanket.

"General," Longstreet yawned, "any word from Wheeler."

"Joe Wheeler can take care of hisself," Forrest said. He stuck his hand under the blanket, pulled out a stick, and with a snort of disgust threw it on the fire.

"I have no doubt."

"Since you're askin' me about Wheeler, I suppose you ain't heard from Pemberton or Hardee." His hand found another stick, which also found its way into the fire. Now satisfied with his bed, Forrest stretched out.

"Hardee's here. He arrived about an hour ago."

Forrest didn't reply. Had he gone to sleep? Suddenly, he sat up. "Do you want me to go find Pemberton for ya?"

"No."

Forrest lay back down. This time he went to sleep. Longstreet rolled over and did the same.

A hand on his shoulder. Longstreet sat straight up and glanced wildly about. A thousand evil scenarios swamped his mind. His gaze finally settled on Sorrel.

"General Lee is here," the adjutant said.

In his sleep-addled mind, Longstreet believed it was Lee, come from Virginia to save his old war horse. The thought burst and he almost wept in despair. Of course, Sorrel meant Stephen D. Lee. He threw off the blanket and went to greet the corps commander. "General Lee, I am so glad to see you. Have you heard from General Pemberton?"

Lee shook his head. "Not since early yesterday morning. He ordered my corps on the road before the Yankees attacked. I tried to get back, but we were cut off. So, I just headed south. My men are coming in now."

Longstreet heard the exhaustion Lee's voice. "Is there anything you need?" He asked compassionately.

"Just a place for my bed roll," Lee replied.

"Come, join me. There's a fire, though the cold has it licked." Longstreet led the way back to the fire.

Lee unrolled his blanket. Forrest snored away. "General Longstreet, I'm sorry I was unable to help General Pemberton."

"Get some sleep," Longstreet said. Lee lay down. "General Lee, how many men are following you into camp?"

"I only have a rough count." In the firelight, Longstreet could see Lee's frosty breath. "About 9,000 maybe 10,000."

Longstreet put his head in his hands. Lee had lost over 5,000 men. He saw movement out of the corner of his eyes. Forrest was awake and watching him.

"I'll go find Pemberton at first light," Forrest said.

Longstreet nodded in appreciation.

★ ★ ★

The cold woke him. Longstreet sat up and shivered. In the gray light of dawn, he noticed Forrest's bedroll was missing. Longstreet shivered again. The fire had died. He struggled to his feet, wrapped a blanket around his shoulders, and poked at the ashes with a stick until the fire sputtered back to life.

"General!" It was Goree.

Longstreet put a finger to his lips. Lee was still sleeping and Longstreet didn't want to wake him.

"Sorry," Goree whispered. "Cook has coffee and biscuits prepared."

He gestured to Goree to lead him toward the coffee.

Longstreet cupped the cup in both hands, warming them against the hot tin. "T.J., let's get the senior officers up. We might have to contend with the Yankees this morning, and I need to know what shape this army is in."

Goree swallowed the rest of his biscuit and went to do as he was told.

The weary army manned a horseshoe perimeter around Lovejoy Station, waiting for the attack that never came. Morgan sent word that the Yankees were still at Jonesboro and were making no preparations to march. Longstreet could hear his army's collective sigh. Morning disappeared into early afternoon. The word from Morgan didn't change. The Yankees wouldn't be attacking today.

Longstreet was relieved. The ground around Lovejoy Station was impossible to defend. He needed to head toward Macon immediately. This presented its own unique set of problems. Macon was filled to bursting with refugees. Longstreet didn't want to compete for the roads with a panicked public who was sure to abandon Macon as readily as they had abandoned their homes. He sent his engineers to find a place to plant the army but ordered them to find that ground north of Macon.

Late afternoon saw the first of Loring's men hobble into camp from the east. They were without arms, canteens, winter coats, and supplies. The only news the soldiers relayed was that they had been whipped. Longstreet ordered the cook fires lit, and the army feasted on the last of the cattle captured from the Yankees. By nightfall the aroma of roasting beef caused Longstreet's stomach to growl with hunger. It had been almost forty-eight hours since he last ate.

He was demolishing a large steak when horse hooves interrupted his meal. He looked up. Forrest dismounted and joined him at the fire. Longstreet smiled. Behind Forrest was Pemberton.

★ ★ ★

Washington City
January 31, 1865

"Mr. President, General Grant is here to see you."

194

Lincoln peered over the rim of his spectacles and saw John Hay framed in the doorway. He frowned at the mantle clock. It was after ten. His heart dropped. There must be news from Atlanta. But for Grant to come this late. He sighed and lifted his eyes upward. *Let it be good news.* "Tell the General to come in."

Grant burst through the door. Lincoln sized him up. Grant's expression gave nothing away. He would just have to wait until Grant revealed his secrets.

"General, what brings you here so late?" Lincoln gestured toward the large chairs in front of the fire place.

Grant fell into the one closest to the fire. With his foot he maneuvered a spittoon next to the chair. He took out a cigar and lit it. Once he was satisfied that the cigar would remain lit, he reached into his jacket pocket and pulled out a telegram. "I knew you'd want to see this right away." He handed the telegram to Lincoln.

As he took the paper, Lincoln suddenly felt giddy. There was no tension in Grant. In fact, as Grant puffed away on his cigar, he looked positively ebullient. Lincoln read the telegram: *Atlanta is ours, and fairly won.* Tears of joy flooded his eyes. Could the end of the war finally be at hand? He wiped at his eyes with a handkerchief and blew his nose. Grant continued to smoke his cigar.

"What of Longstreet?" Lincoln asked when he could speak again.

"He escaped, but not without being severely damaged," Grant said. He threw the butt of the cigar into the spittoon.

"How damaged?" Lincoln asked, staving off the disappointment that swamped him at the news that the Rebs had escaped.

"Sherman reports that he has taken over 7,000 prisoners, most of them from the Army of Mississippi. The Rebs have also suffered a tremendous number of wounded and dead."

"What of our wounded and dead?" Lincoln asked.

"It was a hard fought battle," Grant said slowly. "Sherman puts his dead at 5,000 and his wounded at double that."

Lincoln closed his eyes and sighed. Eighteen Sixty Five was only thirty-one days old and already the year was costly in blood. "Is General Sherman requesting more soldiers?"

Grant shook his head. "No, he has numerical superiority over the Rebs. He can make do."

The answer satisfied Lincoln. "When will Sherman get after the Rebs?"

Grant removed a leather cigar case from his pocket and carefully selected another cigar.

"Does General Sherman plan to get after the Rebs?" Lincoln asked, perturbed at Grant's non-answer.

"General Sherman plans to occupy Atlanta and rest his men."

"Is that necessary?" Lincoln asked harshly. The Army of the Potomac was stuck in Washington because of the miserable conditions of the roads as was the Army of the Cumberland in North Carolina. Now Sherman was going to stop and rest. How would that play in the papers?

Grant blew out a stream of smoke. "Yes, it is."

"For how long?" Again Lincoln was harsh.

Grant didn't seem to notice. "A couple of weeks."

"I don't understand why General Sherman is letting the Rebs up." Lincoln read the telegram again, but this time the words did not bring him comfort.

"I understand your frustration," Grant replied diplomatically, "but resting the men, especially after a hard campaign is the right course of action. They deserve the rest."

"Do you believe that or are you defending your man's decision."

"The men deserve the rest," Grant repeated.

Lincoln let his anger go. He trusted Grant and so far Grant had not disappointed him. He would not start second guessing him now.

"But I'll urge General Sherman to be on his way as soon as practicable." Grant smiled.

"Is it almost over?"

"The war?" Grant asked.
Lincoln nodded.
"Yes, it is," Grant said.
Lincoln believed him.

Chapter Twenty Five

Henry County, Georgia
April 3, 1865

Forrest ducked down behind a row of scraggly hedges and watched a dozen Union soldiers terrorize a woman and her three children. The soldiers didn't speak to the woman but made trip after trip into the large farmhouse, returning with their hands full of the family's possessions. The family's livestock had already been slaughtered and slung across saddles. Sorry looking chickens and a half-starved pig. From behind the house, black smoke rose. The Yankees had set fire to the cotton. They had also ridden their horses through the small family garden, destroying any hope of a spring crop.

Two soldiers fought over a jewelry box. The winner took out a pair of ear-bobs and held them up. Sunlight danced off the diamonds. He pocketed them. A gold chain and bracelet followed. The loser gestured to the woman and spoke harshly. At first the woman refused, but the soldier motioned with his pistol. The woman removed a ring from her left hand.

Forrest seethed in anger. Them low-down, dirty Yankees were stealing the woman's wedding rings! Beside him, Colonel Kelley seethed as well. Forrest put a gauntlet finger to his lips. Keeping low, he hurried to the end of the hedge, passing twenty troopers with their hands on their revolvers, waiting for him to give the word. Forrest knelt next to the driveway, careful to remain hidden. He turned back and held up his hand. His men slid their revolvers from holsters.

The sound of hooves. The varmints were coming. Just another fifteen feet... Forrest sprang into the driveway. He took aim at the lead rider and fired. The Yankee dropped from the saddle and slammed to the ground. Forrest's men burst through the hedges.

A blonde Yankee reached for his pistol.

"You better not," Forrest warned.

The Yankee stared at Forrest. Slowly, he moved his hand away from the pistol and into the air. He barked something in a language Forrest had never heard before. The rest of the Yankees raised their hands in the air.

Forrest motioned with his pistol for them to climb down from their horses. They did as directed. "Any of you fellers speak English?"

"I do," one of the Yankees declared with a thick accent. He held the rank of the captain.

"Tell your men to empty their haversacks. Right here." Forrest pointed to the ground.

The Yankee turned and spoke a long sentence that Forrest didn't understand, but his men lined up and emptied their bags onto the grass. Jewelry, a gold thimble, and even a little girl's doll tumbled onto the lawn.

Forrest's face was thunderous. He picked and poked through the pile but didn't find what he was looking for. "Where are the rings?" He questioned with a shout.

"What rings?" The captain spluttered.

Forrest searched the line of Yankees until he spied the soldier he was looking for. "You there!" He barked. "Empty your pockets!"

The blue-coated soldier gestured that he didn't understand what Forrest had said. Forrest pointed to the captain. "Tell him to empty his pockets." Pockets were emptied and the rings revealed. "Have all your men empty their pockets!" The pile of goods doubled in size.

Forrest gestured with his gun toward the house where the woman and her children watched from the porch. His troopers drove the soldiers before them. "Now you apologize for thievin'," Forrest commanded the captain.

"Sorry, ma'am."

Forrest gestured with his pistol. "All of you."

"Entschuldigen Sie bitte," the Yankees said in unison.

"Colonel Kelley, tell the men to get their ropes," Forrest said. Kelley whispered something to a private, who ran full speed down the driveway.

"Ma'am, send the children to gather up your possessions." Forrest was courteous.

The mother bent down and whispered to the children. They refused to move.

"Them Yankees ain't gonna hurt ya," Forrest said. He smiled. "Now do as your mama says."

The children, a young boy of eight, and two girls, maybe five and four, sidled off the porch, their eyes never leaving the Yankees. Holding hands, they walked rapidly down the driveway. They scooped up their treasures and returned.

Three troopers came down the driveway, leading horses.

"Now, ma'am, go on into the house. You don't want the children to witness what happens next."

The woman's eyes widened. "Are you going to hang them?"

"Yes, ma'am, I am," Forrest replied.

"Good!" She gathered her children. "Let's go into the house." She shut the front door after them.

"Colonel Kelley, there are some good trees on the road."

Kelley gave the order and marched the Yankees down the driveway. Forrest had the dead Yankees dragged onto the road. Ropes were fashioned into nooses and thrown over large branches.

"You mean to hang us?" The captain asked fearfully.

"Not you," Forrest replied. "You're goin' back to General Sherman to tell him what happened to your men."

"You don't need to hang them," he implored.

"Yes, I do. Let's call it an object lesson. Get 'em up on their horses!" He commanded.

When the nooses went around their necks, the prisoners babbled incoherently.

"They are begging for their lives," the captain informed Forrest.

Forrest glared at the Yankee. "I don't care."

He turned and slapped the rump of the horse closest to him. The horse bolted; the Yankee swung back and forward. In quick succession, the rest of the Yankees joined the first.

Forrest returned his gaze to the captain. "Now, git on back to General Sherman and tell him that General Forrest says to fight it out like a man. Tell him when he's found his courage, I'll be right here, waitin' for him." Forrest waved the pistol at Kelley. "Let him go."

Terrified, the captain ran down the road.

Forrest watched him go. "Gather up the Yankees' horses. No use good horseflesh gonna to waste." He swung up on King Philip and rode in the opposite direction of the captain.

"Have a seat, General Forrest," Longstreet said severely.

Forrest plopped in the seat Longstreet had indicated. He stifled a yawn then peeled off his gauntlets.

Longstreet reached into his portfolio and pulled out an envelope. "Do you know what I have here?" Longstreet knew he was shouting, but he didn't care. Forrest shrugged. "It's a letter from General Sherman."

"Yeah," Forrest said through a yawn.

"He's protesting the hanging of his soldiers."

Forrest sat up a little straighter. "They ain't soldiers. They're a bunch of lowdown, thievin' cowards."

Longstreet scratched his brow. "You can't go around the countryside hanging…"

Forrest interrupted. "Why not? Them Yankees have been sent by Sherman to terrorize women and children. Stealin' everything their grubbin' hands can grab."

"It's recognized practice that an army in enemy territory will confiscate supplies from the countryside," Longstreet replied as patiently as possible.

"The first set of Yankees I hung stole a little girl's dolly. That's hardly a supply necessary to maintain an army."

Longstreet's mind could barely comprehend Forrest's words. *The first set!* "How many Yankees have you hung?" He blurted out.

"Not near enough," Forrest said. "'Cause Morgan reports this mornin' that he ran into some Yankees just east of here whose saddlebags were filled with women's underwear. What could Sherman possibly be needin' with those?"

Longstreet didn't reply. Of course, Forrest was right. The Yankees were taking more than necessary supplies, but it still didn't give Forrest cause to hang them. But he wasn't going to debate the cavalry leader on the finer points of supply collection, so he changed tack. "Why did you let some of the soldiers go?"

"To send a message," Forrest declared.

Longstreet held up the letter. "Message received." Forrest snorted in triumph and smugly folded his arms across his chest. "But I don't think it's the message you were trying to send."

Arms were unfolded. "Whatcha mean?"

"General Sherman has made it clear that he will retaliate your attacks on his men by hanging any of ours that come into his lines."

Forrest snorted again. "Deserters deserve to be hung."

Longstreet shook his head in disbelief. "You're a hard man, Forrest."

"Why turn insultin?" Forrest asked with a hurt voice.

"I didn't mean to be insulting," Longstreet responded, surprised at Forrest's reaction. He didn't think mere words could pierce the cavalry leader's thick skin.

Forrest cleared his throat. "Perhaps you should publish Sherman's note throughout the army. It'd stop desertions cold."

Longstreet chuckled. "Perhaps." He grew somber. "You can't hang any more Yankees."

Forrest scowled. "They cain't be allowed free reign to ride around the country scarin' women and children. If we hang enough of 'em, they'll stop."

"No, they won't," Longstreet replied. "If I thought it would stop them, I would tell you to continue."

Forrest blazed to anger. He pointed his finger at Longstreet. "You're retreatin' again."

The accusation caught Longstreet by surprise. There was no way Forrest could have known. He had just reached the decision to retreat early this morning.

Forrest leapt to his feet, his face red with rage. "I've been beggin' you to attack the Yankees, but for the last year, you've let every chance pass you by. The time to fight was when Thomas left, but right now will have to do."

"I don't have to justify my command decisions to you." Longstreet was yelling again.

"What a disappointment you've turned out to be," Forrest shot back.

"You're dismissed," Longstreet said, holding back the rage threatening to engulf him. Without a word, Forrest started toward the tent door.

"If I hear that you've hung, shot, knifed, or executed a Yankee by any other means, I will have you arrested. Do you understand me?"

"Oh, yes, I do." This time it was Forrest who was insulting. Then he was gone.

Chapter Twenty Six

Macon, Georgia
End of April, 1865

As soon as the head of Hardee's columns marched into Macon, panic ensued. Those who had refugeed from Atlanta packed their belongings and lit out for Savannah. Wheeler described the roads south as a sad and sore trial. Ladies trudged along with weary children by their sides. The elderly were heaped in wagons along with the baggage. The roads were lined with items that told of a civilization lost. But those who had retreated from Dalton to Resaca to Atlanta and finally to Macon simply refused the army's edict that they evacuate the city for safer regions. They had gone as far as they were going. If the army abandoned Macon to the Yankees, they were prepared to throw themselves on Sherman's mercy.

Longstreet dug in, extending his lines east and west in preparation of the flanking movement he knew was coming. His problem remained the same: manpower. The latest reinforcements up from Savannah and Florida didn't inspire confidence: old men who should be sitting under shade trees telling stories to their grandchildren; old campaigners who had already sacrificed arms, legs, and eyes but were now returning to the army because they knew just how desperate the fight had become.

But most were young boys, not even old enough to shave. These recruits Longstreet sent home. Oh, how they protested his order and swore up and down that they could fight as good as their fathers and brothers. Longstreet assured them that he knew that, but their future lay in the rebuilding of the South once the war ended.

It was the first time Longstreet admitted to himself that the South would lose the war. He didn't know how his depleted army would hold off the Yankees once Sherman gave the order to attack. He wished Bragg was here to advise him. Pemberton didn't have the experience and neither did Polk – the new commander of the Army of Tennessee. Actually, Polk's advancement was the only bright light in an otherwise dismal winter. Polk took his promotion seriously and executed his orders with a diligence that made Jackson look like a slacker. During sleepless nights, Longstreet wrote letter after letter to Lee asking for advice, but he couldn't bring himself to send them. He couldn't admit that all he wanted to be was Lee's old war horse again.

He even considered Forrest's advice to attack, but in the end decided against it. He would defend Macon until those blue lines snaked around his own. Then he would retreat to fight another day.

April turned to May. The Union army burned Atlanta to the foundation stones and headed south. Forrest begged to be allowed to attack. Longstreet acquiesced fully expecting Forrest to come skedaddling back to the safety of the breastworks, but Forrest whipped the Yankees and sent them skedaddling instead. Then Sherman did a surprising thing. He stopped his march and threw up defensives.

The armies stared at each other for the next couple of days – waiting... watching. Sherman ended the stalemate by putting his army on the move. Forrest plunged in again but soon found himself in quite a scrape. It took three orders from Longstreet before Forrest obeyed and broke off the attack. He rode back to the defenses and received the shouts and acclamation of the men. The first real emotion Longstreet had ever heard from the army, and he was jealous of the fiery cavalry leader.

Schofield attacked Pemberton on the right. With shouts of "Remember Atlanta!" Lee and Loring held their ground and sent the Yankees reeling back across the clover dotted meadow. Supper celebrated a victory that had been sorely lacking in the retreat through Georgia.

The next morning Blair's Army of the Tennessee came screaming across the field. Cleburne's corps met them with a scream of their own. Cleburne prevailed. The Yankees limped back to their camps.

The week's end saw alternating attacks on the flank, but on a drizzly Monday morning, the Yankees hit the entire line. The collapse happened so quickly that Longstreet didn't have time to get the large stores of food and ammunition on the trains. He ordered the warehouses open. Hungry citizens mobbed the rail yard, shouting and pushing each other like waves rolling on and off the shore, clawing to the front of the line desperate to come away with just some of the supplies the army was abandoning. Old men labored under the burden of flour sacks. Children wrestled hams down the street. The crowd reminded Wheeler, who tried to keep the chaos from descending into anarchy, of the frantic activity of an anthill that had been disrupted by a careless foot.

When the warehouses were emptied, Longstreet ordered the ammunition depots destroyed. Large explosions rocked the city. Windows shattered in the concussion and buildings near the depots collapsed, showering the retreating soldiers with brick dust.

The Yankees pursued through the burning city but ventured no further. Forrest prowled the city's edge daring the Yankees to attack. They refused to take Forrest up on his challenge. Days passed. The Yankees remained ensconced in the city. A multitude of train whistles announced why. Sherman was bringing up supplies.

May slipped away. June arrived.

Chapter Twenty Seven

Near Jeffersonville, Georgia
June 5, 1865

Longstreet sat outside his tent drinking the last of the apple cider. The Yankees had departed Macon this morning, but as the temperature soared, they went into bivouac. So, tomorrow or the next day, the two armies would clash again.

He drained the tin cup. What was it about cider that made him thirstier? He strode over to the table and plunged his finger into a bucket. The water was somewhat cool. He fished out the dipper. He slopped more water down the front of his shirt than made it into his mouth, but he didn't mind. In this heat, the water felt good.

He heard footsteps. "Who's there?" He asked the darkness.

"It's Major Goree." Goree's voice was strangled. He practically staggered into the firelight.

"What's wrong, T.J.?" Longstreet asked. "Are you sick?"

"Telegram..." Goree held out a slip of paper.

Suddenly, Longstreet felt apprehensive. Something in that telegram had struck Goree speechless. He held up his hand as if to ward off bad news. "Just tell me, T.J."

Goree gulped. Tears flowed down his cheeks. "General Lee..."

Lee was dead! It was the first thought that popped in his mind. He sat down heavily in the nearest chair. He couldn't bear to hear anymore. He closed his eyes. Tears gathered behind his eyelids. "What about General Lee?" He slipped his handkerchief out of his pocket and wiped at his eyes.

"He surrendered the Army of Northern Virginia," Goree announced. He wept unashamedly. "What's going to happen to General Lee? Or General Jackson and General Stuart?"

Longstreet didn't know the answer. "May I have the telegram?" Goree handed it over. With heavy legs, Longstreet walked over to the fire. He read the telegram in the fire's light. The telegram was from Seddon. Richmond had fallen, the Cabinet had fled the city, the Army of Northern Virginia had been disbanded, and if all that news wasn't devastating enough, the Army of the Cumberland was headed south.

The trains coming into Macon! Were they filled with Thomas' army?

"T.J., I need to see Generals Pemberton, Polk, and Forrest." Goree wiped his eyes with his jacket sleeve. "And T.J., don't tell them the news. Okay?"

"Yes, sir."

What to do? That question attacked Longstreet's mind like a swarm of bees. Lee had surrendered. Jackson had let him.

What to do? He asked himself again. If Thomas was returning, then Sherman's army would be almost triple the size of his own. With Lee now surrendered, what would prevent the Army of the Potomac from joining Sherman. Then what?

"General Longstreet?"

Longstreet looked up and saw Pemberton. "General Pemberton. Would you like a cup of coffee?"

"It's too hot for coffee," Pemberton replied.

"There's water on the table. But I'm afraid it's not very cold." Pemberton declined. "We're waiting for General Polk and General Forrest."

The sound of hard riding announced Forrest's arrival. He jumped off King Philip and bounded over. "That there water cold?" He pointed at the bucket on the table. He didn't wait for an answer. The dipper made a loud splash. Forrest slurped it down then made a face. He emptied the bucket on the ground and thrust it at the nearest corpsman. "Bring it back with cold water." The corpsmen hustled to obey.

"What's up?" Forrest asked. "Your aide looked like someone kilt his dog."

"We'll wait until General Polk arrives," Longstreet replied.

They didn't have to wait long. Polk arrived and joined the group. The corpsman returned with the bucket. Forrest hurried over. In went the dipper. Forrest drank noisily. He smacked his lips. "That's much better." He turned his attention to Longstreet. "Well?"

"There's news from Richmond," Longstreet began. He fought back the tears that pooled in his eyes. The three generals turned somber eyes on him. "Lee has surrendered." This produced gasps of shocks. "Richmond has fallen and Davis and the government are on the run." Longstreet waited for some kind of reaction, but all three generals just sat in stunned silence. "The Army of the Cumberland is on its way south. I think we can also expect the Army of the Potomac to follow shortly."

Pemberton whistled.

"Then we should attack before them other Yankees git here," Forrest said.

"Why? The war's over," Pemberton said.

"For Lee, yes, but not for us," Forrest replied sharply. "We still got an army that could damage the enemy if it would just get out from behind these breastworks and fight as the Yankees come up tomorrow."

Pemberton shook his head. "Do we have the right to sacrifice any more lives for a Cause that is lost?"

"Then perhaps you better run on home to Pennsylvania…"

"General Forrest, don't you finish that sentence," Longstreet ordered harshly. Forrest went silent. "We have a decision to make and turning on each other is not the way we're going to arrive at an answer."

Forrest sat down, folded his arms against his chest, and glowered first at Pemberton and then at Longstreet.

"I agree with General Pemberton about the useless sacrifice of life," Longstreet said. Forrest swelled up in anger. Longstreet pointed a warning finger at Forrest. "But I don't think the time has come to surrender. As long as Thomas hasn't arrived." Longstreet glanced at the generals. "But my fear is that the trains we've heard for the last week haven't been bringing in supplies like I thought but Thomas' army. General Forrest, do you think you can manage to get some spies into Macon."

"I know some men who could blend in," Forrest said.

"Good. If Thomas hasn't arrived, then he's on his way. That means we need to get in the Yankees' rear and tear up the railroad. General Forrest, that's a job for you."

"No!" Forrest yelled. "You need me here. To put steel in your spine."

Longstreet grew angry. "There's nothing wrong with my spine. And I'm not going to tell you again to watch what you say."

Once more Forrest folded his arms and glowered.

To cool his anger, Longstreet turned to Polk. "General, you've been awfully quiet."

"I have to admit, it does look grim. But if Thomas hasn't arrived, then we still have a small window of opportunity to defeat Sherman..."

Pemberton interrupted. "What will be gained? Lee is still surrendered. His men are either in prison or paroled. The Army of Northern Virginia can't help us anymore."

"If the men are paroled, they'll join us," Forrest insisted.

"Not unless General Lee gives them permission," Longstreet stated. Forrest started to argue. "It's true whether you believe it or not."

"Do you think this army can defeat the combined Union forces? Especially if Grant retakes command?" Pemberton wouldn't let go of his argument.

"Sherman, Grant, it doesn't matter," Polk said. "What happens in the next few days will decide this army's fate. General Forrest is correct. We need to attack Sherman as he brings up his army."

"It's a waste of life," Pemberton insisted.

"Okay, thank you gentlemen for your counsel," Longstreet said. "I don't want the men to know Lee has surrendered. It will just open the floodgates of desertions. General Forrest, I know you think you need to babysit me, but I need you to get behind the Union lines and slow Thomas down." Longstreet addressed Polk and Pemberton. "Colonel Sorrel will deliver your orders before dawn. That's all, gentlemen."

"Yes, sir."

Polk and Pemberton headed toward their horses. Forrest hung back.

Longstreet sighed in exhaustion. "What is it, General?"

"I want you to reconsider sending my men. General Morgan is more than able."

"Yes, he is. But if the day should go against us…"

"That's why I should be here," Forrest insisted.

Longstreet held up his hand. "If the day should go against us, then I want you as far away from Yankee justice as I can get you."

Forrest's face revealed his shock. "Why do I need to be avoidin' Yankee justice?"

"For the hangings. Just in case."

Forrest didn't say anything. He paced back and forth deep in thought. "I'll get my men into Macon immediately. I'll have them report directly to you. My men will head out at first light."

"Thank you, General," Longstreet held out his hand.

Forrest took it. "It's been a pleasure. Now fight them hard and don't let them up."

"I will."

★ ★ ★

Dawn approached. Longstreet collapsed in the bed and stretched out. Hopefully he could sleep for an hour. He closed his eyes. The tent flap opened. "What?" He snapped.

"General Longstreet," Forrest said.

"Why are you still here?"

"A messenger under white flag entered our lines. Wheeler's pickets stopped him. He had this." Forrest held out a piece of paper.

Longstreet sat up with a groan. He took the paper, walked over to his desk, and lit a candle.

> *3:30 a.m.*
> *June 6, 1865*
>
> *General Longstreet,*
>
> *Lee has surrendered. General Thomas will arrive in the next day or two. I expect the Army of the James to arrive by the end of the week. Why risk further bloodshed and needless deaths? I've been authorized to offer you the same generous terms General Grant gave General Lee. Let us end this war.*
>
> *General Sherman*
> *Major General Commanding.*

Longstreet folded the paper. "I guess that answers the question about Thomas."

"Yes, sir, it does," Forrest agreed.

Longstreet wrote rapidly and handed a note to Forrest. "For the courier. I assume he's waiting for a reply."

"Yes, sir," Forrest said. "Good luck, General."

"You, too."

Once outside, Forrest opened the note. *Not yet* was all Longstreet had written.

Chapter Twenty Eight

Sherman read Longstreet's answer. He shook his head in disbelief. What did Longstreet hope to gain by remaining in the field? Three more hours, days, weeks, or months of fighting wasn't going to change the fact that the Confederacy was dead. Sherman wadded up Longstreet's reply and threw it on the ground.

Anger goaded him to get on the road, find the Rebs, and hammer them into surrender. But reason won out over anger. Thomas was in Atlanta, loading his troops on the trains. He would wait the forty-eight hours it would take the Virginian to arrive, then he would launch his final attack.

The time for Thomas to arrive came and went. Twelve hours. Twenty-four hours. No telegram. (The lines had been cut.) No courier. Nothing. Atlanta might as well have been an island in the Pacific for all the information Sherman was receiving.

Forrest! It had to be! Sherman sent orders to Stanley: don't come back until that devil was dead. It was well after midnight before Stanley returned. Sherman took one look at the exhausted cavalry leader to know that he had been whipped again.

Sherman seethed in wordless fury. Once communications were re-established, he was going to wire Washington and ask Grant to send Sheridan to Georgia. Sheridan would disperse Forrest's troops like confetti on the breeze.

With no idea when Thomas would arrive, Sherman wheeled Blair's troops behind Schofield and launched a dawn attack on the Reb fortifications. By time the sun reached its zenith, the two armies were locked in a death match. *What made these Rebs fight so hard for a Cause that was lost?* Schofield's men staggered back across the field. Disappointed, Sherman lowered his glasses.

Then this morning, an answer to prayer – Thomas rode into camp.

"I'm sorry I was delayed," Thomas apologized. "Reb cavalry dogged my steps the entire trip."

"Understood," Sherman replied. When this war was over, he would personally track down Forrest and see him hung. "Will your men be ready to fight tomorrow morning?"

"I'll only have about a third of the army," Thomas responded. He accepted a cup of coffee from the corpsmen.

"It will have to do. Tomorrow, we end this."

June 14, 1863
Jeffersonville, Georgia

The parlor in the small house was stifling in the afternoon heat. Longstreet paced back and forth, feeling trapped within the confines of its four white walls. This morning, the room had been a bevy of activity as orders went out in anticipation of battle. Now, the parlor had been stripped of all traces that the Commanding General of the Armies of Tennessee and Mississippi had occupied this room as his headquarters. All that remained was the furniture and Sorrel and Goree, who were sitting on the horsehair couch.

The clock on the mantle ticked away the seconds. With each tick, the room grew smaller and hotter. Longstreet stuck his head out of the window and breathed deeply. He withdrew back into the room. He turned and his eyes fell on his two aides. Poor Moxley and T.J. They hadn't said a word since they had arrived. Their faces just grew paler and their eyes wider as they sat and waited for Sherman to arrive.

Longstreet returned to the window. Even now, he was surprised at how easy it was to make the decision to surrender. When he had first come west, he had only seen bright horizons. But he had learned through the long retreat that Mars wasn't going to crown him with success. It was a bitter pill to swallow and, at first, he gagged on it. But Bragg died and he realized that there were more important things than his own ambition.

He watched this morning's battle with his heart in his throat. His gallant men struggled to keep back the blue tidal wave. Then, in a blink of an eye, Pemberton's flank gave way. The Yankees swamped the line. It was over. He wouldn't ask his men for any more sacrifices. What was needed now was life. He would send the men who had followed him faithfully during the long retreat home to their wives and family so they could rebuild their lives under the Stainless Banner that they had so valiantly fought for. "T.J.! Find me a white flag." Goree stood rooted in place. "Go on, T.J."

The mantle clock chimed the hour. Five o'clock. Longstreet glanced at his aides. They looked as if they were preparing to meet death face-to-face. He wanted to speak comforting words to them but didn't know of any.

Horses came down the street. If it were possible, Sorrel and Goree turned paler. Longstreet peered out the window. Union officers dismounted and poured into the yard. Their behavior puzzled him. Each and every officer was slumped in despair. There was no air of victory, no lightness from accomplishment – just a weary sadness.

The front door opened. The floor in the foyer squeaked under the weight of boots. A red-haired man appeared in the doorway. "General Longstreet?"

Longstreet turned from the window. "Yes."

"I'm General Sherman."

Longstreet extended his hand but Sherman brushed past it.

Sherman pointed at the desk. "Can I sit there?"

Longstreet nodded.

Two armed guards took position at the door. Their presence was not lost on Sorrel and Goree, who sat up at attention, color rapidly reappearing in their faces. Longstreet peeked out the window and saw armed guards spreading out in the yard and street.

"It's nice to finally meet, General." Longstreet took a seat in a wing-back chair. "I'm here to surrender the Army of Tennessee and the Army of Mississippi."

"Are you alone?" Sherman questioned brusquely.

"My adjutant, Colonel Sorrel and my aide-de-camp, Major Goree are with me." Longstreet gestured toward the couch.

Sherman didn't acknowledge them. Longstreet observed Sherman's demeanor. He appeared to be a man who had suffered some sort of blow.

"Are General Bragg and General Pemberton still with their armies?" Sherman reached into his jacket and withdrew a gold pen.

"General Bragg is dead," Longstreet answered. "He died in the battles around Atlanta, but General Pemberton is with his army."

"And I suppose Forrest is somewhere in the rear destroying my supply line?" Sherman snapped.

Longstreet was glad to hear anger in Sherman's voice. It helped to settle some of the uneasiness coursing through his body. He nodded in response.

"General Grant…" Sherman paused. Tears flooded his eyes.

Longstreet wanted to ask Sherman what was wrong, but before he could, the Union commander took a breath and continued. "General Grant offered General Lee the following terms. For the unconditional surrender of the Army of Northern Virginia, the men would be paroled to their homes provided they do not to take up arms against the United States Government. He allowed the cavalry and the artillerymen to keep their animals. He insisted on a formal surrender parade where colors and weapons were surrendered. These are the terms I offer you."

"They're very generous." Longstreet was pleased. No prison for his men.

"Perhaps too generous," Sherman barked.

Longstreet didn't know how to respond. He glanced again at his aides. Uncertainty filled their eyes. Sherman settled back in the chair. He was done speaking.

"I accept the terms," Longstreet said.

The guards at the door whispered to each other.

Sherman slid two pieces of paper across the desk. "I've already written them out. I'll give you a moment to read them."

Longstreet read without comprehension. He reached the end of the page. "Focus," he whispered to himself. He shut his eyes and started over. The words were a jumbled mess on the page. When he reached the bottom of the page, he still didn't understood what he had read.

"Are the terms acceptable?" Sherman questioned sharply.

"Of course," Longstreet agreed.

"Then I need a signature." Sherman rolled the pen across the desk.

On the desk was an ink pot. Longstreet popped the lid off and dipped the pen. He only paused briefly before signing the bottom of the paper. He was satisfied with his signature, for he had signed with a strong hand. He slid the first page to Sherman. He signed the second page, blew on his signature, and handed the page to Sorrel.

Sherman snatched up his pen, wiped the nib on the blotter, and stowed it in his pocket. "I placed General Blair in charge of organizing the surrender ceremony. Who will be your army's representative?"

"Me," Longstreet replied.

"No, you won't be here," Sherman said.

Longstreet glanced back at the couch. Sorrel and Goree moved to the edge of the couch, alert and on-guard. The soldiers snapped to attention.

"Where will I be?" Longstreet asked.

"You're under arrest."

Longstreet found his feet. "Why am I under arrest?" His voice was calm.

"For planning the assassination of President Lincoln and the murder of General Grant." Sherman voice was anguished.

The news hit Longstreet like a sledgehammer. His knees buckled and he gasped. *Dear Sam was dead.* "Surely, you don't think I had anything to do with Sam's death?"

"What I think doesn't matter," Sherman snapped. "The order comes from President Hamlin. Guards, arrest him."

Longstreet backed up until he hit the window. He was trapped. The only escape was through the soldiers, but even if he got passed them, he would still have to contend with the guards in the yard.

"Stay back!" Sorrel's voice suddenly filled the room. He jerked his revolver from its holster. Goree followed in kind. "Or I'll shoot."

"Order your men to stand down!" Sherman barked at Longstreet.

"Colonel…"

Sorrel pulled back the hammer. "No, General, I won't let them arrest you for something you didn't do."

"Moxley!" Sorrel glanced at him and Longstreet saw murder in his adjutant's eyes. Sorrel was prepared to die to protect him. "Please."

Sorrel reacted to the plea in Longstreet's voice. He lowered his pistol. The guard raised his rifle butt and struck Sorrel in the stomach. The adjutant doubled over and received a rifle blow to the head. He fell to the ground in a heap. Goree rushed to Sorrel's defense, hand on his pistol. The guards pointed their rifles at Goree.

"T.J., stop!" Longstreet said.

Goree stood still: defiant and helpless at the same time.

Longstreet whirled about and appealed to Sherman. "I've been up to my knees in red clay since December, same as you. I had no hand in the murder of General Grant. He was my friend."

218

Sherman gestured to the guards. "Place General Longstreet under arrest."

Goree helped Sorrel to his feet. Woozy, the adjutant collapsed on the couch. Blood oozed from a cut on his forehead.

"You know I'm telling the truth," Longstreet said to Sherman.

"I have my orders. That's all I care about."

The guard produced manacles. Quickly, he shackled Longstreet's ankles and wrists. He jerked on the chain.

Longstreet lost his balance and stumbled forward. He managed to keep his feet. He turned toward Sherman. "General Sherman, give me a moment."

Sherman gestured to the guard.

"Moxley, are you okay?" Sorrel nodded in response. "T.J., tell General Pemberton that he's in command. Give him the surrender terms. I need both of you to do this for me."

"Yes, sir," Goree said.

Sherman gave another gesture.

"Let's go," the first guard ordered. He gave another jerk on the chain.

Longstreet hobbled out of the room.

Chapter Twenty Nine

The cell door clanged shut. Longstreet stood still, afraid to move in the suffocating darkness. He had no idea where he was. From the small house in Jeffersonville, he had been hustled onto a waiting train and chained to the side of what was once a cattle car. In the hot, humid sun, the car stank to high heaven. Day after long day the train rattled onward to some secret destination. In the evening he was given a small scrap of bread and a swallow of water. Not once did he see the sun or the stars or feel solid ground beneath his feet. Just the ever swaying train car as it raced north.

Tonight the train had rolled to a stop. The door slid open and an armed escort waited for him. Two guards took him by the elbows, hauled him down a wooden ramp to a covered wagon, and tossed him in the back like a rag doll. The wagon rumbled through the streets. Longstreet heard horses riding along side.

The wagon jerked to a halt, pitching him forward. He groaned in pain as his shoulder slammed into the side. The canvas flap was pulled back, and he was yanked from the wagon and deposited onto the ground. In the torch flames, he saw the outline of stone walls and barred windows. He took a deep breath of fresh air. Guards came forward, grabbed the chains, and hauled him inside. Navigating the stairs was difficult. He slipped and crashed to the ground. Unkind hands dragged him to his feet. His ankle throbbed with every step, but he ignored the pain. He saw two Union soldiers standing guard at a door at the end of the hall. He wondered what desperate creature was imprisoned in there.

"Halt!" A large, fat corporal shouted. He produced a key and unlocked the chains around his prisoner's wrists and ankles. A key now scraped in the lock and the next thing Longstreet knew he was pushed into a black cell. The door slammed shut behind him. He stood still until his eyes could adjust to his new surroundings.

"Who's there?" A familiar voice queried him. "I said who's there?" The voice demanded an answer this time.

Longstreet smiled. The voice belonged to Joe Johnston. "Joe!" Happiness surged through him. "It's me. Pete."

"Pete!" Johnston's voice was filled with relief.

Longstreet could finally see. In the faint moonlight that dripped in through the high window, he made out the shadow that was Johnston standing by a bed. Longstreet extended his hand.

Johnston brushed the hand aside and hugged him close. "I'm so glad to see you. Not that I'm glad you've been arrested, but I'm glad that I'm no longer alone."

Another bed stood against the opposing wall. Longstreet crossed to it and collapsed. The straw ticking was wet and so was the blanket. He pushed the blanket onto the floor. "Who else is here?"

Johnston sat on his bed. "General Lee and General Jackson are somewhere, but I haven't seen them since we were brought here."

"When was that?"

"I've lost track of the days," Johnston confessed. He sighed. "Oh, Pete, if you're here, then it means the war is finally over." His voice wobbled.

Longstreet felt his own throat tighten. To keep from talking about the surrender, he changed the subject to one that had nagged at him all during the long trip from Georgia. "Did General Lee have anything to do with the murder of General Grant?"

Johnston stiffened with rage. "General Lee would never consent to something like that!"

"General Jackson?" Longstreet queried.

"You know better than that, Pete."

Longstreet did know better than that, but he had to be sure. After all, Grant had been a good friend.

"None of us had anything to do with it," Johnston continued, his voice still heated with indignation. "An actor shot Lincoln and Grant. The Federal government grabbed onto it as an excuse to have us arrested."

"The Yankees going to hang us, aren't they?" Longstreet asked flatly. That first night in the rail car, Longstreet accepted the fact that this journey would end in his death. He allowed that reality free reign for the night and wept hot tears because he would never see his wife or darling children again. He made a solemn promise not to think of his family until he climbed the gallows. Then he would flood his heart with their memories.

"After they have their show trial, I suppose so," Johnston said in resignation.

"If I had known what they had planned for me, I would have never surrendered," Longstreet declared.

"I'm sure General Lee shares your sentiments."

Suddenly Longstreet had to know. "How is General Lee?"

"He was fine the last time I saw him."

"And General Jackson?"

Johnston laughed. "General Jackson remains the same. Trusting in his ever kind Providence."

"I wish the Yankees had the good sense to arrest General Stuart. Then we would have had some entertainment while we waited for them to hang us." Longstreet laughed as well.

"Actually, General Stuart slipped through the Yankees' grasp. At least he did the night we were all arrested."

Longstreet smiled. It was the first bit of good news he heard since his arrest. Stuart was still out there.

"Tell me, Pete, how did you find the West?" Johnston asked.

Longstreet strained to hear resentment in Johnston's voice, but there wasn't any. "I felt as safe as Julius Caesar on the Ides of March," Longstreet said. The laugh that followed was bitter.

"I suppose you did," Johnston agreed. "I was sorry to hear about General Bragg, though. He was a good man for all his ill temper."

Longstreet's throat tightened. Bragg's death was still a gaping wound. "We lost a lot of good men."

They went silent.

"Breakfast arrives at dawn. How about we get some sleep," Johnston said.

Longstreet stretched out on the bed. The straw reeked of mildew.

"I'm glad you're here, Pete."

The sound of joy in Johnston's voice warmed Longstreet. He closed his eyes and dropped off to sleep.

★ ★ ★

The rain leaked through the holes in the roof. Forrest moved the crushed pot under the newest leak and listened as the water plinked against the metal. Thunder shook the shack. He peered out the window, through the mist covering the mountains, at the gray sky. The war was over. It had ended with Longstreet's surrender and arrest five weeks ago. The Yankees were accusing Longstreet of Lincoln's murder, a man, in Forrest's opinion, who needed killing. Same with Grant, though Grant had won Forrest's reluctant respect.

When Forrest first heard the news of the surrender, he encouraged his men to return home and abide by the surrender terms. He was on his way home when word reached him that Sherman had put a $5,000 bounty on his head. That was a lot of money to resist, especially for a soldier arriving home after four years of war only to find his house burned to the ground, his fields destroyed, and his livestock stolen.

Forrest retreated to the mountains to plot his strategy. He didn't plan to hide forever. He was eager to see his wife and son. At first, he thought he would just lay low until the Yankees got occupied with some new, shiny thing and gave up the search. But the weeks rolled by and the Yankees hadn't given up. In fact, they were closing in. He would have to move soon. The folks on the bottom of the mountain knew he was up here.

He heard a horse. He peeked out and saw Kelley dismount. Kelley ran toward the house. Forrest met the adjutant on the porch.

"It's really coming down," Kelley said. He shed his great coat and shook the water from it.

Forrest sat down on a barrel and watched the rain splash the puddles. "Did you git coffee?"

Kelley shook his head. "There were Yankees in the store. They were asking questions about you and flashing greenbacks."

"Then I guess we need to hi-trail it out of here." Perhaps it would be easier if he just went down the mountain and forced a confrontation with the Yankees. If they could take him alive, they were welcomed to him.

Kelley sat on the porch step. "When I was leaving, I was stopped by a man who had fought with Jackson. He had some interesting news about Stuart."

Forrest made a face. "I don't care to hear what that dandy is up to."

"He's forming an army to mount a rescue of our men."

"Really?" Forrest's opinion of Stuart instantly improved.

"Yeah, the man claims that Stuart is leading raids against the Yankees in Virginia."

Forrest whistled. "Well, I was gettin' a little tired of the scenery around here."

"Me, too," the adjutant agreed with a smile.

Forrest could feel excitement welling up again. Surrender hadn't been his idea. Now, here he was, plotting to get back in the fight. He stood. "Well if we're goin', let's git goin'." He walked off the porch and went to saddle King Philip.

Chapter Thirty

The War Department
Washington City

Sherman sighed loudly. Secretary Stanton stopped his filibuster long enough to glare his disapproval. Sherman sighed again, softer this time, and placed his elbow on the desk and his chin in his hand. An hour ago, he had been standing at the train station, ticket home in hand. Before he could climb up into the passenger car, a messenger had arrived from Stanton. He had almost disobeyed Stanton's order to report to the War Department. Listening to the Secretary of War rant and rave about the evils of Lee and Jackson, he wished he had listened to his instincts and bolted the city while the getting was good.

Stanton took a breath.

"I don't want the job," Sherman declared hastily. The job was Grant's old position as general in chief of the army, which also came with the Grant's rank. "The war's over. I want to go home."

Stanton's face turned bright pink. He huffed and puffed. "President Hamlin was very specific."

"Sheridan can get the job done."

"Sheridan is a good, little watchdog," Stanton said, "but he doesn't command the respect of the men like you do."

"Then give the job to John Reynolds."

Stanton's eyes narrowed. "Reynolds doesn't command my respect."

"Well, he should." Stanton glowered but didn't reply. "For he's right."

"I didn't bring you here for your opinions on politics." Stanton was snide.

Sherman's hand slammed down on the table. "Well you're getting my opinions," he said angrily. "I know you have at least one innocent man in the Washington Arsenal. Longstreet would never acquiesce to the death of Grant. They were friends. What I know of Lee, neither would he."

"Again, not your decision to make," Stanton retorted. "President Hamlin has ordered you to take the promotion. And you will agree or find yourself in a cell next to Longstreet. Your choice."

Sherman dropped his head in defeat. "What do you need me to do?"

"Jeb Stuart is a fugitive and seems intent on restarting the war. The President wants you to stop him."

Sherman raised his head. "Is that all?" Stanton nodded. "Then let Lee and the rest of them go. I'm sure Stuart will happily return to whatever home he has left."

Stanton raised his hands in a placating nature. "Let's be pragmatic, shall we."

How he hated politicians! They were a dishonorable bunch of rapscallions.

"The faster you capture Stuart; the faster you go home."

Sherman unclenched his jaw. That was the first reasonable thing Stanton had said during the entire meeting. "Do I have a free hand?"

"Within limits."

Sherman dismissed the restriction. As long as he delivered a political acceptable result, Stanton could care less how he achieved it. "Is that all?" Sherman stood.

"You're dismissed."

Sherman turned on his heel, slamming the door with all his might as he exited the office.

✮✮✮

Stars blanketed the night sky, lighting the open meadows and revealing silhouettes of small animals foraging for food. Starlight also created deep shadows in the surrounding woods. Jeb Stuart waited in one of those shadows now. Centurion shifted impatiently underneath him.

"Quiet boy," Stuart said, petting the thoroughbred. He peered down the small hill toward an unimportant road in the Virginia wilderness. The road was empty. He reached into his pocket and withdrew his watch. He opened it but couldn't read the time. He moved it around trying to find a glimmer of light but could find none in the shadows that hid him. So great was his anxiety about the time that he considered riding out of the trees' shelter and into the moonlight. Reason took hold of him. He slipped the watch back into his pocket and returned to watching the road at the bottom of the hill.

This afternoon a small boy had ridden into his small camp in the Shenandoah Valley. Joe Morrison had brought him to Stuart's tent.

"I was to give you this, General." The boy's voice quivered. He held out an envelope sealed with red sealing wax. There was no imprint in the wax.

Stuart opened the envelope.

> *I have news regarding your men in the Washington*
> *Arsenal. If you want to save their lives, please meet me.*
> *Come alone.*

There was no signature, but the handwriting looked familiar. Stuart couldn't place it, but he was positive he had seen it before. When that was would come to him sooner or later. At the bottom of the note were a time and a map of the road now under his surveillance.

A rider came into view – a silhouette against the black sky. Stuart stiffened and patted Centurion. "Here we go, boy." The rider pulled up. He appeared to be alone. Stuart waited a few minutes to make sure. He urged Centurion forward and slipped out from the trees and into the open. The rider saw him. He turned from the road and started up the hill. Stuart remained where he was.

As the rider came closer, Stuart was once again struck by something familiar. He knew the man just like he knew the handwriting.

"General Stuart."

Stuart reeled back in his saddle. It was John Reynolds! "General Reynolds!" He gasped. Reynolds became visible in the starlight.

"I know it must be quite a shock to see me under these circumstances," Reynolds laughed.

"To say the least."

"Let me start off by saying how sorry I am about the arrest of your men. Did you know that General Longstreet has also been arrested?"

"I know that," Stuart said severely. "What I don't know is why you're here."

"I want to help," Reynolds said.

Stuart erupted in anger. "The time to help was before my men were hauled from their beds in the middle of the night."

Reynolds calmly received Stuart's rebuke. "I did my best, but when I refused to arrest innocent men, President Hamlin had me removed from command."

Stuart repented of his anger. "I'm sorry."

Reynolds smiled. "I just wished I could have done more."

All the kind feelings Stuart ever held for Reynolds bubbled to the surface. The Union commander had always been an ally, a friend. The fear that gripped him since Joe Morrison first informed him of the arrest eased just a bit. The Lord had provided someone on the inside. "Can I get a message to General Lee?"

"I don't think that would be wise. But I did share your recent activities with him. It cheered him considerably."

"So, you've seen him. How is he?"

Reynolds hesitated. Stuart's heart dropped into his stomach. "He's ill," Reynolds said. "The doctor likens it to a bad summer cold."

"Is he alone?" Stuart asked, troubled by the idea of Lee suffering alone in a cold, dark cell.

"No, General Jackson is with him."

Stuart exhaled loudly. His good and gallant Jackson! He would make sure Lee was well cared for.

"I risked meeting you tonight because the trial is starting next week," Reynolds said.

"Who can I get in there?"

"The courtroom will be closed."

"Are they going to receive a fair trial?" Reynolds' silence said it all. "I'm not going to let Sheridan hang them!" Stuart declared. "I'll start the war again before I let him hang those good men."

"That's why I've come," Reynolds said matter-of-factly. "I'm here to make sure that you get your men back without having to restart the war."

On top of the hill, a horse whinnied. Startled, Reynolds wheeled about. "You're not alone!" He accused Stuart.

"I'm sure you're not alone either," Stuart accused right back.

Reynolds relaxed and chuckled. "Colonel Rosengarten is hidden in the bushes over there." He pointed behind him.

"Then I shall be properly terrified," Stuart laughed.

"I'll let him know," Reynolds grinned. "In the meantime, I need to get back before I'm missed. I'll keep you informed."

"I can't thank you enough." Stuart meant it. Reynolds was proof that God had heard Stuart's many prayers.

"It's my name on your parole. I mean to keep my word," Reynolds said quietly. "Look for my messages." He trotted down the hill and started down the road. Another silhouette joined him and, together, they disappeared into the night.

Stuart gave Centurion the signal. The stallion climbed up the hill.

Chapter Thirty One

Longstreet woke with a start. He sat up on the cot, his heart beating out of his chest. What had wakened him? Over his own deep breaths, he heard Johnston's soft snores. He pulled the blanket around his shoulders and shivered. Slowly, his heart settled down. In the hall, he was surprised to hear the guards. Usually they didn't stir until an hour after daybreak. He waited for them to enter the cell, but they walked by. Intrigued by this change of routine, he crept to the door and peered through the small barred window. He couldn't see anything. Suddenly, a face appeared in the window.

"Get back!" The guard snarled.

Johnston bolted up in the bed. "What's going on?" He demanded.

"Shut-up!" The guard turned his back on the cell.

"What's going on?" Johnston asked again, but softer.

Longstreet shrugged. "Your guess is as good as mine but..." Longstreet went still. From the hall came the sound of chains. They listened until the clanging faded away.

The door swung open. A torch flooded the room with light. Longstreet held up his hand and shielded his eyes. The torch disappeared. Longstreet waited until his eyes readjusted to the semi-darkness of the cell. A tray sat on the floor. He went to see what was for breakfast.

"Oatmeal," he announced to Johnston.

The oatmeal was thick and sticky. Longstreet put half in one bowl and passed it to Johnston. He scraped the rest in his bowl and took a bite. It was tasteless and dry. In disgust, he set the bowl down on the tray. No matter how hungry he was, he couldn't eat that swill. Johnston doggedly gagged down his breakfast.

Longstreet grabbed one of the cups of water and crossed to the window. He and Johnston only received a cup of water at breakfast and another at dinner, leaving their thirst unquenched. Longstreet fought the urge to swallow the cup's contents in one gulp. He sipped and sipped until he had to tip the mug upside down to get the last drop.

The sound of chains echoed down the hall. The guard was at the door again. When the hall was quiet, the door swung open.

"Let's go!" The guard barked.

"Where are we going?" Johnston asked.

"You don't ask questions. Now, let's go."

When they were returned to their cell, fresh linens were laid out on their cots. Longstreet picked through the small pile of white garments. He held up a shirt. "We're going to be put on display," he said, sliding the shirt over his head. It was made from coarse cotton and scratched his skin. Whereas his shirt fit, Johnston's shirt was two sizes too big.

Longstreet gathered the extra material in his fist. "We could make you another shirt."

Johnston laughed. It struck Longstreet that this was the first time he had heard Johnston laugh since the night he had arrived. When Johnston had the army, before his wounding at Seven Pines and before Lee took command, he had been a bright light in the camp. A sudden sadness gripped Longstreet at the memory.

Johnston sobered. "Guards."

Longstreet listened. The guards were moving down the hall. They went past the cell. The door opened at the end of the hall. Longstreet waited, expecting to see the back of the head of some guard. No one appeared. Chains echoed in the stone passageway. Longstreet stole to the door. He stood on one side so as not to be seen and glanced down the hall. Lee came into view. Shackled, he was barely able to walk. Lee passed then there was Jackson.

"What are you doing?" The fat corporal barked through the barred window. "Get back!"

Longstreet backed away. The door crashed opened. The corporal burst into the cell, his rifle raised high. He thrust it at Longstreet's face. Longstreet held up his hands in surrender. Two more guards entered, chains clanking in their hands. Longstreet stretched out his arms and was quickly shackled. With prods of rifle butts on their backs, Longstreet and Johnston were ushered from the cell.

They reached the yard in time to see a covered wagon pull out of the small courtyard. Longstreet suspected that the wagon contained Lee and Jackson, but the canvas was lashed down tight, and he couldn't see in. Another covered wagon pulled up. The tailgate was lowered. The guards man-handled both generals into the back. Longstreet crashed down onto the floor. He groaned in pain. A long bench rested against one of the wagon's side. He rolled over and used his elbows and knees to drag himself to the bench. Exhausted, but finally seated, he gasped for breath. Johnston sat next to him, also gasping for breath. The tailgate slammed shut and the canvas was tied down. The heat was unbearable. Sweat ran down Longstreet's face and spine like many rivers. He didn't know where he was going, but his fresh cotton shirt wouldn't be fresh by time he arrived.

Horses rode along side the wagon. "The Yankees must think we're terrifying," Longstreet whispered to Johnston.

"I don't understand what this overwhelming display of force is supposed to convey," Johnston whispered back. He shrugged then withdrew into his own thoughts.

The wagon rolled to a stop and the canvas was thrown back. Longstreet sucked in the fresh air. Breath after breath. He saw a squat, brick building encircled by a ring of soldiers.

Hands reached up and helped him down. Up the stairs he went. In the semi-dark foyer, his manacles were removed.

"There's no escape from this place," the fat corporal informed him. "So don't even try. If you do, I'll have to shoot you, and I'll count that as a pleasure not a crime." The smile that followed confirmed that he meant his threat.

Rifle butts pressing against Longstreet's back was the signal to move. He followed Johnston into a makeshift courtroom. Chairs lined a large center aisle. The seats were already filled. Necks craned to catch a glimpse of the prisoners. Whispers cascaded up and down the rows of spectators. Longstreet glanced at each face but recognized no one.

In the front of the room, perched high on a raised dais, sat the judge's bench. Directly in front of the dais was another table with files piled high. Two tables fronted the rows of chairs. Longstreet's eyes flew open. Lee had a glass of water in his hand! And there was a pitcher of water on the table. Longstreet quickly glanced at the table he was being corralled to. There was a pitcher of water at that table also.

As soon as they were seated, Longstreet reached over, filled a glass full of the precious liquid, and drank it down. A second glass followed. He became aware of Johnston holding out a glass. Longstreet filled Johnston's glass.

"Do you think we can get more?" Johnston whispered. He pointed at the pitcher that was already three quarters empty.

"I hope so," Longstreet replied. "Because if the Yankees are intent on hanging us, I don't want to die thirsty."

He turned his attention to the other table. Lee smiled hello. Longstreet's own smile faded. Lee looked ill. His face was gray and his cheeks were bright red with fever. The hand holding the glass shook. Longstreet's eyes sought Jackson, but those blue-gray eyes gave nothing away.

Jackson swiveled in his chair and scanned the courtroom. Longstreet's own gaze followed. Whoever Jackson sought must not have been in the courtroom, for with a disappointed sigh, he gave up and turned to face the front of the room. Longstreet was preparing to do the same when the door opened. Sherman walked through the door accompanied by a smaller man, a major general, with a scowl on his face. For the first time since his arrest, Longstreet felt a surge of hope. Perhaps Sherman had come to finally set the record straight.

"Sherman's here," he whispered to Johnston.

Johnston whipped his head around. "Which one?"

"The tall officer in the back of the room. The one with red hair."

"On the left?" Johnston questioned.

"That's him. He knows I had no part in killing Lincoln or Grant."

Johnston went rigid with anger. "Sheridan's with him," he hissed.

"Who's Sheridan?"

"The general standing next to your Sherman."

Longstreet noted that Sheridan was the scowler.

"He's the ringleader of this affair," Johnston continued. Longstreet had never heard such hatred in Johnston's voice. "And he knows we didn't do it either. That didn't stop him from having us arrested." Johnston turned back around. The vein in his forehead throbbed in anger.

Longstreet chanced another look. Jackson was staring also. Old Jack's face revealed his contempt for the small man. Sheridan said something to Sherman then left the room. Sherman took a seat at the back of the room.

A corpsmen walked by the table. Longstreet held up his hand. "Could we – and with a wave of his hand that included Jackson and Lee – have some more water, please." The corpsman snatched the pitchers from the tables. He disappeared out the back door.

As the back door swung shut, a door at the front of the room opened. A colonel, dressed in a blue uniform covered with more braid than Jeb Stuart would ever think of putting on a jacket, marched in. He pivoted like he was on the parade ground at West Point. One more step and he reached the table. He sat in the chair ramrod straight and eyes front. A large man in a black silk robe appeared through the door.

The colonel jumped to his feet. "All rise!" He ordered.

Longstreet stood and watched Jackson help Lee to his feet. Lee smiled his thanks, and in Stonewall's smile in return, Longstreet felt his old irritation toward Jackson resurface.

"Quiet in the court!" The colonel barked.

The nervous chatter humming through the room instantly quieted. The judge climbed the dais and sat down behind the desk. "You can be seated," he said. Chairs scraped and the hum restarted, lower in intensity this time. The judge banged the large gavel. "Quiet." The room obeyed. "Colonel Braverman, you have the floor."

Braverman stood and smoothed his jacket. "The prisoners are accused of conspiring with John Wilkes Booth in the assassination of our beloved President Lincoln and the murder of General Grant." He picked up an envelope and held it in the air. "This letter written to Lee by the murderer Booth exhorts Lee to retake the field and win the war."

"Is that all they have?" Johnston mumbled.

"I'm surprised they have that much," Longstreet replied. He glanced back at Sherman, but the Union general's expression gave nothing away. He returned his attention to Colonel Braverman.

"I call General Lee to the stand."

Lee stood and Jackson stood with him. Jackson offered Lee his arm and helped him to a chair next to the dais.

"You'll have to excuse my weakened state," Lee apologized, "but I've been ill."

The judge frowned. "Have you been seen by a doctor?"

"I have. He gave me some medicine, but it is working very slowly."

The judge frowned again but said nothing else.

"Please state your name for the court," Braverman ordered.

"Robert Edward Lee."

"You were the commanding general of the Army of Northern Virginia."

"I am," Lee answered quietly. He began to cough – body racking coughs that were painful to listen to.

"Could we get some water!" The judge said in exasperation.

Jackson's voice pierced the courtroom. "They took away our water pitchers."

"General Sherman, let's get the prisoners some water."

Longstreet's attention focused again on the back of the room. Sherman barked an inaudible order to a soldier standing by the door. The soldier slipped out of the courtroom. Lee extracted a graying handkerchief from his pocket and coughed into the cloth. The corpsman who had disappeared with the pitchers now returned. He set a pitcher on Jackson's table before bringing the second pitcher to Longstreet. Johnston claimed it and filled his glass. Jackson poured water into a glass and pulled a wax paper from his jacket's pocket. He emptied the container's content into the water. Having no spoon, he stuck his index finger in the water and stirred. He rose but the judge stopped him.

"Corpsman, please bring the glass to the prisoner."

The corpsman took the glass from Jackson and brought it to Lee. Lee drank it down. Slowly, the coughing eased. Lee sat the glass at his feet and wiped his mouth with his handkerchief.

"Do you need a minute?" The judge asked.

Lee shook his head. The judge gestured to Braverman to continue.

"Have you ever met John Wilkes Booth?"

"No."

"Are you sure?"

"Yes."

Colonel Braverman's expression was one of disbelief. He returned to his desk and searched through a file. "Are you an honest man?" He questioned Lee.

"He's an honest man," Johnston said, loud enough for the judge to hear.

The gavel banged heavily on the desk. "Quiet!"

One glance at Johnston and Longstreet knew Johnston was going to ignore the judge's warning. He placed a hand on Johnston's arm. "No, Joe. You'll only make it worse."

Lee pulled on his sleeve's cuff. "I don't think I can answer that."

"Why not?" Braverman challenged.

"It would be up to others to inform you if I'm an honest man." Lee pulled on his cuff again.

"So you never met with Booth?"

"No." Anger tinged Lee's voice.

"Okay," Braverman relented. "Do you know the whereabouts of Jeb Stuart?"

Lee laughed. "I have no idea."

"Has he been in contact with you?"

Lee's face filled with astonishment. "No," he laughed again.

"What's so funny, General?"

"I've been chained to a wall in a cell for weeks. How could General Stuart communicate with me?"

This revelation sat Longstreet back in his seat. Lee was chained to a wall! What had he done to warrant such drastic punishments? Had he tried to escape?

"I don't know where General Stuart is," Lee continued tightly. "I just pray he's safe."

"I have nothing further for the witness."

Jackson started out of his seat, but Lee shook his head. He walked slowly back to the table and sat down. He leaned into Jackson and whispered something. Jackson nodded in agreement.

"Your next witness, Colonel," the judge said.

"I call Corporal Andrew Whitman to the stand," Braverman called.

A young man, not more than twenty, stood, or rather tried to. He fell back in his chair. Another try brought him to his feet, but he lurched forward and grabbed the chair in front of him, almost knocking the woman seated there onto the floor. Whitman then lurched into the aisle and staggered down the center aisle. He bumped into Longstreet's table. Longstreet could smell the whiskey on him. Not that the stench was needed to verify the fact that Braverman's witness was very drunk.

It took the corporal several tries and all his concentration to pour himself into the witness chair.

"Thank you for coming," Braverman said. His tone was solicitous and friendly.

The witness mumbled something unintelligible.

"Did you serve in the Army of Northern Virginia?"

The movement of the witness' head didn't signify yes or no. Braverman repeated the question, this time more firmly.

"Yes," Whitman blurted out.

"Were you in the infantry?" Braverman asked. The young man wasn't paying any attention. He was staring at the judge's gavel. "Corporal Whitman!"

Whitman dragged his eyes from the gravel and focused on Braverman. "Were you in the infantry?" The colonel replied.

"No, I served in General Lee's headquarters."

That could have been true. Longstreet didn't know all the corpsmen who rotated in and out of his headquarters. Sorrel might, but T.J. would know for sure.

Braverman squared his shoulders. "When did you serve in General Lee's headquarters?"

"In the spring of 1865," Whitman hiccupped.

"Did General Lee have any unexpected guests?"

"Yes. After dinner, I was…clearing… the dishes…" Whitman's voice trailed away. He stared blankly at Braverman.

"You were clearing the dishes? Were they supper dishes?" Braverman led the witness.

"Yes, supper dishes." Whitman smiled in triumph.

Longstreet dropped his head. He knew where the testimony was headed. The unexpected guest would be Booth. Jackson and Johnston would be present at the meeting. The only thing he couldn't figure out is how Braverman would link him to the conspiracy.

"So, you saw John Wilkes Booth in General Lee's tent?"

Longstreet glanced at Lee, but Lee's expression revealed nothing. He couldn't see Jackson, hidden as he was behind Lee.

Johnston nudged his arm. "That's not true."

"I know."

"And who was there with Lee?" Braverman asked.

Whitman's finger pointed at Jackson, but when he swung his arm toward the other table, his finger stopped on Longstreet.

"I was in Georgia," Longstreet said. He pointed toward the back. "General Sherman can vouch for me."

The audience broke into nervous laughter. The back door slammed shut. Longstreet spun around in his chair. Sherman was gone. Disappointment slashed at him. An empty chair appeared to be Sherman's sole commentary on this travesty.

"Let the record show that Corporal Whitman has identified both General Jackson and General Johnston," Braverman crowed. The audience murmured approvingly. "Were there any other name mentioned?"

"Yes, a General Longstreet," Whitman chirped. He burped loudly then giggled.

Braverman shot Whitman a glare, which sobered the witness. "What did General Lee say about Longstreet?"

"General Longstreet was to make sure Booth escaped into Florida," Whitman said. Braverman smiled in victory.

Longstreet took the accusation in stride. All hope, foolish as it might have been to still have hope, dissipated. The Yankees were going to hang them. This mockery of a trial was the window dressing necessary to justify the politicians' refusal to accept the paroles granted by Grant and Sherman in the field.

"I have no more questions." Braverman dismissed the witness.

Chapter Thirty Two

Shenandoah Valley
August, 1865

Forrest dismounted. In the shadows of a copse of trees, he saw a white tent that must belong to Jeb Stuart. It was a miracle he had found it at all. Stuart was a man who sure knew how to cover his tracks. He led King Philip toward the tent. Correction, tents. Hidden in the trees, Forrest counted two more. A shout drew him up. A colonel approached on the run.

"Can I help you?" The colonel was stern and deferential at the same time. Must be an adjutant.

"I've come to see General Stuart."

The colonel looked him over. "I don't know you."

Forrest drew himself up to his full height. "Do as you're told, Colonel!"

The colonel pursed his lips then slowly turned and headed toward the tents. Forrest followed. With one more stare at Forrest, the colonel disappeared into the tent.

Forrest didn't blame the colonel for his suspicion. Stuart was a wanted man. When Forrest had crossed into Virginia, he had instantly seen an increased Union presence. There were Yankee patrols everywhere – on the main and secondary roads. The towns he by-passed was filled to the brim with blue-uniformed soldiers. He would never get the 400 men who had joined him along the way to a location that he didn't know of, in a country that he was unfamiliar with. He told Kelley to take the men back to Tennessee and wait for word. He'd find Stuart and get help from the Virginians in getting his men across the border and to safety.

How the men found him was a mystery. Coming down off the mountain, he had to swing west to avoid a Yankee patrol. He discovered a forgotten bridle path and traveled throughout the night.

When the moon set, he found a place to hide and sleep. Kelley went into town for supplies. He returned with four men ready to ride. They woke at twilight to find three more men waiting. Slowly they came, in drips and drabs, until his command was too large to hide even at the night.

Ten days after he and Kelley started out, the Yankees picked up his trail. He turned his men around, set an ambush, and waited. Fifteen minutes later the Yankees had been dispensed. But the next morning, a new pack of Yankees dogged his steps. He fought them everyday from Sweetwater to Knoxville.

He also stole from them. Union garrisons became prime targets of his raids. He stole guns, ammunition, food, and other supplies. Now that he was openly defying the Yankees, word of his passing spread like wildfire. By time he reached Johnson City, he had close to 400 men. He was also skirmishing with the Yankees every day.

He crossed into Virginia at Bristol. Fifteen miles up the road, he came across a Union regiment. Skirmishing was one thing, but an out-and-out battle with well-armed Yankees was a different matter altogether.

"Colonel Kelley, take the men across the border."

"Where are you going?" Kelley asked.

"I'm going to find Stuart."

"Not alone!" Kelley protested. Forrest glared at the argumentative adjutant. "You don't even know where he is!"

It took a direct order and a few choice words to turn Kelley around. But the adjutant was right about one thing. Forrest had no idea where Stuart was. A week of aimless wandering convinced him of that. He was no closer to Stuart's location now than when he entered Virginia.

He walked into a small tavern on the crossroads to nowhere and glanced around at the gray jacketed men. He crossed to the rickety structure that served as a bar. "Whiskey." The barkeep placed a chipped glass in front of him and filled it with brown liquid. "To the

Army of Northern Virginia!" Forrest said in a loud voice, raising his glass high into the air.

"To General Lee!" Returned half dozen voices.

"To Stonewall!" Returned the rest.

Forrest tossed his whiskey down. It burned his throat. "My name is Nathan Bedford Forrest! I believe you know who I am." The bar went silent and all eyes were fastened on him. "I'm looking for General Stuart." Then he waited.

The customers returned to their drinks. Forrest tapped the bar. The barkeep refilled his glass.

"I need someone to tell me where I can find General Stuart." No response. He smiled suddenly. "Don't make me make it an order."

From the back of the crowded room, Forrest heard laughter. A tall soldier stood. "Sir, that won't be necessary. None us know where General Stuart is exactly."

"Can you get me close?" Forrest sipped the whiskey.

The soldier nodded. "I can get you close."

"What's your name?" Forrest dropped a coin on the bar.

"Captain Griggs, sir."

Forrest headed toward the door. Griggs followed behind. "I can trust you, right, Griggs?"

"Yes, sir."

"I want you to run an errand for me. Do you have a horse?"

"It's not much of a horse, but I got one," Griggs said.

Forrest had sent Griggs to Kelley, while he followed the map Griggs had sketched. The captain had gotten him within a mile of Stuart.

The colonel reappeared. "General Stuart is asking for a name."

"Just tell him that I'm one of Longstreet's generals."

The colonel disappeared again. A moment later, he was back and waving Forrest into the tent.

★ ★ ★

The final witness lurched down the aisle: a captain who had worked in Johnston's headquarters and had charge over Johnston's personal billet. Except Johnston didn't know him. But Johnston wasn't asked, so the drunken captain was able to spin his tale of conspiracy and murder until all four generals were implicated. Once that was done, Braverman dismissed him.

"The prosecution rests," Braverman announced.

The enthralled spectators clapped, prompting the judge to wake up from his nap and pound his gavel on the desk. "Quiet! I say Quiet!"

Braverman returned to his small desk and handed up four files. The judge put on his spectacles and read each file slowly.

"When do we have our say?" Johnston asked sardonically.

Longstreet gave him a small smile.

The judge laid the last file down. "Will the prisoners stand?" He directed his gaze at Lee. "Robert Edward Lee, I find you guilty of treason and conspiracy to overthrow the United States Government. Do you have anything to say in your defense?"

"No."

Longstreet marveled. How is it that a simple word from Lee could contain such dignity, innocence, and contempt at the same time?

Jackson and Johnston were both found guilty. In Jackson's "no" Longstreet could hear the quiet acceptance of his fate. Johnston's "no" was defiant and angry.

Now, it was his turn. How would he answer? He hoped his "no" would be like Lee's. His throat grew tighter. The contradiction wasn't lost on him. He had chafed and fought against Lee's leadership like it had been a noose around his neck, holding him back from achieving his potential and, now, here, at the end, he wanted to emulate Lee.

He remembered back to the night Atlanta fell, when Sorrel had awakened him and informed him that General Lee had arrived. In that moment, he had hoped with all his might that it was Lee come to save him. But Lee hadn't come and Bragg was dead and he was all alone. And standing in this court room, he still felt alone.

Tears burned his eyes. He closed them. He didn't want anyone getting the wrong idea.

"Do you have anything to say in your defense?"

Longstreet opened his eyes. "No." It didn't have the innocence or contempt that Lee's "no" did, but his reply had the dignity. He chanced a glance at Lee, but Lee looked straight ahead.

The judge handed the files to Braverman. "Then I sentence each of you to be hanged by the neck until dead at a date to be determined by the Secretary of War." The gavel crashed down one last time. "This court is dismissed."

The spectators spilled into the center lane blocking the rear exit. The fat corporal and his cohorts beat their way through, shoving and pushing, earning glares from the men and gasps of outrage from the ladies.

Longstreet stretched out his hands and felt the cold iron around his wrists. Lee passed in front of him, close enough to touch. How he desired a moment with Lee, to tell Lee... A tug on the chain interrupted his musings.

The guards led him out the front door near the judge's bench and thrust him into an anteroom.

"There's to be no talking!" The fat corporal warned. He waved the rifle butt in Longstreet's face to emphasize his warning. "I'll be right outside." He slammed the door.

Longstreet turned and almost fainted with surprise. He wasn't alone, and it wasn't his usual cellmate in the room with him. It was Lee. Thanks be to Jackson's ever kind Providence.

"General Lee."

"Pete."

Now that he had his wish, Longstreet didn't know were to begin. "How are you feeling?" He blurted out.

"I'm tired." Lee was gracious.

Longstreet sat down opposite Lee. "I was so sorry to hear about Rooney. I know how much it hurts to lose your children." He stretched out his hand. Sadness overtook Lee. He gripped Longstreet's hand. "It's something we should never have to know." Lee untangled his hand. "I don't think we have much time..." Longstreet trailed off, afraid to give words to the feelings churning within him.

"I'm surprised we have this time at all."

"Will you give General Jackson my warm regards?" Longstreet didn't know why he said it. It was just something to say until he screwed up his courage and said the things he had wanted to say since Atlanta.

"I will." Lee gave him a smile filled with friendship and warmth. "Pete, I must say, I have missed you. My old war horse. I'm just sorry that you've been caught in this... farce. Is that the right word?"

Tears welled up in Longstreet's eyes. "It will do." It was now or never. He took a deep breath and plunged in. "I just wanted to tell you that..."

The door crashed opened. The fat corporal burst into the room, his rifle raised high in the air. This time, Longstreet knew the Yankee meant to carry out his threat. He jerked to his feet and used his massive body to protect Lee.

"CORPORAL!" The angry voice spun the corporal around like a top. "That is enough of that!"

Longstreet saw an angry, dark-haired Union general in the door.

"General Reynolds," the corporal whimpered.

Reynolds strode into the room. "General Lee, are you okay?" Lee indicated that he was. "General Longstreet?"

"I'm alright," Longstreet said tightly.

Reynolds beckoned the corporal. "If you ever hit...

The corporal interrupted. "General Sheridan says to keep order by any means necessary.

"You think clubbing defenseless men with your rifle butt is a necessary means?"

The corporal swelled up. "I said no talking. They – he gestured at Lee and Longstreet – were talking."

"You're excused." Reynolds pointed at the door.

"General Sheridan..."

"You're excused!" The tone of his voice gave the corporal no choice but to leave the room.

"I apologize," Reynolds said. He held out his hand to Longstreet. "We've never met. I'm John Reynolds."

"It's nice to meet you," Longstreet shook the hand offered. "Thank you."

Lee stood. "General Reynolds, is there any news of General Stuart?" He whispered.

Longstreet stared at the Union general. Had he news about Stuart?

Guards entered the room. "It's time to go."

Lee hadn't received an answer to his question. Longstreet didn't want to leave until he did. But the guards were jerking on his chains.

At the door, Longstreet gave one more frantic look at both men. Lee was stoic and Reynolds was looking down at the floor.

Chapter Thirty Three

Trenton, New Jersey
August, 1865

George McClellan laid down the newspaper that contained the recent editorial he had penned. Anonymously. Since his release from prison and his resignation from the army, he had been a prisoner in his home and unpopularity had been his most zealous warden. No one wanted to be seen with him. No one even wanted to hear from him.

For almost a year he had waited patiently for the people to come to their senses and realize that he was the only one who could save this nation from the perils threatening to swamp it. Then Lee surrendered and the war was over. While the nation celebrated the news, McClellan locked himself in his office and wept tears of despair.

Yes, he was proud of the army he had created and commanded. His loyal men had won a great victory. But he had been wrong; about everything. He wasn't God's appointed savior. The Union didn't need him. Didn't want him. Didn't even remember him. This revelation broke both his heart and his unwavering faith in himself. For the first time in his life, he didn't know what to do.

Then Lincoln was assassinated – cut down while celebrating Grant's great victory. National joy turned into national gnashing of teeth and rending of garments. This unpopular president, who had to suspend the election because he was about to lose his office, now became a beloved martyr dead on the altar of a grateful nation.

The Trenton newspapers blamed McClellan's impromptu speech on the porch for giving John Wilkes Booth the idea of assassination. A howl of righteous indignation rose throughout the city. So great was the public outrage that McClellan expected angry citizens armed with pitchforks and torches to storm his house, drag him from it, tar and feather him, and run him out of town on a rail. In self-defense, he wrote a letter to the editor, but not in his name. He wrote as if he was a spectator who was on the lawn that afternoon and heard the speech. It was the defense he never had. Point-by-point he went over the speech, emphasizing that he didn't call for Lincoln's assassination, but, in fact, had vehemently eschewed that course of action.

What would be the response? McClellan waited impatiently every morning for the papers to arrive. Three days later, the paper published his letter along with an editorial that vindicated him. He should have been overjoyed. But in the weeks that followed, no one came to his door. Yes, the truth about the speech was out, but the letter's goal was to relieve his isolation and, in that regard, the letter had failed.

One morning McClellan opened his newspaper and received a gift from Heaven. Jeb Stuart had raided Fort Monroe and had liberated a battery of artillery and other weapons. McClellan took out a clean sheet of paper and began to write. When he was through, his editorial was a condemnation of Stanton. Who was in charge in Washington? Stanton or Hamlin? The nation had a right to know. Again, he didn't sign his name. Five letters later and others were beginning to ask the same questions.

A knock on the door startled him. The door opened and James stood in the doorway. "Sir, Henry Bicknell is here."

Shocked that Bicknell would be the first person to arrive at his door, he spluttered a show him in. He swallowed hard and collected himself.

The door swung open wide and the portly Bicknell burst into the room. "General!" He hailed boisterously.

"Not any more," McClellan said bitterly.

"That was an injustice." Bicknell was compassionate. "May I?" He pointed at the red leather chair.

"First, tell me why I shouldn't throw you out of my house?" McClellan asked severely. Bicknell's hands fluttered helplessly in the air. "It's been months since I was released from prison. Not one note or letter."

Bicknell eased into the chair. "That was wrong."

McClellan's pent-up anger burst like a dam. He jumped to his feet. "Wrong? How about cowardly? How about scurrilous?" He ranted, gesturing wildly. "You sat in my office and drank of my hospitality and when the chips were down," he pointed an accusing finger at the pudgy man, "you turned tail and ran for the hills." To his credit, Bicknell took the dressing down like a soldier. Curiosity extinguished McClellan's anger. Why had Bicknell come? What news did he bring with him? Bicknell still held an influential position in New Jersey state politics. He returned to his seat. "James!"

The door opened and the butler appeared. "Could we have some coffee, please?" The door closed. McClellan turned to Bicknell. "The coffee should be here in a moment."

"I didn't come for coffee," Bicknell said. He reached in his pocket and pulled out pieces of newspaper. He laid them, one by one, on the desk. McClellan gathered them up. They were his letters to the editors. "You wrote them?" Bicknell's question wasn't really a question.

McClellan smiled. "Yes."

Bicknell nodded. "I thought so. I told the party you had. They didn't believe me, so they sent me to find out."

A knock on the door announced the arrival of the coffee. James slipped into the room and laid the silver tray and coffee on a low table.

"What interest does the party have in my letters?" McClellan asked.

"As you know, the Democratic nominating convention is next week in Philadelphia."

251

McClellan's head reeled. Had Bicknell come to ask permission to work for his nomination? "I did know that."

"The party wants you to come to Philadelphia and make a speech." Bicknell gestured toward the editorials. "On those."

"A speech?" McClellan inquired in disappointment. All Bicknell wanted was a speech that any politician could give. But he dare not refuse. Make the right speech at the right time and in four years, the presidential nomination could be his. "I'd be honored."

Bicknell stood. "Thank you, General."

"George," McClellan reminded him.

"General," Bicknell repeated. "I'll see myself out."

★ ★ ★

A self-conscious McClellan stood in the wings, waiting his turn to speak. In his black broadcloth suit, he felt underdressed. There was no gleaming sword in a gleaming scabbard. No red sash with fringe dancing above polished boots as he walked. Would the suit remind the delegates of his fall from grace? He swallowed hard and took stock of what he knew. His destiny *was* to save this nation, and that destiny hadn't changed despite his momentary season of doubt. Even though his name had not been placed in nomination, he was being given the opportunity to shape policy. If he could galvanize the delegates with this speech, he might even be able to shape the next presidency.

Applause began as the New Jersey chairman wrapped up his introduction. McClellan gauged the applause's intensity. The applause was more than polite but less than enthusiastic. His work was cut out for him. He swallowed again and stepped out onto the stage and to the podium.

The applause did not build when he appeared. He cut it off as quickly as he could by raising his hand and asking for quiet. The delegates quickly obeyed. He took his time and surveyed the room.

He had addressed thousands of soldiers, Congress, and even Cabinet officials. He was no stranger to the power of the spoken word. He was in his element, for he knew how to sway a room.

"Jeb Stuart is outraged and he has every right to be." There was a smattering of applause and some boos, but mostly the audience sat silent. "When General Lee surrendered the Army of Northern Virginia, he, his staff, and his army received paroles permitting them to return home in peace so long as they did not take up arms against the United States Government. They went home in good faith. In Georgia, General Longstreet surrendered the Army of Tennessee and the Army of Mississippi and received the same generous terms.

"We all know what happened in between the surrenders in Virginia and Georgia. President Lincoln was brutally assassinated and General Grant was brutally murdered. The assassin was shot on site. He was deranged actor and in his pocket he had a letter begging Lee to retake the field. Or so we are told.

"Under the cover of night, soldiers arrested Lee, Jackson, and Johnston and threw them in prison. Longstreet was arrested when he surrendered. The trial was conducted in secret. You and I were forbidden to see the evidence Secretary Stanton had gathered. And now those men are going to hang for a crime they did not commit. For if the Rebels were guilty, why didn't Stanton try them openly. Was there something Stanton didn't want us to know?"

This time the audience's reception was positive. McClellan's heart began to race.

"If we don't demand accountability from our leaders, this bloody war just ended will begin again. And those who fought and survived will be forced to return to the field of battle. This time, not to preserve the Union, but to preserve Stanton's power. Since Lincoln's assassination, the Secretary of War has placed the capital under martial law. He has ordered Union soldiers to terrorize the citizens of the Shenandoah Valley in the hopes of extracting the location of Jeb Stuart and the army that is quickly rallying around him.

"If Stanton's goal is to stop Stuart, then I suggest an easier way. Release the prisoners. Release them and Stuart will stop!" Applause drowned out McClellan's next few sentences. He didn't mind. To him, cliché though it was, the applause was like a drink of water to a thirsty man. He drank it in until he believed he was going to drown.

By time he finished his speech, the delegates were eating out of his hand. If he had had the apparatus in place, the men to wrangle delegates' votes, and a powerful state like New Jersey behind him, he would have left the hall the Democratic party nominee for president. He wanted to shout in victory. All those months alone, when he thought his life was over, had been wiped away with a single speech. He had returned to the national stage covered in glory. He closed his eyes and heard the delegates shouting his name.

"General McClellan! General McClellan!"

McClellan opened his eyes and saw Henry Bicknell weaving his through the passengers waiting on the train platform with him. Bicknell drew up, put his hands on his knees, and caught his breath. "I'm glad I caught you before you went back to Trenton." Sweat dripped off the edge of tip nose.

"What's wrong?" McClellan asked.

"The delegates have voted," Bicknell wheezed.

That was fast. Too fast. "Is it Senator Pendleton?" McClellan asked.

"No," Bicknell replied. He wiped the sweat from his nose and broke into a smile. "They voted for you."

Chapter Thirty Four

The sun was rising. Longstreet stood at the window and watched the sky turn red, pink, orange, and every shade in between. He marveled at the beauty, wishing it would never end. After all, this was his last sunrise.

In the days following his brief visit with Lee, he had pondered long and hard on why Lee would ask a Union general, of all people, about Stuart. He could only come up with one answer that made any sense. Stuart was out there, planning a rescue, and the Yankees knew about it.

So every morning Longstreet woke expecting to hear the sound of gunfire that would announce Stuart's arrival. Every night he went to bed frustrated and angry. What was Stuart doing? When he could no longer hold back his wrath, he said as much to Johnston.

"Pete, Stuart loves Lee like a father, and Jackson..." Johnston smiled. "Those two are more like brothers. We were spirited away in the night and have been locked up here ever since. Perhaps Stuart doesn't know where we are."

Longstreet refused to believe that. Stuart always had spies in the highest places of the Union War Department. Why didn't he just pressure one of those contacts now to tell him where they were being held? Longstreet raged against Stuart for days until his anger finally turned against Johnston for constantly defending the cavalry leader. But Johnston's words finally penetrated his anger. Joe was right. Stuart might not risk all to rescue the occupants of this cell, but he would risk all to rescue Lee and Jackson.

In the interminable, sleepless nights, he wondered where were his friends were? Friends he had gone to West Point with and had fought alongside during the Mexican War. Played poker and drank whiskey with. Why weren't they protesting this travesty? Well, it didn't matter any more. He would be dead by noon.

The sun was almost up. The room turned golden. Longstreet heard Johnston stirring. "I wish Jackson was here." Longstreet's voice was loud in the cell.

Johnston stretched his arms. By the looks of the dark circles under his eyes, Johnston didn't get much sleep last night either. "You do?"

"I need him to tell me about Heaven. Don't get me wrong, I'm a believing man. I know where my hope lies. But this morning, my fear is crowding out my faith."

Johnston came to the window. "Are you afraid?"

"Not of dying," Longstreet said. "I think I've seen too much death to be afraid of it. But I'm afraid for my wife and children. They'll be all alone. How will they survive in this hostile world?"

Johnston laid a reassuring hand on Longstreet's arm. "They won't be alone."

"We're alone." Longstreet's tone was bitter.

"No, we're just lost. But our men and our country won't forget our widows and our children. They won't ever forget our leadership in the field or our murders."

They were silent for a moment.

"Do you have any regrets?" Johnston asked.

Longstreet didn't even have to think. "I should have done as Forrest advised. I should have come out from behind my trenches and hit Sherman the day Thomas pulled out. I had the numbers." He shrugged. It wasn't important now. "What about you, Joe?"

Johnston's eyes filled with tears. "My regret is that I allowed my wounded pride over the loss of the army to steal from me the things I valued most."

Johnston's word caused Longstreet's heart to ache with regret. He was guilty of this very sin. His wounded pride had caused him to stab Johnston in the back and steal armies from him. When Davis had asked if Johnston was able to handle the command of both armies, Longstreet gave a diplomatic answer, but he knew if Davis had pressed him, he would have sold Joe out. Surely, Joe had to know. Yet, for their entire imprisonment, he never brought it up. Not even hinted at it. "What things?" There was a catch in Longstreet's voice.

"Friendships, peace of mind, and self-respect."

Longstreet swallowed hard. "Joe, I need to confess something."

Johnston shook his head. "No, you don't." He smiled kindly.

Tears welled up in Longstreet's eyes. Suddenly, he was sorry; sorry for it all. "Please..."

"Don't you think I know." Johnston smile remained kind. "Of course, I was angry. At first. But in my demotion, I found the peace and blessing of God."

Longstreet didn't stop his tears from falling. Joe had known all this time and had treated Longstreet as he always had – with respect and friendship.

"Now we're going to meet the blessed Savior." Johnston fished in his pocket and produced a handkerchief. "And I'm so grateful that I can meet Him with a clean conscience and heart." He wiped his eyes.

"Even though you don't need to hear it, I need to say it. I'm so sorry." Longstreet began to weep. Johnston hugged him. "It's okay," Johnston murmured.

The key turned in the door. The moment had arrived.

A verse came to Longstreet. One he had heard at his childrens' funeral. He whispered it in Johnston's ear. *"And God shall wipe away all tears from their eyes; and there shall be no more death, neither sorrow, nor crying, neither shall there be any more pain..."*

The door swung open. The guards invaded the cell. "Let's go!"

"We're ready," Johnston said. He flashed Longstreet a smile then gestured for Longstreet to go first.

They left the cell. The fat corporal was waiting. "No talking!" He commanded.

Longstreet gave him a bored look.

There came a commotion from down the hall. Lee and Jackson approached. Lee's arm was threaded through Jackson's.

The fat corporal hit Longstreet on the back with the rifle. No, he wasn't afraid to die, but he would do so on his own time. He refused to move. Beside him, he saw Johnston smile. He smiled back and started down the hall. He stepped outside, into the sunlight, and breathed deeply.

Stuart stared across the Potomac and saw the newly installed dome on the Capitol glimmering in the rising sun. Centurion waded into the river and drank thirstily. Stuart looked to his right, toward Greenleaf Point, at the confluence of the Potomac and Anacosita Rivers. He raised his fieldglasses and focused on the brick walls of the Washington Arsenal. Behind those walls were his men.

Right now, a hundred Confederates were sneaking into Alexandria, singularly and in pairs, trying not to look like the raiding party they were. So far they hadn't been discovered. For that Stuart offered a prayer of thanksgiving. General Rodes waited outside the city with another fifty men. When the shooting started, Rodes would take the city and the roads. General Early was waiting in Maryland just in case Stuart couldn't make it back to the Long Bridge and had to escape the city by a different route.

Forrest approached. "It's time you git goin'."

Stuart glanced at his watch. "Not yet."

Forrest frowned. "The longer we hang around, the more likely we'll be spotted."

"We'll have to take that chance. I want to make sure our men are out of their cells before I attack." Stuart slipped the watch back into his vest pocket. "Are you ready?"

Forrest's eyes gleamed. "Don't you worry none about your escape. I'll keep the Long Bridge open for ya."

Stuart smiled. "I have no doubt. But just in case, don't hesitate to call on General Rodes. He's from Alabama, and he can fight."

"I will."

Stuart extended his hand. Forrest gave it a quick shake before striding away.

Centurion nudged him. Stuart laughed and gave the thoroughbred a lump of sugar. His watch made another appearance. It was time. Stuart gathered up Centurion's reins and swung up in the saddle. "Let's go get our men!"

To be continued...

Historical Notes
After Chancellorsville:

During the war, **Francis P. Blair, Jr.** commanded a division during the siege of Vicksburg and the battle of Chattanooga. He commanded the XVIII Corps during the Georgia Campaign. After the war, Blair returned to politics, running unsuccessfully for vice president in 1868 and entered the Senate in 1871. He died from a fall in 1875. He was fifty-four years old.

Braxton Bragg was relieved of command in February, 1864, and assumed the role of Jefferson Davis' military advisor. After the war, he held many jobs, including supervisor of the New Orleans Waterworks, Alabama's chief engineer, and a railroad inspector. Bragg died in Galveston, Texas at the age of fifty-nine.

Patrick Cleburne was known as the Stonewall of the West. He died from wounds received during the Battle of Franklin. He was thirty-six years old.

After the Battle of Chickamauga, **Nathan Bedford Forrest** was given independent command in Mississippi. He captured Fort Pillow and won again at Brice's Crossroads before losing at Tupelo. He surrendered his forces on May 9, 1865. After the war he settled in Memphis and found employment with the Marion and Memphis Railroad, eventually becoming the railroad's president. Forrest died in 1877 at the age of fifty-six.

Ulysses S. Grant capitalized on his fame by running for president in 1868. After his post-war fortune was stolen by his business partner, he wrote his memoirs to provide for his family. He completed them a few days before he died. Grant was sixty-three.

After the Union army captured Atlanta, **William J. Hardee** requested a transfer from the Army of Tennessee. He was reassigned to the Department of South Carolina, Georgia, and Florida and was responsible for opposing Sherman's March to the Sea. When the war ended, he moved to Alabama. Hardee died of an illness at the age of fifty-eight.

Thomas "Stonewall" Jackson was severely wounded at Chancellorsville. He developed pneumonia and died on May 10, 1863. Jackson's last words were, "let us cross over the river and rest under the shade of the trees."

After recovering from the wounds sustained during the Peninsula campaign, **Joseph Johnston** took command of the Department of the Mississippi. He opposed Sherman during the long march through Georgia and was replaced by John Bell Hood during the Atlanta campaign. In the last days of the war, Lee requested Johnston be returned to command. Johnston died of pneumonia at the age of eighty-four.

On April 9, 1865, **Robert E. Lee** surrendered the Army of Northern Virginia at Appomattox Court House. After the war, he served as president of Washington College in Lexington. He died of heart failure in 1870. Lee was sixty-three years old.

When the Confederate forces surrendered at Vicksburg, **Stephen Dill Lee** became a prisoner of war. After his exchange, Lee commanded the Department of Alabama and East Louisiana and participated in the Georgia campaign. Lee died in 1908. He was seventy-four years old.

Abraham Lincoln was re-elected for a second term. Less than a week after Lee surrendered at Appomattox, Lincoln was assassinated by John Wilkes Booth.

After the war **James Longstreet** joined the Republican Party, endorsing his friend Grant for president, which caused his reputation to slip among many Southerners. He died of pneumonia at the age of eighty-two.

George B. McClellan lost the 1864 election to Lincoln. He used his biography, *McClellan's Own Story*, to justify his war record. It was published posthumously. McClellan died suddenly in 1885 at the age of fifty-nine.

John Hunt Morgan conducted the longest raid of the war through southern Indiana and Ohio before surrendering at Salineville, Ohio. Morgan escaped from prison and returned to the Confederacy where he was hailed a hero. On September 4, 1864, Morgan was killed in Tennessee during a Union raid. He was thirty-nine years old.

James McPherson commanded the Army of the Tennessee during Sherman's Georgia Campaign. He was killed in action on July 22, 1864 while reconnoitering the Confederate position near Atlanta. McPherson was thirty-five.

John Pemberton surrendered Vicksburg to Ulysses S. Grant on July 4, 1863. Exchanged in October, 1863, he returned to Richmond. He resigned his commission only to accept a lieutenant colonelcy of artillery three days later. He manned the artillery during the defense of Richmond. After the war, he lived in both Virginia and Pennsylvania. He died at the age of sixty-six.

Leonidas Polk was transferred from the Army of Tennessee to command both the Department of Mississippi and East Louisiana and the Department of Alabama and East Mississippi. He participated in the Georgia Campaign and was killed in action while scouting enemy positions at Pine Mountain. He was sixty years old.

After Chancellorsville, **John Fulton Reynolds** was offered command of the Army of the Potomac, which he turned down because of Lincoln's penchant for meddling. Reynolds commanded the First Corps during the Gettysburg campaign. Reynolds was killed on the first day of battle. He was forty-two.

Philip Sheridan was promoted to lieutenant general in 1869. Two months after sending his memoirs to his publisher, he suffered a massive heart attack. Sheridan is buried at Arlington in front of the Custis-Lee Mansion. Sheridan was fifty-seven.

After the war, **William T. Sherman** was promoted to lieutenant general. When Grant won the presidency, Sherman was appointed Commanding General of the United States Army. Sherman died in New York City on February 4, 1891. He was seventy-one years old.

Alexander P. Stewart fought in the Georgia Campaign and replaced Leonidas Polk at the head of the Third Corps after Polk was killed in action. After the war, Stewart served as Chancellor of the University of Mississippi and was the commissioner of the Chickamauga and Chattanooga National Military Park. He died in 1908 at the age of eighty-six.

James Ewell Brown Stuart was wounded at Yellow Tavern on May 11, 1864. He died the next day in Richmond. Stuart was thirty-one years old. Lee wept bitterly when he heard the news.

George Thomas participated in the Georgia Campaign and was the Union commanding general at both the Battle of Franklin and the Battle of Nashville. After the war, Thomas commanded the Department of the Cumberland and the Division of the Pacific. He suffered a stroke and died at the age of fifty-two.

During the Spanish-American War, **Joe Wheeler** received an appointment as major general of volunteers and assumed command of the cavalry, which included Theodore Roosevelt's Rough Riders. Wheeler died at the age of sixty-nine and is buried in Arlington Cemetery

The Story Concludes

Save In Defense

Four condemned Confederate generals are herded at gunpoint to the large gallows erected in the prison yard at the Washington Arsenal.

Two Confederate cavalry leaders battle Union troops in a desperate attempt to reach the condemned men before they hang for crimes they did not commit.

One Union general bows his head and prays that the rescue mission has aided will succeed and prevent another war.

Army of Northern Virginia ✶ Army of Mississippi
Army of Tennessee ✶ Army of Trans-Mississippi

Lee, Jackson, Stuart, Longstreet, Forrest, Bragg,
Pemberton, Johnston, Cleburne, Hampton, Polk,
Hood, Kirby-Smith, and more...

Manassas, Perryville, Fredericksburg, Chancellorsville,
Chickamauga, Fort Stedman, Franklin, Missionary
Ridge, Fort Henry, Gettysburg, and
Appomattox Court House

THE STAINLESS BANNER
an e-zine dedicated to the armies of the Confederacy.

Subscription is free.

To subscribe, visit our website
www.thestainlessbanner.com

www.ingramcontent.com/pod-product-compliance
Lightning Source LLC
Chambersburg PA
CBHW031117030726
47496CB00002BA/577